NOT *AGAIN!*

"Emergency!" The address system blared across the recreation level. *"Code Blue, AUGL ward. All named personnel report immediately to the AUGL ward. Chief Psychologist O'Mara, Charge Nurse Hredlichli, Trainee Cha Thrat. Code Blue—"*

Cha Thrat missed the rest because Cresk-sar was glaring down at her. It wasn't laughing.

"Move yourself," it said harshly. "I'll acknowledge and go with you. As your tutor, I am responsible for your medical misdeeds. Hurry."

As they were leaving the recreational level the tutor continued, "A Code Blue is an emergency involving extreme danger to both patients and staff. Untrained personnel are usually ordered to stay clear. But they have paged you.

"What have you *done*—?"

By James White
Published by Ballantine Books:

AMBULANCE SHIP

ALL JUDGMENT FLED

CODE BLUE—EMERGENCY!

THE DREAM MILLENNIUM

FUTURES PAST

HOSPITAL STATION

MAJOR OPERATION

SECTOR GENERAL

STAR HEALER

STAR SURGEON

CODE BLUE—EMERGENCY
(A SECTOR GENERAL NOVEL)

JAMES WHITE

A Del Rey Book

BALLANTINE BOOKS • NEW YORK

A Del Rey Book
Published by Ballantine Books

Library of Congress Catalog Card Number: 87-91136

ISBN 0-345-34172-4

Manufactured in the United States of America

First Edition: July 1987

Cover Art by David B. Mattingly

Chapter 1

THE ruler of the ship sat beside Cha Thrat at the recreation deck's viewscreen while the fuzzy blob of light that was the space hospital grew into a gigantic, complex structure ablaze with every color and intensity of light that her eyes could detect. She had strong feelings of awe, wonder, excitement, and great embarrassment.

Ruler Chiang, she had learned, carried the rank of major in the Monitor Corps Extraterrestrial Communications and Cultural Contact division. But the ruler seriously confused her at times by behaving like a warrior. Now it was sitting beside her because it felt some strange, Earth-human obligation to do so. It had wanted to pay her the compliment of allowing her to watch the approach to the hospital from its control deck, but as she was physiologically unable to enter that small and already crowded compartment, it had felt obliged to desert its post and sit with her here.

The compliment was a completely unnecessary piece of time-wasting nonsense, considering wide disparity in the social and professional levels of the people involved, but Chiang seemed to derive some pleasure from the foolishness and it had, after all, been a patient of hers.

The muted conversation in Control was being relayed with the image on the repeater screen and, while Cha

Thrat's translator gave her the equivalent of every word, the particular technical jargon that the ship's warriors were using made the total meaning of what they were saying unclear. But suddenly there was a new, amplified voice whose words were simple and unambiguous, accompanied by a picture of the disgustingly hairy being who was speaking them.

"Sector General Reception," it said briskly. "Identify yourself, please. Patient, visitor, or staff; degree of urgency; and physiological classification, if known. If uncertain, please make full visual contact and we will classify."

"Monitor Corps courier vessel *Thromasaggar*," a voice from Control responded. "Short-stay docking facilities to unload patient and staff member. Crew and patient classification Earth-human DBDG. Patient is ambulatory, convalescent, treatment nonurgent. Staff member is classification DCNF and is also a warm-blooded oxygen-breather with no special temperature, gravity, or pressure requirements."

"Wait," the obnoxious creature said, and once again the image of the hospital filled the screen. A definite improvement, she thought.

"What *is* that thing?" she asked the ruler. "It looks like a . . . a *scroggila*. You know, one of our rodents."

"I've seen pictures of them," the ruler said, and made the unpleasant barking sound that denoted amusement with these people. "It is a Nidian DBDG, about half the body mass of an Earth-human with a very similar metabolism. Its species is highly advanced technologically and culturally, so it only looks like an outsize rodent. You'll learn to work with much less beautiful beings in that place—"

It broke off as the image of the Nidian returned.

"Follow the blue-yellow-blue direction beacons," the receptionist said. "Debark patient and staff member at Lock One Zero Four, then proceed to Dock Eighteen via the blue-blue-white beacons. Major Chiang and the Sommaradvan healer are expected and will be met."

By what? she wondered.

The ruler had given her a great deal of helpful advice and information about Sector Twelve General Hospital, most of which she did not believe. And when they entered the lock antechamber a short time later, she could not believe that the smooth, waist-high hemisphere of green jelly occupying the deck between the two waiting Earth-humans was a person.

Ruler Chiang said, "This is Lieutenant Braithwaite of the Chief Psychologist's Office, and Maintenance Officer Timmins, who is responsible for preparing your accommodation, and Doctor Danalta, who is attached to the ambulance ship, *Rhabwar*..."

Except for minor differences in the insignia on their uniforms, she could not tell the two Earth-humans apart. The large blob of green stuff on the floor, she guessed, was some kind of practical joke, or perhaps part of an initiation ritual for newcomers to the hospital. For the time being she decided not to react.

"...And this is Cha Thrat," it went on, "the new healer from Sommaradva, who is joining the staff."

Both Earth-humans moved their right hands up to waist level, then lowered them as the ruler shook its head. Cha Thrat had already told Chiang that grasping a strange person's appendage was considered quite vulgar where she came from, and it would have been much more considerate of them if they had given her some indication of their status. Ruler Chiang had spoken to them as equals, but then it had often done that while addressing subordinates on the ship. It was very careless of the ruler and most confusing for her.

"Timmins will see that your personal effects are moved to your quarters," the ruler went on. "I don't know what Danalta and Braithwaite have in mind for us."

"Nothing too onerous," Braithwaite said as the other Earth-human was leaving. "On hospital time it is the middle of the day, and the healer's accommodation will not be ready until early evening. In midafternoon you are due for a physical, Major. Cha Thrat is expected to be present, no doubt to receive the compliments of our medics for what was obviously a very tidy piece of, for a Sommaradvan, other-species surgery."

It looked in her direction and for some reason inclined its head forward from the neck, then went on. "Immediately following the examination both of you have appointments in Psychology: Cha Thrat for an orientation talk with O'Mara, and you for an investigation, purely a formality in your case, to ensure that there is no non-physical trauma resulting from your recent injuries. But until then . . . Have you eaten recently?"

"No," said Chiang, "and I would welcome a change from ship food."

The other Earth-human made soft barking sounds and said, "You haven't tasted a hospital meal yet. But we try hard not to poison our visitors . . ."

It broke off to apologize and explain hastily that it was making an in-hospital joke, that the food was quite palatable, and that it had been given full instructions regarding Cha Thrat's dietary requirements.

But she was only vaguely aware of what it was saying because her attention was on the hemisphere of green stuff, the surface of which had begun to ripple and pucker and grow pseudopods. It wobbled sluggishly and heaved itself upright until it was as tall as she was, its skin coloration became mottled, the wet gleam of what could only be eyes appeared, the number of short, crudely formed appendages increased until it looked like something a young child on Sommaradva might make from modeling clay. She felt sudden nausea, but her feelings of curiosity and wonder were even stronger as the body firmed out, became more finely structured, and the features appeared. Then the clothing and equipment pouch grew into place, and there was standing before her the figure of another female Sommaradvan identical in every detail to herself.

"If our Earth-human friends intend subjecting you to the environment of a multispecies dining hall within minutes of your arrival," it said in a voice that was not, thankfully, hers, "I must counteract their lack of consideration by providing you with something familiar, and friendly, to whom you can relate. It is the least I can do for a new member of the staff."

"Doctor Danalta," Braithwaite said, barking again, "is not as altruistic as it would have you think, Cha Thrat. Due to the incredibly savage environment of its planet of origin, the species evolved protective mimicry of a very high order. There are few warm-blooded oxygen-breathing life-forms in Sector General that it cannot accurately reproduce within a few minutes, as you've seen. But we suspect that any new, intelligent life-form to arrive at the hospital, be it patient, visitor, or staff, is regarded by Danalta as a challenge to its powers of physical mimicry."

"Nevertheless," she said, "I am impressed."

She stared eye to eye at her utterly alien but identical twin, thinking that the being had displayed concern for her present mental well-being by using its incredible talent to make her feel more comfortable. It was the action of a healer of rulers, and it might even be a ruler itself. Instinctively she made the gesture of respect to superiors, then belatedly realized that neither the Earth-humans nor her Danalta-copy would recognize it for what it was.

"Why, thank you, Cha Thrat," said Danalta, returning the gesture. "With protective mimicry there is an associated empathic faculty. While I don't know what the limb gesture means exactly, I could feel that I was being complimented."

Danalta, she had no doubt, was also aware of her embarrassment, but as they followed the two Earth-humans from the compartment the shape-changer did not speak of it.

The corridor outside was thronged with a menagerie of creatures, a few of whom resembled, in shape if not in size, nonintelligent species found on Sommaradva. She tried not to flinch as one of the small, red-furred bipeds of the species she had seen in charge of Reception brushed past, and she felt acutely anxious when enormous, six-limbed, multitentacled monsters of many times her body mass bore down on her. But not all of the creatures were frightening, or even ugly. A large crustacean with a beautifully marked carapace and hard exoskeletal limbs clickedpast, its pincers opening and closing slowly as it talked to a truly lovely being who had at least thirty short, stubby legs and an overall coat of rippling, silvery fur. There were others she could not see clearly because of their protective envelopes and, in the case of the occupant of a mobile pressure vessel from which steam was escaping, she had no idea what weird or wonderful shape the vehicle was concealing.

The cacophony of hooting, chirping, gobbling, and moaning conversation could not be described, because it was totally unlike anything she had previously experienced.

"There is a much shorter route to the dining hall," Danalta said as a spiney, membraneous being who looked like some kind of dark, oily vegetable shuffled past, its physical details clouded by the thick yellow fog inside its transparent suit. "But it would mean a trip through the water-filled Chalder wards, and your protective envelopes won't be ready for another six, maybe seven days. How do you feel, and what do you think of the place so far?"

It was disconcerting and embarrassing to have Danalta, who could be nothing less than a wizard-healer of rulers, ask such questions of a mere warrior-surgeon. But the questions had been asked, and answers were expected. If the being wished to practice its art in the middle of a crowded corridor, it was certainly not her place to criticize.

Promptly she replied, "I feel confused, frightened, repelled, curious, and unsure of my ability to adapt. My confusion is such that I am unable to be more specific. I'm beginning to feel that the two Earth-humans walking in front of us, member of a species that a short time ago I would have considered totally alien, have an almost welcome normality about them. And I feel that you, because you have made yourself the most familiar and reassuring entity in the hospital, are by your very nature the most alien of all. I haven't had enough time, nor have I sufficient direct experience, to form any useful impressions or opinions about the hospital, but it may well be that the empathic faculty you possess has already made you aware of my feelings.

"Is the environment of the dining hall," she added worriedly, "much worse than this?"

Danalta did not reply at once, and the two Earth-humans had been silent for some time. The one called Braithwaite had fallen slightly behind the other, and its head was turned to one side so that the fleshy protuberance that was one of its auricular organs would be better able to pick up her words. It seemed that her feelings were of interest not only to the shape-changer. When Danalta did speak, its words resembled a lecture rather than a simple reply to her question.

"A low level of empathy is common in most intelligent life-forms," it said, "but only in one species, the natives of Cinruss, is there a perfect empathic faculty. You will meet one of them soon because it, too, is curious about newly discovered life-forms and will want to seek you out at the first opportunity. You can then compare my limited empathic faculty with Prilicla's.

"My own limited faculty," it went on, "is based on the observation of body movements, tensions, changes in skin coloration, and so on, rather than the direct reception of the subject's emotional radiation. As a healer you, too, must have a degree of empathy with your patients, and on many occasions are able to sense their condition, or changes in their condition, without direct physical investigation. But no matter how refined the faculty may be, your thoughts are still private, exclusively your own property, and it is simply your stronger feelings that I detect—"

"The dining hall," Braithwaite said suddenly. It turned into the wide, doorless entrance, narrowly avoided colliding with a Nidian and two of the silver-furred beings who were leaving, and barked softly as they made derogatory remarks about its clumsiness. It pointed. "Over there, an empty table!"

For a moment Cha Thrat could not move a single limb as she stared across the vast expanse of highly polished floor with its regimented islands of eating benches and seats, grouped by size and shape to accommodate the incredible variety of beings using them. It was much, much worse than her experience of the corridors, where she had encountered the creatures two or three at a time. Here there were hundreds of them, grouped together into species or with several different life-forms occupying the same table.

There were beings who were terrifying in their obvious physical strength and range of natural weapons; others who were frightening, horrifying, and repugnant in the color and slime-sheen and nauseous growths covering their teguments; and many of them were the phantasms of Sommaradvan nightmare given frightful solidity. At a few of the tables were entities whose body and limb configurations were so utterly ridiculous that she had trouble believing her eyes.

"This way," said Danalta, who had been waiting for Cha Thrat's limbs to stop trembling. It led the way to the table claimed by Braithwaite, and she noticed that the furiture suited neither the physiologies of the Earth-humans nor the trio of exoskeletal crustaceans who were vacating it.

She wondered if she would ever be able to adapt to the ways of these chronically disorganized and untidy beings. At least on Sommaradva the people knew their place.

"The mechanism for food selection and delivery is similar to that on the ship," Braithwaite said as she lowered herself carefully into the dreadfully uncomfortable chair and her weight made the menu display light up. "You tap in your physiological classification and it will list the food available. Until the catering computer has

been programmed with details of the combinations, con-
sistencies, and platter displays you favor, it is likely to
come in unsightly but nutritious lumps. You'll soon get
used to the system, but in the meantime I'll order for
you."

"Thank you," she said.

When it arrived the biggest lump looked like an uneven block of *tasam.* But it smelled like roasted *cretsi,*
had the consistency of roasted *cretsi,* and, she found
after trying a small corner, it tasted like roasted *cretsi.*
She realized suddenly that she was hungry.

"It sometimes happens," Braithwaite continued, "that
the meals of your fellow diners, or even the diners themselves, are visually distressing to the point where it is
affecting your appetite. You may keep one eye on your
platter and close all the others; we won't be offended."

She did as it suggested, but kept one eye slightly open
so that she could see Braithwaite, who was still watching
her intently while pretending, for some odd, Earth-
human reason, not to do so. While she ate, her mind
went back to the incident with the ship ruler on Sommaradva, the voyage, and her reception here, and she
realized that she was becoming suspicious, and irritated.

"On the subject of your stronger feelings," Danalta
said, seemingly intent upon resuming the lecture it had
broken off at the entrance, "do you have any strong feelings against discussing personal or professional matters
in the presence of strangers?"

The ship ruler, Chiang, paused with what looked like
a piece of what had once been a living creature halfway
to its eating orifice. It said, "On Sommaradva they prefer
to hear directly what other people think of them. And
conversely, the presence of interested witnesses during a
discussion of their affairs is often considered beneficial."

Braithwaite, she saw, was concentrating too much attention on its disgusting meal. She turned as many eyes as would bear on the shape-changer, ignoring the many things she did not want to see in the background.

"Very well," Danalta said, turning its alien mimic's eyes on her. "You must already have realized, Cha Thrat, that your situation is unlike that of the other staff members who join the hospital for a probationary period. Appointments to Sector General are much sought after, and candidates must pass rigorous professional examinations and deep psychological investigation on their home worlds to ensure that they will have a fair chance of adapting to a multispecies hospital environment so that they will profit from our training.

"You were not screened in this manner," her alien twin went on. "There were no professional examinations, no birth-to-maturity psych profiles, no objective measure of your worth as a healer. We know only that you come with a very high recommendation, from the Cultural Contact department of the Monitor Corps and, presumably, your professional colleagues on Sommaradva, a world and society about which we know little.

"You appreciate our difficulty, Cha Thrat?" it continued. "An untrained, unprepared, single-species-oriented being could cause untold harm to itself and to the hospital staff and patients. We have to know what exactly it is that we're getting, and quickly."

The others had stopped eating and so did she, even though there was a mouth free for speaking. She said, "As a stranger arriving and expecting to take up an appointment here, I thought that my treatment showed a lack of sensitivity, but I decided that alien behavior patterns, of which I have very limited experience, were to blame. Then I began to suspect that the harsh and insensitive treatment was deliberate, and I was being tested in some fashion. You have confirmed this suspicion, but I am seriously displeased that I was not informed of the test. Secret tests, to my mind, can often show a failure in the examiner."

There was a long silence. She looked at Danalta and away again. The shape-changer's body and features and expression were the mirror of her own, and told her nothing. She turned her attention to Braithwaite, who had been taking such a continuous and covert interest in her, and waited for a reaction.

For a moment the Earth-human's two recessed eyes looked calmly into her four, and she began to feel very sure that the being was, in fact, a ruler and not a warrior as it said, "A secret test is sometimes given to avoid the unpleasantness of telling a candidate that it has failed. By pretending that no test took place, another and more acceptable reason, one that does not imply any lack of professional competence or psychological or emotional weakness, can be given for refusing the candidate an appointment. I'm sorry that you are displeased by the covert nature of the test, but in the circumstances we decided that it was better to ... to ..."

It broke off and began to bark quietly, as if there was something humorous in the situation, then went on. "We Earth-humans have an expression that covers your position very well. We threw you in at the deep end of the pool."

"And what," Cha Thrat said, deliberately omitting the gesture of politeness due a ruler, "did you discover from this secret test?"

"We discovered," Braithwaite said, and this time it did not bark, "that you are a very good swimmer."

Chapter 2

BRAITHWAITE left before the others had finished eating, saying that O'Mara would have its intestines for hosiery supports if it was late back from lunch two days in a row. Cha Thrat knew nothing of the entity other than that it was a greatly respected and feared ruler of some kind, but the punishment for tardiness sounded a bit extreme. Danalta said that she should not worry about it, that Earth-humans frequently made such ridiculously exaggerated statements, that there was no factual basis to the remark, and that it was some kind of linguistic code they used among themselves which had a tenuous connection with the mental associative process they called humor.

"I understand," Cha Thrat said.

"I don't," Danalta said.

Ship ruler Chiang barked quietly but did not speak.

As a result, the shape-changer was their only guide on an even longer and more complicated journey to the place where Chiang was to undergo its examination—one of the casualty reception and observation wards, she was informed, reserved for the treatment of warm-blooded, oxygen-breathing patients. Danalta had returned to its original body configuration of a large, dark-green, uneven ball that guided itself, with surprising speed and accuracy, through the wheeled and walking traffic in the corridors. Was the Sommaradvan form too difficult to maintain, she wondered, or did it now feel that such psychological props were no longer necessary?

It was a surprisingly large compartment, rendered small by the number and variety of examination tables and associated equipment covering the floor and walls. There was an observation gallery for the use of visitors and trainees, and Danalta suggested that she choose the least uncomfortable chair while they were waiting. One of the silver-furred beings had already taken Chiang away to be prepared for the examination.

"We shall be able to see and hear everything that is happening," Danalta said, "but they will not hear us unless you press the transmit button, just there, on the side of your chair. You may have to use it if they ask questions."

Another silver-furred being, or perhaps it was the same one, undulated into the compartment, performed a seemingly purposeless act on an as-yet incomprehensible piece of equipment, then looked up at them briefly as it was leaving.

"And now we wait," Danalta went on. "But you must have questions, Cha Thrat. There is enough time to answer a few of them."

The shape-changer had retained the form of a lumpy green hemisphere, featureless except for one bulbous eye and a small fleshy protuberance that seemed to combine the functions of hearing and speech. In time, she thought, one could become used to anything—except the lack of discipline among these people, and their unwillingness to define properly their areas of authority and responsibility.

Choosing her words with care, she said, "As yet I am too ignorant and confused by all this to ask the right questions. But could I begin by asking for a detailed clarification of your own duties and responsibilities, and the class of patient you treat?"

The answer left her feeling more confused than ever.

"I don't treat patients," Danalta replied, "and unless there was a major surgical emergency, I would not be asked to do so. As for my duties, I am part of the medical team on *Rhabwar*. That is the hospital's special ambulance ship, which carries an operational crew of Monitor Corps officers and a medical team that assumes overall authority once the ship has reached the location of the vessel in distress or, as the case may be, the site of the disaster.

"The medical team," it went on, ignoring Cha Thrat's confusion, "which is led by the Cinrusskin empath, Prilicla, also comprises Pathologist Murchison, an Earth-human female; Charge Nurse Naydrad, a Kelgian experienced in space rescue work; and myself. My job is to use the shape-changing ability to reach and render first aid to casualties who might be trapped in areas inaccessible to beings of limited physical adaptability, and do whatever I can to help the injured until the rescue crew is able to extricate and move them to the ambulance ship for rapid transfer to the hospital here. You will understand that by extruding limbs and sensors of any required shape, useful work can be done in the very restricted conditions found inside a badly damaged space vessel, and there are times when I can make a valuable contribution. But in honesty I must say that the real work is done by the hospital.

"And that," it concluded, "is how I fit into this medical madhouse."

With every word, Cha Thrat's confusion had increased. Able and physically gifted this entity might be, but was it, in truth, merely a servant? But if Danalta had sensed her confusion, it mistook the reason for it.

"I have other uses, too, of course," it went on, and made a very Earth-human barking sound with its un-Earthly mouth. "As a comparative newcomer to the hospital, they send me to meet new arrivals like you on the assumption that—Pay attention, Cha Thrat! They're bringing in your ex-patient."

Two of the silver-furred beings, identified by Danalta as Kelgian operating room nurses, moved Chiang in on a powered litter, even though the ship ruler was quite capable of walking and was constantly reminding them of this fact. The Earth-human's torso was draped in a green sheet so that only its head was visible. Chiang's protests continued while they were transferring it to the examination table, until one of the nurses, in a manner completely lacking in the respect due a ruler, reminded it that it was a fully grown, mature entity who should stop acting like an infant.

Before the nurse had finished speaking, a six-legged, exoskeletal being with a high, richly marked carapace entered and approached the examination table. Silently it held out its pincers and waited while a nurse sprayed them with something that dried into a thin, transparent film.

"That is Senior Physician Edanelt," Danalta said. "It is a Melfan, physiological classification ELNT, whose reputation as a surgeon is—"

"Apologies for my personal ignorance," Cha Thrat broke in. "Beyond the fact that I am a DCNF, the Earth-human is a DBDG, and the Melfan is an ELNT, I know nothing of your classification system."

"You'll learn," the shape-changer said. "But for now, just watch and be ready for questions."

But there were no questions. While the examination

proceeded, Edanelt did not speak and neither did the nurses or the patient. Cha Thrat learned the purpose of one of the mechanisms, a deep scanner that showed in minute detail the subdermal blood supply network, musculature, bone structure, and even the movement of the deepest underlying organs. The images were relayed to the observation gallery's screen, together with a mass of physiological data that was presented graphically but in a form that was completely unintelligible to her.

"That is something else you will learn," Danalta said.

Cha Thrat had been watching the screen closely, so captivated by Edanelt's meticulous charting of her surgical repair work that she had not realized that she had been thinking aloud. She looked up in time to see the arrival of yet another and even more incredible being.

"That," Danalta said simply, "is Prilicla."

It was an insect, an enormous, incredibly fragile, flying insect that was tiny in comparison with the other beings in the room. From its tubular, exoskeletal body there projected six pencil-thin legs, four even more delicately formed manipulators, and four sets of wide, iridescent wings that were beating slowly as it flew toward the examination table and hovered above it. Suddenly it flipped over, attached its sucker-tipped legs to the ceiling, and curved its extensible eyes down to regard the patient.

From somewhere in its body came a series of musical clicks and trills, which her translator relayed as "Friend Chiang, you look as if you've been in a war."

"We're not savages!" Cha Thrat protested angrily. "There hasn't been a war on Sommaradva for eight generations—"

She stopped abruptly as the long, incredibly thin legs and partly folded wings of the insect began to shake. It was as if there were a strong wind blowing through the room. Everyone on and around the examination table was staring at the little being, and then they were turning to look up at the observation gallery. At her.

"Prilicla is a true empath," Danalta said sharply. "It feels what you are feeling. Please control your emotions!"

It was very difficult to control her emotions: not only her anger at the implied insult to her now unwarlike race but also the feeling of utter disbelief that such control was necessary. She had often been forced to hide her feelings before superiors or patients, but trying to *control* them was a new experience. With a great effort, which in some obscure fashion seemed to be a negation of effort, she made herself calm.

"Thank you, new friend," the empath trilled at her. It was no longer trembling as it returned its attention to Chiang.

"I'm wasting your valuable time, Doctors," the Earth-human said. "Honestly, I feel fine."

Prilicla dropped from the ceiling to hover above the site of Chiang's recent injuries, and touched the scar tissue with a cluster of feather-light digits. It said, "I know how you feel, friend Chiang. And we are not wasting our time. Would you refuse us, a Melfan and a Cinrusskin who are both keen to enlarge our other-species experience, the opportunity of tinkering with an Earth-human, even a perfectly healthy one?"

"I suppose not," Chiang said. It made another soft, barking sound and added, "But you would have found it more interesting if you'd seen me after the crash."

The empath returned to the ceiling. To the Melfan it said, "What is your assessment, friend Edanelt?"

"The work is not as I would have performed it," the Melfan replied, "but it is adequate."

"Friend Edanelt," the empath said gently, with a brief

glance in the direction of the gallery, "we are all aware, with the exception of the newest member of our staff, that you consider as merely adequate the kind of surgery which Conway himself would describe as exemplary. It would be interesting to discuss the pre- and postoperative history."

"That was my thought as well," the Melfan said. There was a rapid, irregular tapping of its six boney feet, and it turned to face the observation gallery. "Will you join us, please."

Quickly Cha Thrat disentangled herself from the alien chair and followed Danalta into the ward and across to the group at the table, aware that it was now her turn to undergo an even more searching examination, one that would establish her professional rather than her physical fitness to practice in Sector General.

The prospect must have worried her more than she realized because the empath was beginning to tremble again. And it was disconcerting, even frightening, to be so close to the Cinrusskin. On Sommaradva, large insects were to be avoided because they invariably possessed lethal stings. Her instincts told her to swat or run away from this one. She had hated insects and always avoided looking closely at them. Now she had no choice.

But there was a subtle visual attraction in the intricate symmetry of the extraordinarily fragile body and trembling limbs, whose dark sheen seemed to be reflecting colors that were not present in the room. The head was an alien, convoluted eggshell, so finely structured that the sensory and manipulatory organs that it supported seemed ready to fall off at the first sudden movement. But it was the complex structure and coloration of the partially folded wings, seemingly made of iridescent gossamer stretched across a framework of impossibly thin twigs, that made her realize that, alien or not, this insect was one of the most beautiful creatures she had ever seen—and she could see it very clearly because its limbs were no longer trembling.

"Thank you again, Cha Thrat," the empath said. "You learn quickly. And don't worry. We are your friends and are wishing for your success."

Edanelt's feet were making irregular clicking noises against the floor, a sound that might possibly be indicating impatience. It said, "Please present your patient, Doctor."

For a moment she looked down at the Earth-human, at the pink, oddly formed alien body that, as a result of the accident, had become so familiar to her. She remembered how it had looked when she first saw it: the bleeding, open wounds and the fractured, protruding bones; the general condition that strongly indicated the immediate use of comforting medication until casualty termination. Even now she could not find the words to explain why she had not ended this Earth-human's life. She looked up again at the Cinrusskin.

Prilicla did not speak, but she felt as if waves of reassurance and encouragement were emanating from the little empath. That was a ridiculous idea, of course, and probably the result of wishful and not very lucid thinking, but she felt comforted nonetheless.

"This patient," Cha Thrat said calmly, "was one of three occupants of an aircraft that crashed into a mountain lake. A Sommaradvan pilot and another Earth-human were taken from the wreck before it sank, but they were already dead. The patient was taken ashore and looked at by a healer who was insufficiently qualified, and, knowing that I was spending a recreation period in the area, he sent for me.

"The patient had sustained many incised and lacerated wounds to the limbs and torso caused by violent contact with the metal of the aircraft," she went on. "There was continuing blood loss. Differences in the appearance of the limbs on the right and left sides indicated the presence of multiple fractures, one of which was visible where it projected through the tegument of the left leg. There was no evidence of blood coming from the patient's breathing and speaking orifices, so it was assumed that no serious injuries had been sustained in the lung and abdominal areas. Naturally, very careful consideration had to be given before I agreed to take the case."

"Naturally," Edanelt said. "You were faced with treating a member of an off-planet species, one possessing a physiology and metabolism of which you had no previous experience. Or had you previous experience? Did you consider sending for same-species medical assistance?"

"I had not seen an Earth-human before that time," Cha Thrat replied. "I knew that one of their ships was in orbit around Sommaradva and that the process of establishing friendly contact was well advanced. I had heard that they were traveling widely among our principal cities, and that they often used our air transport, presumably to gain some experience of our level of technology. I sent a message to the nearest city hoping that they would relay it to the Earth-humans, but it was unlikely that it would arrive in time. The area is remote, mountainous, heavily forested, and thinly populated. The facilities were limited and time was short."

"I understand," Edanelt said. "Describe your procedure."

Remembering, Cha Thrat looked again at the network of scars and the dark, contused areas where the subdermal bleeding had not completely dispersed.

"At the time of treatment I was not aware of the fact that native pathogens have no effect on life-forms which evolved on a different planet, and it seemed to me that there was a grave danger of infection. It was also thought that Sommaradvan medication and anesthetics would be ineffective if not lethal. The only indicated procedure was to thoroughly irrigate the wounds, particularly those associated with the fractures, with distilled water. While reducing the fractures, some minor repairs were required to damaged blood vessels in the area. The incised wounds were sutured, covered, and the fractured limbs immobilized. The work was done very quickly because the patient was conscious and . . ."

"Not for long," Chiang said in a low voice. "I passed out."

". . . and the pulse seemed weak and irregular," she went on, "even though I didn't know the normal rate. The only means available to counteract shock and the effects of blood loss were external heating, provided by wood fires placed downwind so that smoke and ash would not contaminate the operative field, and pure water given intravenously when consciousness was lost. I was unsure whether our saline solution would be beneficial or toxic. I realize now that I was being overcautious, but I did not want to risk losing a limb."

"Naturally," Edanelt said. "Now describe your postoperative treatment."

"The patient regained consciousness late that evening," Cha Thrat went on. "It appeared to be mentally and verbally lucid, although the exact meaning of some words were unclear since they referred to the consigning of the faulty aircraft, the whole current situation, and myself to some hypothetical but extremely unpleasant afterlife. Since the native edible vegetation was likely to prove harmful, only water administered orally could be given. The patient complained of severe discomfort at the site of the wounds. Native pain-relief medication could not be given because it might prove toxic, so that the condition could only be treated, however inadequately, by verbal reassurance and encouragement—"

"For three days she never stopped talking," Chiang said. "Asking questions about my work, and what I would be doing after I returned to active duty, when I was pretty sure that I would be returning in a box. She talked so much, sometimes, that I just fell asleep."

There was a slight tremor apparent in Prilicla's limbs. Cha Thrat wondered if the Cinrusskin was sensitive even to the Earth-human's remembered pain.

She resumed. "In response to several urgent requests, five members of the patient's species, one of whom was a healer, arrived with supplies of suitable food and supportive medication. Progress toward recovery was rapid thereafter. The Earth-human healer gave advice on diet and medication dosage, and it was free to examine the patient at any time, but I would not allow further surgical intervention. I should explain that on Sommaradva, a surgeon will not share or in any other way avoid personal responsibility for a patient. There was strong criticism, both personal and professional, of my standpoint, particularly from the Earth-human healer. I would not allow the patient to be moved to its ship until eighteen days after the operation, when I was convinced that full recuperation was assured."

"She watched over me," Chiang said, barking softly, "like an old mother hen."

There was silence for what seemed to Cha Thrat to be a very long time, during which everyone looked at the Melfan while it regarded the patient. It was tapping one hard-tipped leg against the floor, but the sound it made was a thoughtful rather than an impatient one.

Finally it said, "Without immediate surgical attention you would undoubtedly have died as a result of your injuries, and you were fortunate indeed to receive the necessary attention from an entity completely unfamiliar with your physiological classification. Fortunate, too, in that the entity concerned was not only skilled, resourceful, and deeply concerned with your aftercare, but made the proper use of the limited facilities available to it. I can find no serious fault with the surgical work performed here, and the patient is, indeed, wasting the hospital's time."

Suddenly they were all looking at her, but it was the empath who spoke first.

"From Edanelt," Prilicla said, "that is praise indeed."

Chapter 3

THE private office of the Earth-human O'Mara was large, but the floor area was almost entirely covered by a variety of chairs, benches, recliners and frames designed for the use of the entities having business with the Chief Psychologist. Chiang took the indicated Earth-human chair and Cha Thrat chose a low, convoluted cage that looked as if it might not be too uncomfortable, and sat down.

She saw at once that O'Mara was an old Earth-human. The short, bristling fur covering the top and sides of its head, and the two thick crescents above its eyes, were the gray color of unpainted metal. But the heavy muscle structure apparent in the shoulders, upper limbs, and hands was not that of the other aged Earth-humans she had seen. The flexible, fleshy covers of its eyes, which were similar in color to its hair, did not droop as it studied her in every physical detail.

"You are a stranger among us, Cha Thrat," it said abruptly. "I am here to help you feel less strange, to answer questions you have been unable or unwilling to ask of others, and to see how your present abilities can be trained and extended so that they may be put to the best possible use by the hospital."

It turned its attention to Chiang. "My intention was to interview you separately, but for some reason you wish to be present during my initial talk with Cha Thrat. Can it be that you have heard, and believed, some of the things the staff say about me? Do you have delusions of being a gentleman and Cha Thrat a lady, albeit of a different physiological classification, who if not actually in distress is a friend in need of moral support? Is that it, Major?"

Chiang barked quietly but did not speak.

"A question," Cha Thrat said. "Why do Earth-humans make that strange barking sound?"

O'Mara turned its head to regard her for a long moment, then it exhaled loudly and said, "I had expected your first question to be more ... profound. But very well. The sound is called laughing, not barking, and in most cases it is a psychophysical mechanism for the release of minor degrees of tension. An Earth-human laughs because of a sudden relief from worry or fear, or to express scorn or disbelief or sarcasm, or in response to words or a situation that is ridiculous, illogical, or funny, or out of politeness when the situation or words are *not* funny but the person responsible is of high rank. I shall not even try to explain sarcasm or the Earth-human sense of humor to you, because we don't fully understand them ourselves. For reasons that will become clearer the longer you stay here, I rarely laugh."

For some reason Chiang barked—laughed—again.

Ignoring it, O'Mara went on. "Senior Physician Edanelt is satisfied regarding your professional competence and suggests that I assign you to a suitable ward as soon as possible. Before that happens you must become more familiar with the layout, operation, and work of the hospital. You will find that it is a very dangerous and frightening place to the uninformed. At present, that is you."

"I understand," Cha Thrat said.

"The people who will impart this very necessary information," it went on, "are of many different physiological types and medical and technical specialities. They will range from Diagnosticians, Senior Physicians, and healers like, or totally unlike, yourself, to nursing staff, and laboratory and maintenance technicians. Some of them will be your medical or administrative superiors, others will be nominally subordinate to you, but the knowledge they impart is equally valuable. I'm told that you are averse to sharing patient responsibility. While learning you may, at the discretion of the doctor in charge, be allowed to practice, but under close supervision. Do you understand, and agree?"

"I do," Cha Thrat said unhappily. It was going to be her first year in the School for Warrior-Surgeons on Sommaradva all over again but, hopefully, without the attendant nonmedical problems.

"This interview," O'Mara went on, "will not decide whether or not you are accepted as a permanent member of the hospital staff. I cannot tell you what or what not to do in every situation that will arise; you must learn by observation and attention to the words of your tutors and decide that for yourself. But if there are really serious problems that you are unable to solve for yourself, you may come to me for guidance. Naturally, the fewer visits you make to this office the better disposed I shall feel toward you. I shall be receiving continuous reports on your progress, or lack of it, and it is these that will decide whether or not you remain here."

It paused briefly and moved the digits of one hand through the short gray head-fur. She watched carefully but saw no sign of dislodged parasites, and decided that the movement was an unthinking one.

"This interview," O'Mara continued, "is intended to explore some of the nonmedical aspects of your treatment of Chiang. In the short time available I would like to learn as much as possible about you as a person: your feelings, motivations, fears, likes, and dislikes, that sort of thing. Is there any area in which you would not want to answer questions, or would give obscure or false answers, because of moral or parental or community tribal conditioning during childhood or maturity? I must warn you that I am capable of detecting a lie, even the weird and wonderfully complicated lies that some of our extraterrestrials tell, but it takes time and I have none of that to waste."

She thought for a moment, then said, "There are matters involving sexual encounters that I would rather not discuss, but all other answers will be complete and truthful."

"Good!" O'Mara said. "I have no intention of entering that area and, hopefully, may never have to do so. At present I am interested in your thoughts and feelings between the time you first saw your patient and the decision to operate, any relevant discussion between the healer who was first on the scene and yourself, and the reason for the delay in starting the operation when you did take charge. If you had any strong feelings at that time, please describe and explain them if you can, and speak as the thoughts come to you."

For a moment Cha Thrat tried to recall her exact feelings at the time, then she said, "I was spending but not enjoying an enforced vacation in the area, because I would have preferred to continue working in my hospital instead of trying to devise ways of wasting time. When I heard of the accident I was almost pleased, thinking at first that the survivor was a Sommaradvan, and there was proper work for me to do. Then I saw the Earth-human's injuries and knew that the local healer would not dare touch it because he was a healer of serviles. Even though the survivor was not a Sommaradvan warrior, it was plainly a warrior injured in the course of its duty.

"I am uncertain about your units of time measurement," she went on. "The crash occurred just before sunrise, and I reached the shore of the lake where Chiang had been placed shortly before the time of the morning meal. Without proper medication or knowledge of the body structure, many things had to be considered. The sensible course would have been to allow the survivor to bleed to death or, out of kindness, expedite matters by immersing it in the lake . . ."

She stopped for a moment because O'Mara seemed to have a temporary blockage of the breathing passages, then she resumed. "After several examinations and evaluations of the risks, surgery was begun early in the afternoon. At the time I did not know that Chiang was the ruler of a ship."

The two Earth-humans exchanged looks, and O'Mara said, "That was five, maybe six hours later. Do you usually take as long as that to reach a professional decision? And would it have made any difference if you had known of Chiang's importance?"

"There were many risks to consider—I did not want to risk losing a limb," she replied sharply, sensing a criticism. "And yes, it should have made a difference. A warrior-surgeon is in the same position to a ruler as the servile-healer is in relation to a warrior. I am forbidden to practice beyond my qualifications. The penalties are most severe, even allowing for the increasingly lax standards so prevalent these days. But in this instance, well, it was a unique situation. I felt frightened, and excited, and I would probably have acted in the same way."

O'Mara said, "I'm glad you don't normally practice surgery beyond your level of competence..."

"It's a good thing she did," Chiang said softly.

"...And your tutors will be relieved as well," O'Mara went on. "But I'm interested in this stratification of the Sommaradvan medical profession. Can you tell me about that?"

Puzzled by what seemed to be a nonsense question, she replied, "We are not forbidden to talk about anything. On Sommaradva there are three levels of persons —serviles, warriors, and rulers—and three levels of healers to care for them..."

At the bottom were the serviles, the people whose work was undemanding and repetitious—important in many respects, but completely without risk. They were a contented group, protected from gross physical damage, and the healers charged with their care used very simple procedures and medication such as herbs, poultices, and other traditional remedies. The second level, less numerous than the serviles, were the warriors, who occupied positions of responsibility and often great physical danger.

There had been no war on Sommaradva for many generations, but the warrior class had kept the name. They were the descendants of the people who had fought to protect their homelands, hunted for food, raised city defenses, and generally performed the dangerous, responsible jobs while the serviles saw to their physical needs. Now they were the engineers, technicians, and scientists who still performed the high-risk jobs associated with mining, power generation, large-scale construction, and the protection of rulers. For that reason the injuries sustained by warriors were and always had been traumatic in nature, requiring surgical intervention or repair, and this work was the responsibility of the warrior-surgeons.

The ruler-healers had even greater responsibilities and, at times, much less reward or satisfaction in their work.

Protected against all physical accident or injury, the ruler class were the administrators, academics, researchers, and planners on Sommaradva. They were the people charged with the smooth running of the cities and the continents and the world, and the ills that affected them were invariably the phantasms of the mind. Their healers dealt in wizardry, spells, sympathetic magic, and all the other aspects of nonphysical medicine.

"Even from the earliest times the practice of healing has been so divided," Cha Thrat concluded, "into physicians and surgeons and wizards."

When she finished speaking, O'Mara looked down for a moment at its hands, which were placed palms down on its desktop, and said quietly, "It's nice to know that I would rate the top level of the Sommaradvan medical profession, but I'm not sure that I like being called a wizard." It looked up suddenly. "What happens if one of your warriors or rulers gets a simple tummyache, instead of a traumatic injury or an emotional problem? Or if a servile should accidentally break a leg? Or what if a ser-

vile or a warrior is dissatisfied and wants to better itself?"

"The Cultural Contact people sent you a full report on
all this," Chiang broke in, "as background material on
the new medic." Apologetically it added, "The decision
to send Cha Thrat was taken at the last moment, and
possibly the report arrived with us on *Thromasaggar*."

O'Mara exhaled loudly, and she wondered if it was an
expression of irritation at the interruption, then said,
"And the hospital's internal mail system operates at a
speed considerably less than that of light. Please go on,
Cha Thrat."

"In the highly unlikely event of a servile having such
an accident," she said, "a request for treatment would be
made to a warrior-surgeon who, depending on assessment of the injuries, would or would not agree to do the
work. Responsibility for a patient is not taken lightly on
Sommaradva, as is shown by the delay in treating
Chiang, and the loss of a life, an organ, or a limb has
serious repercussions for the surgeon.

"Should a warrior or ruler require simple medical attention," she continued, "a servile-healer would be instructed, and would indeed be honored, to provide the
necessary assistance.

"If a discontented servile or warrior is able as well as
ambitious," she went on, "elevation to a higher level is
possible. But the examinations are wide-ranging and difficult, and it is much easier to remain at the level tradi-
tionally occupied by the family or tribe or, if a release
from problems and responsibilities is desired, to go down
a level. Promotions, even minor promotions within a
level, are not easy on Sommaradva."

"Nor are they easy here," O'Mara said. "But why did
you come to Sector General? Ambition, curiosity, or a
release from problems at home?"

This was an important question, Cha Thrat knew, and the quality and accuracy of the answer would have an important bearing on whether or not she was accepted by the hospital. She tried to frame the answer so that it would be accurate, truthful, and brief, but before she could reply the ship ruler was talking again.

"We were grateful to Cha Thrat for saving my life," Chiang said, speaking very quickly, "and we told her colleagues and superiors so in no uncertain language. The subject of treatment by other-species medics came up, and Sector General, where it was the rule rather than the exception. It was suggested to us, and we agreed, that Cha Thrat should come here. The Sommaradvan cultural contact is going very well and we didn't want to risk offending, perhaps insulting, them by refusing.

"I realize that we bypassed the normal candidate selection procedure," it continued. "But her already-proven ability to perform other-species surgery, on me, made us sure that you would be interested in—"

O'Mara was holding up one hand, and it had not taken its attention from Cha Thrat while the other Earth-human had been speaking. It said, "Is this a political appointment, then, which we must accept whether we like it or not? But the original question remains. Why did you want to come here?"

"I didn't want to come here," she replied. "I was sent."

Chiang covered its eyes suddenly with one hand, a gesture she had never seen it make before. O'Mara looked at her for a moment, then said, "Explain."

"When the warriors of the Monitor Corps told us of the many different intelligent species who make up the Galactic Federation," she replied, "and talked to me at great length about Sector General, where I could meet and work with many of these life-forms, I was curious, interested, but much too frightened by the prospect of meeting not one but nearly seventy different species to risk undergoing an experience that might give me a ruler's disease. I told everyone who would listen my feelings, and reminded them of my utter lack of competence in relation to the level of surgery practiced here. I was not pretending to modesty. I really was, and am, ignorant. Because I was warrior level, I could not be forced, but it was strongly suggested by my colleagues and local rulers that I come."

"Ignorance can be a temporary condition," O'Mara said. "And it must have been a pretty strong suggestion. Why was it made?"

"In my hospital I am respected but not liked," she went on, hoping that the anger in her voice was not reproduced by the translator. "In spite of being one of the first female warrior-surgeons, an innovation in itself, I am a traditionalist. I will not tolerate the reduced standards of professional behavior that are becoming increasingly prevalent, and I am critical of colleagues and superiors alike if they become lax. It was suggested to me that if I did not take advantage of the opportunity being offered by the Earth-humans, there would be a continuing increase of the nonmaterial pressures associated with my work as a surgeon. The situation was too complex for me to describe briefly, but my rulers made suggestions to the Monitor Corps, who were very reassuring and persuasive. The Earth-humans pulled while my superiors pushed, and I am here.

"Now that I am here," she ended, "I shall use my limited abilities, under direction, as best I can."

O'Mara was looking at the ship ruler now. Chiang had taken its hand away from its eyes, but its pink face was a deeper color than she had ever seen before.

"The Sommaradvan contact was widening nicely,"

Chiang said, "but it was at a delicate stage. We didn't want to risk refusing what seemed to them to be such a small favor. And anyway, we were pretty sure that they were giving Cha Thrat a hard time and we—I—thought she would be happier here."

"So," O'Mara said, still looking at the ship ruler, whose face was now an even deeper shade of pink, "we have not only a political appointee but an unwilling volunteer and possibly a misfit. And, out of a misplaced sense of gratitude, you tried to conceal the true situation from me. That's great!"

It turned to face Cha Thrat again and said, "I appreciate your truthfulness. This material will be useful in the preparation of your psych profile but it does not, in spite of what your misguided friend may think, preclude your acceptance by the hospital provided the other requirements are satisfied. Those you will learn during training, which will begin first thing in our morning."

The words were coming faster than before, as if O'Mara's time for talking were limited, as it went on. "In the outer office you will be given an information package, maps, class schedules, general rules, and advice, all printed in the most widely used language on Sommaradva. Some of our trainees will tell you that their first and most difficult test was finding their rooms.

"Good luck, Cha Thrat."

As she was picking her way between the alien furniture toward the door, O'Mara was saying "I'm primarily interested in your postoperative emotional condition, Major Chiang. Have there been any waking fears, recurrent nightmares, unexplained episodes of tension, with or without accompanying perspiration, associated with the operation? Any feelings of drowning, strangulation, increasing and unreasoning fear of the dark? . . ."

Truly, she thought, *O'Mara was a great wizard.*

In the outer office, the Earth-human Braithwaite gave verbal as well as printed advice together with a white band to wear on one of her upper arms. It signified to all that she was a trainee, it said, laughing, and likely to become confused and lost. Should that happen she could ask any member of the hospital staff for directions. It, too, ended by wishing her well.

Finding the way to her room was a nightmare worse, she was sure, than any that Chiang might be relating to O'Mara. She needed directions on two occasions, and each time she asked groups of the silver-furred Kelgians who seemed to be everywhere in the hospital, rather than any of the great, lumbering monsters or the squishy beings in chlorine envelopes who crowded past her. But on both occasions, in spite of the respectful manner of her request, the information was given in a most rude and abrupt fashion.

Her immediate feeling was one of severe personal offense. But then she saw that the Kelgians were rude and short-tempered even to other members of their own species, and she decided that it might be better not to upbraid them for their extreme lack of politeness toward a stranger.

When she at last located her room, the door was wide open and the Earth-human Timmins was lying prone on the floor and holding a small metal box that was making quiet noises and winking its lights.

"Just testing," Timmins said. "I'll be finished in a moment. Look around. The operating instructions for everything are on the table. If there is anything you don't understand, use the communicator to call Staff Training, they'll help you." It rolled onto its back and got to its feet in a way that was physically impossible for a Sommaradvan, and added, "What do you think of the place?"

"I'm—I'm surprised," Cha Thrat said, feeling almost

shocked by its familiarity. "And delighted. It's just like my quarters at home."

"We aim to please," Timmins said. It raised one hand in a gesture she did not understand, and was gone.

For a long time she moved about the small room examining the furniture and equipment, not quite believing what she saw and felt. She knew that photographs and measurements had been taken of her quarters in the warrior-surgeon level at the Calgren House of Healing, but she had not expected such close attention to detail in the reproduction of her favorite pictures, wall coverings, lighting, and personal utilities. There were differences, too, some obvious and others subtle, to remind her that this place, despite appearances to the contrary, was not on her home world.

The room itself was larger and the furniture more comfortable, but there were no joints visible in the construction. It was as if every item had been fabricated in one piece. All the doors and drawers and fastenings in the replicas worked perfectly, which the originals had never done, and the air smelled different—in fact, it did not smell at all.

Gradually her initial feelings of pleasure and relief were being diluted by the realization that this was nothing more than a tiny, familiar bubble of normality inside a vast, alien, and terrifyingly complex structure. The fear and anxiety she was beginning to feel were greater than she had ever experienced on her incredibly distant home planet, and with them was a growing degree of loneliness so acute that it felt like an intense, physical hunger.

But she was not liked or wanted on far Sommaradva, and here, at least, they had taken positive measures to welcome her, so much so that she had to remain in this terrible place if only to discharge the obligation. And she would try to learn as much as she could before the hospital rulers decided that she was unsuitable and sent her home.

She should start learning now.

Was the hunger real, she wondered, rather than imaginary? She had not been able to eat to repletion during the earlier visit to the dining hall because her mind had been on matters other than food. She began to plan the route there, and to the location of her first lecture in the morning, from her present position. But she did not feel like another trip along the hospital's weirdly populated corridors just yet. She was very tired, and the room had a limited-menu food dispenser for trainees who did not wish to interrupt their studies by going to the dining hall.

She referred to the list of foods suited to her metabolism and tapped for medium-to-large portions. When she was feeling comfortably distended, she tried to sleep.

The room and the corridor outside were full of quiet, unidentifiable sounds, and she did not know enough to be able to ignore them. Sleep would not come and she was beginning to feel afraid again, and to wonder if her thoughts and feelings were of the kind to interest the wizard O'Mara, and that made her even more fearful for her future at Sector General. While still lying at rest, physically if not mentally, she used the ceiling projection facility of the communicator to see what was happening on the entertainment and training channels.

According to the relevant information sheet, ten of the channels continuously screened some of the Galactic Federation's most popular entertainment, current interest, and drama programs with a translator output, if required. But she discovered that while she could understand the words that the different physiological types were saying to and about each other, the accompanying actions were in turn horrifying, mystifying, ridicu-

lous, or downright obscene to Sommaradvan eyes. She
switched to the training channels.

There she had a choice of watching displays of currently meaningless figures and tabulations on the temperatures, blood pressures, and pulse rates of about fifty
different life-forms, or surgical operations in progress
that were visually disquieting and not calculated to lull
anyone to sleep.

In desperation, Cha Thrat tried the sound-only channels. But the music she found, even when the volume
was reduced to bare audibility, sounded as if it were
coming from a piece of malfunctioning heavy machinery.
So it was a great surprise when the room alarm began
reminding her, monotonously and with steadily increasing volume, that it was time to awaken if she required
breakfast before her first lecture.

Chapter 4

THE lecturer was a Nidian who had been intro-
duced as Senior Physician Cresk-Sar. While it was
speaking, it prowled up and down the line of trainees like
some small, hairy, carnivorous beast, which meant that
every few minutes it passed Cha Thrat so closely that
she wanted to either fold her limbs in defensive mode or
run away.

"To minimize verbal confusion during meetings with
other-species entities," it was saying, "and to avoid in-

advertently giving offense, it is assumed that all members of the medical and support staff who do not belong to your own particular species are sexless. Whether you are addressing them directly or discussing them in their absence, you will always think of them as an 'it'. The only exception to this rule is when an other-species patient is being treated for a condition directly related to its sex, in which case the doctor must know whether it is male or female, or one of the multisexed species, if the proper treatment is to be carried out.

"I am a male Nidian DBDG," Cresk-Sar went on, "but do not think of me as 'he' or 'him'. Think of me as 'it'."

As the disgusting, hairy shape moved to within a few paces of her before turning away again, Cha Thrat thought that she would have no difficulty in thinking of this Senior Physician as "it."

With the intention of finding someone less repulsive to look at, she turned her eyes toward the trainee closest to her—one of the three silver-furred Kelgians attending the lecture. It was strange, she thought, how the Nidian's fur made her cringe inwardly while the equally alien covering of the Kelgian relaxed and calmed her like a work of great art. The fur was in constant motion, with long, slow ripples moving from the creature's conical head right down to its tail, with occasional cross-eddies and wavelets appearing, as if the incredibly fine pelt was a liquid stirred by an unfelt wind. At first she thought the movements were random, but a pattern of ripples and eddies seemed to be developing the more closely she watched.

"What are you staring at?" the Kelgian said suddenly, its translated words overlaid by the moaning and hissing sounds of its native speech. "Do I have a bald patch, or something?"

"I'm sorry, I had not meant to give offense," Cha Thrat said. "Your fur is beautiful and I couldn't help admiring it the way it moves—"

"Pay attention, you two!" the Senior Physician said sharply. It moved closer, looked up at each of them in turn, then went prowling down the line again.

"Cresk-Sar's fur," the Kelgian said softly, "is a sight. It makes me think that invisible and no doubt imaginary parasites are about to change their abode. It gives me a terrible psychosomatic itch."

This time Cresk-Sar gave them another long look, made an irritated, snuffling sound that did not translate, and continued with what it was saying.

". . . There is a great deal of illogical behavior associated with sexual differences," it went on, "and I must emphasize once again, unless the sex of a particular entity has a direct bearing on its course of treatment, the subject must be ignored if not deliberately avoided. Some of you may consider that such knowledge of another species would be helpful, conversationally useful during off-duty meetings or, as often happens in this place, when a particularly interesting piece of gossip is circulating. But believe me, in this area, ignorance is a virtue."

"Surely," said a Melfan trainee halfway down the line, "there are interspecies social occasions, shared meals or lectures, when it would be a gross act of bad manners to ignore another intelligent and socially aware person's gender. I think that—"

"And *I* think," Cresk-Sar said with a bark, or laugh, "that you are what our Earth-human friends call a gentleman. You haven't been listening. Ignore the difference. Consider everyone who is not of your own species as neuter. In any case, you would have to observe some of our other-species people very closely to tell the differ-

ence, and that in itself could cause serious embarrassment. In the case of Hudlar life-mates, who alternate
between male and female mode, the behavior patterns
are quite complex."

"What would happen," the Kelgian beside her said,
"if they should go, completely or partly, out of
synchronization?"

From the line of trainees there were a number of different sounds, none of which registered on her translator. The Senior Physician was looking at the Kelgian,
whose fur, for some reason, had begun to move in rapid,
irregular ripples.

"I shall treat that as a serious question," Cresk-Sar
said, "although I doubt that it was intended as such.
Rather than answer it myself, I shall ask one of you to do
so. Would the Hudlar trainee please step forward."

So *that*, Cha Thrat thought, is a Hudlar.

It was a squat, heavy life-form with a hard, almost
featureless dark-gray skin, discolored by patches of the
dried paint she had seen it spraying on itself before they
had entered the lecture theater, and she had decided then
that it was extremely careless in its application of cos-
metics. The body was supported on six heavy tentacles,
each of which terminated in a cluster of flexible digits,
curled inward so that the weight was borne on heavy
knuckles and the fingers remained clear of the floor.

There were no body openings that she could see, not
even in the head, which contained eyes protected by
hard, transparent shells and a semicircular membrane
that vibrated to produce the creature's words as it turned
toward them.

"It is very simple, respected colleagues," the Hudlar
said. "While I am presently male, Hudlars are all sexually neutral until puberty, after which the direction
taken is dependent on social-environmental influences,

sometimes quite subtle influences that do not involve body contact. A picture of an attractive male-mode Hudlar might impel one from neuter toward female mode, or the other way around. A conscious choice can be made if the career one intends to follow favors a particular sex. Unless one is mated, the postpuberty sex choice is fixed for the remainder of one's life.

"When two adults become life-mates," the Hudlar went on, "that is, when they join for the purpose of becoming parents and not simply for temporary pleasure, the sex changes are initiated shortly after conception. By the time the child is born the male has become much less aggressive, more attentive and emotionally oriented toward its mate, while its mate is beginning to lose the female characteristics. Following parturition, the process continues, with the father-that-was taking responsibility for the child while progressing to full female mode, and the mother develops all the male characteristics that will enable it to be a father-to-be.

"There is, of course, a time during which both life-mates are emotional neuters," the Hudlar added, "but this is a period of the pregnancy when physical coupling is contraindicated."

"Thank you," the Senior Physician said, but held up a small, hairy hand to indicate that the Hudlar should remain where it was. "Any further comments, questions?"

It was looking at the Kelgian beside her, the one who had asked the original question, but Cha Thrat spoke on impulse.

"It seems to me that the Hudlars are fortunate," she said, "in that they are not troubled by the situation of the members of one sex considering themselves innately superior to the other, as is the case on Sommaradva . . ."

"And on too many other worlds of the Federation,"

the Kelgian interjected, the fur rising into tufts behind its head.

". . . I thank the Hudlar for its explanation," Cha Thrat went on, "but I was surprised to find that it is presently a male. My first thought, based on observation of what I mistakenly assumed to be cosmetic paint on its body, was that it was female."

The Hudlar's speaking membrane began to vibrate, but Cresk-Sar held its hand up for silence and said, "What are your second thoughts?"

Confused, she stared at the hairy little creature, wondering what she was expected to say.

"Come, come," Cresk-Sar barked. "Tell us what other thoughts, observations, assumptions, mistaken or otherwise, have been going through your Sommaradvan mind regarding this life-form. Think and speak clearly."

Cha Thrat turned all her eyes on it in a way that, had it been a Sommaradvan, would have elicited an immediate verbal and physical response. She said, "My first thoughts were as described. My second was that it might be Hudlar males rather than females, or perhaps both, who wear decorative paint. Then I observed that the being's movements were careful, as if it was afraid of injuring nearby people and equipment, the movements of a gentle being of immense physical strength. That taken in conjunction with the low, squat form of the body, with six rather than two or four limbs, suggested that it was a native of a dense, heavy-gravity world with comparable atmospheric pressure, where an accidental fall would be damaging. The very hard but flexible skin, which is unbroken by any permanent body orifices for the intake or elimination of food, suggested that the paint which I had observed the Hudlar spraying onto itself might be a nutrient solution."

The eyes of Cresk-Sar, and the variegated visual sensors of the other trainees, were watching her steadily. Nobody spoke.

Hesitantly she added, "Another thought, wonderful and exciting but, I expect, pure supposition, is that if this heavy-gravity, high-pressure creature can live unprotected in the hospital surroundings, its body must be capable of containing its own very high internal pressures, and an even lower pressure environment should not inconvenience it.

"It might be possible," she went on, expecting a storm of ridicule from the Nidian Senior, "for it to work unprotected in space. This would mean that—"

"At any moment," Cresk-Sar said, holding its hand up, "you will give me its physiological classification coding, even though we haven't covered that yet. Is this the first time you've seen a Hudlar?"

"I saw two of them in the dining hall," she replied, "but at the time I was too confused to know what I was seeing."

"May your confusion continue to diminish, Cha Thrat," Cresk-Sar said. Turning its head toward the others, it went on, "This trainee has displayed the qualities of observation and deduction that, when trained and refined, will enable you to live among, understand, and treat your other-species colleagues and patients. However, I would advise you not to think of a particular lifeform as a Nidian, a Hudlar, a Kelgian, a Melfan, or a Sommaradvan, that is, by their planets of origin, but by their physiological classifications, DBDG, FROB, DBLF, ELNT, or DCNF. That way you will always be reminded of their pressure, gravity, and atmosphere requirements, basic metabolism and other physiological needs, and know immediately when there is a potential environmental threat to them or to yourselves."

It continued, "Should a PVSJ, a chlorine-breathing

native of Illensa, accidentally rupture its pressure envelope, the risk to the being concerned and to any oxygen-
breathing D, E, and F prefixes in the vicinity would be
extreme. And, if you are ever called to a space rescue
situation, there may be times when an urgent and accurate identification of the casualty's physiological classification, and therefore its life-support requirements, may
depend on a single limb or small area of body surface
glimpsed under shifting wreckage.

"You must train yourselves to be aware, instinctively,
of all the differences of the people around you," Cresk-
Sar went on, giving a low laugh-bark, "if only to know
whom it is safe to jostle in the corridors. And now I will
take you to the wards for your initial patient experience
before my next class in—"

"What about the classification system?" said the
silver-furred Kelgian—the DBLF, Cha Thrat corrected
herself—beside her. "If it is as important as you say it is,
surely you are lacking in the qualities of a teacher not to
have explained it to us."

Cresk-Sar walked slowly toward the speaker, and she
wondered if she could possibly reduce the verbal violence to come by asking the Senior Physician another
and more politely worded question. But for some reason
the Nidian completely ignored the DBLF and spoke instead to Cha Thrat.

"You will already have observed," it said, "that these
Kelgian DBLF life-forms are outspoken, ill-mannered,
rude, and completely lacking in tact . . ."

You should talk, Cha Thrat thought.

". . . But there are good psychophysiological reasons
for this," it went on. "Because of inadequacies in the
Kelgian speech organs, their spoken language lacks mod-
ulation, inflection, and all emotional expression. But
they are compensated by their highly mobile fur that

acts, so far as another Kelgian is concerned, as a perfect but uncontrollable mirror to the speaker's emotional state. As a result the concept of lying, of being diplomatic, tactful, or even polite is completely alien to them. A DBLF says exactly what it means or feels, because the fur reveals its feelings from moment to moment and to do otherwise would be sheer stupidity. The opposite also holds true, because politeness and the verbal circumlocution used by many species confuses and irritates them.

"You will find some of the personalities here as alien as the persons," it continued. "Considering the fact that you have met only one other-species being before your arrival here, your behavior today makes me sure that you will have not trouble in adapting to—"

"Teacher's pet," the DBLF said, its fur tufting into spikes. "I was the one who asked the question, remember?"

"That you did," Cresk-Sar replied, looking at the wall chronometer. "Tapes covering the life-form physiological classification system will be sent to your quarters sometime today. You must study the visual material they contain, carefully and repeatedly, and use your translators on the spoken commentary. But now I have time only to outline the basics of the system."

It turned suddenly and resumed its place facing them. Plainly the answer to the question was being directed toward everyone.

"Unless you have already been attached to one of the smaller, multienvironment hospitals," Cresk-Sar said, "you will normally have encountered off-world patients one species at a time, probably on a short-term basis as a result of a ship accident, and you would refer to them by their planets of origin. But I must stress once again, the rapid and accurate identification of incoming patients is vital, because all too often they are in no condition to furnish the necessary physiological data themselves. Here we have evolved a basic, four-letter physiological classification system that enables us to provide the required life-support and initial treatment pending a more detailed investigation, if that should be necessary, by Pathology. It works like this.

"The first letter denotes the level of physical evolution reached by the species when it acquired intelligence," it continued. "The second indicates the type and distribution of limbs, sense organs, and body orifices, and the remaining two letters refer to the combination of metabolism and food and air requirements associated with the home planet's gravity and atmospheric pressure, which in turn gives an indication of the physical mass and protective tegument possessed by the being."

Cresk-Sar barked softly before saying "Usually I have to remind our other-species trainees at this point that the initial letter of their classification should not be allowed to give them feelings of inferiority, because the degree of physical evolution is controlled by environmental factors and bears little relation to the degree of intelligence . . ."

Species with the prefix A, B, or C, it went on to explain, were water-breathers. On most worlds, life had originated in the sea, and these beings had developed intelligence without having to leave it. D through F were warm-blooded oxygen-breathers, into which group most of the intelligent races of the Federation fell, and the G and K types were also oxygen breathing, but insectile. The Ls and Ms were light-gravity, winged beings.

Chlorine-breathing life-forms were contained in the O and P groups, and after these came the more exotic, the more highly evolved physically, and the downright weird types. Into these categories fell the radiation-eaters, the ultra-cold-blooded or crystalline beings, and entities capable of modifying their physical structure at will. However, those beings possessing extrasensory powers, telekinesis, or teleportation sufficiently well developed to make ambulatory or manipulatory appendages unnecessary were given the prefix V regardless of their size, shape, or environmental background.

"There are anomalies in the system," the Senior Physician continued, "and these must be blamed on the lack of imagination and foresight of the originator. The AACP life-form, for example, has a vegetable metabolism. Normally the A prefix denotes a water-breather, there being nothing lower on our evolutionary coding scale than the piscatorial life-forms. But the double-A prefix, the AACPs, are mobile, intelligent vegetables, and plant life evolved before the fish.

"And now," it said, looking at the chronometer again, "you will meet some of these weird and wonderful and perhaps horrifying creatures. It is the hospital's policy to give you the earliest possible opportunity of getting to know and work with the patients and staff members. Regardless of your position or seniority in your home-planet hospitals, your rank here will be that of Junior or Trainee Nurse—until, that is, you can convince me that your professional competence warrants a higher rating.

"I am not easy to convince," Cresk-Sar added as it began moving toward the exit. "Follow me, please."

It was not easy to follow the Senior Physician because it moved fast for such a small being, and Cha Thrat had the feeling that the other trainees were more experienced in navigating the hospital corridors than she was. But then she noticed that the Hudlar—the FROB—was falling behind as well.

"For obvious reasons," the FROB said as they drew level, "the people here give me plenty of room. If you

were to stay directly behind me, together we might sig-
nificantly increase our speed."

She had a sudden and shocking feeling of unreality, as
if she had been plunged into a nightmare world that was
both terrifying and wonderful, a world in which courtesy
was being shown by a horrendous beast that was capable
of tearing her apart without straining a muscle on one of
its six tentacles. But even if this were a dream, the
proper response had to be made.

"You are most considerate," she said. "Thank you."

The being's membrane vibrated but the sound did not
translate. Then it said, "About the nutrient paint you noticed earlier, to complete your information and to show
how close your deductions were to the actuality, the
paint is not necessary at home. There the atmosphere is
so dense and thickly packed with edible, floating organisms that it resembles a semiliquid soup, a food source
that, because of our high metabolic rate, is absorbed
continuously. As you can see, the last paint application
has almost disappeared and is due for renewal."

Before she could reply, one of the Kelgian DBLFs fell
back and said, "I was nearly walked on by a Tralthan
just now. This looks like a good idea. There's room for
one more."

It moved closer to Cha Thrat so that they were both
protected by the Hudlar's massive body. Choosing her
words carefully, she said, "I do not wish to give offense,
but I cannot tell the difference between one Kelgian and
another. Are you the DBLF whose fur I was admiring
during the lecture?"

"Admiring, you used the right word!" the Kelgian
said, its fur running in concentric waves from head to
tail. "Don't worry about it. If we had more than one
Sommaradvan, I couldn't tell the difference either."

Suddenly the Hudlar stopped and, looking past its

speaking membrane, she saw why. The whole group of trainees had halted and Cresk-Sar was beckoning to a Melfan and the other two Kelgians.

"This is a Tralthan post-op recovery ward," it said. You two will report here after lectures every day until instructed otherwise. You don't need protective suits, the air is breathable, and trace quantities of Tralthan body odor should be ignored. Go in, you're expected."

When the party was on its way again she noticed a few of the trainees detaching themselves without being told, and assumed that they had joined the class earlier and had already been assigned wards. One of them was her Hudlar crowd controller. Very soon the group had shrunk until there was only the DBLF and herself left, and Cresk-Sar was pointing at the Kelgian.

"This is a PVSJ medical ward," it said briskly. "You will be met inside the lock antechamber and instructed in the use of your protective envelope before going through. You will then—"

"But they're chlorine-breathers in there!" the Kelgian protested, its fur standing out in spikes. "Can't you give me a ward where I can at least breathe the air? Do you *try* to make it as difficult as possible for the new people? What happens if I accidentally rupture my suit?"

"To answer your questions in turn," the Senior Physician replied, "No. You've discovered that. And the nearby patients would have their existing injuries complicated by oxygen contamination."

"What about *me*, stupid?"

"You," Cresk-Sar said, "would suffer chlorine poisoning. And what the Charge Nurse would do to you if you recovered doesn't bear thinking about."

She had to concentrate so hard on keeping pace with the Senior Physician as they descended three levels, and traversed seemingly endless and overpopulated corridors, that there was no chance to ask what she would be expected to do. But then Cresk-Sar stopped at an enormous lock entrance that was visually identified in the Galactic Federation's principal written languages—but which did not, of course, include Sommaradvan—and answered the unasked question.

"This is the hospital's AUGL ward," it said. "You will find that the patients, all natives of the ocean world of Chalderescol, are among the most visually fearsome beings you are ever likely to encounter. But they are harmless so long as you—"

"The A prefix," Cha Thrat broke in urgently, "denotes water-breathers."

"Correct," the Nidian said. "What's wrong? Is there a problem O'Mara didn't tell me about? Are you uncomfortable or afraid in water?"

"No," Cha Thrat said. "I enjoy swimming, on the surface. The problem is my lack of a protective garment."

Cresk-Sar barked and said, "There is no problem. The more complex protective equipment for heavy-gravity, high-pressure, and elevated temperature work needs time to produce, but a simple, water-impermeable, contoured envelope with air and communication systems is an easy job for the fabricator. Your suit is waiting for you inside."

This time the Senior Physician went with her, explaining that, as she was a new life-form to the hospital, it had to ensure that her equipment functioned properly and comfortably. But in the event, it was the being waiting for them in the lock antechamber who immediately took charge and did all the talking.

"Cha Thrat," it said briskly, "I am Charge Nurse Hredlichli, a PVSJ. Your protective envelope is in two pieces. Climb into the lower half, pulling on one leg at a time, in whichever order you find most convenient, using the heavier arms encircling your waist. Use the same four arms to pull on the top half, inserting the head and four shoulder-mounted arms first. You will think that the limb end-sections are small, but this is to ensure a tight fit and maximum sensitivity for the digits. Don't seal the waist joint until you know that your air supply is working. When you are sealed in, I'll show you the systems checks that must be performed at every dressing. Then you will remove the envelope and put it on again, repeating the process until we are both happy with your performance. Please begin."

Hredlichli circled her, giving advice and directions during the first three dressings, and then seemed to ignore her while it talked to the Senior Physician. The spiney, membraneous body, looking like a haphazard collection of oily, unhealthy vegetation, was obscured by the yellow chlorine fog inside the being's protective envelope. It was impossible to tell where the Charge Nurse's attention was directed, because Cha Thrat had been unable to locate its eyes.

"We are seriously understaffed at present," Hredlichli was saying, "with three of my best nurses on special post-op recovery cases to the exclusion of all else. Are you hungry?"

Cha Thrat felt that the question was for her, but was unsure of the type of answer to give—the subservient, self-negating reply expected by a ruler or the accurate, truthful kind due a warrior-level colleague. Ignorant as she was of Hredlichli's exact status, she did her best to combine the two.

"I am hungry," she replied, using the opportunity to test her suit's communicator, "but the condition is not yet so advanced that it would impair me physically."

"Good!" said Hredlichli. "As a junior-in-training you will soon discover that practically everyone and everything takes precedence over you. If this causes emotional tension, which may be expressed as verbal resentment or anger, try not to release it until you are out of my ward. You will be allowed to visit your dining hall, for a strictly limited period, as soon as someone returns to relieve you. And now I think you know how your suit works..."

Cresk-Sar turned toward the entrance. Lifting one tiny, hairy hand, it said, "Good luck, Cha Thrat."

"...So we'll go inside to the Nurses' Station," it went on, seeming to ignore the departing Nidian. "Double-check your suit seals and follow me."

She found herself in a surprisingly small compartment that had one transparent wall giving a view into a dim green world where the difference between the inhabitants and the decorative vegetation designed to make them feel at home was unclear. The other three sides of the room were covered by storage units, monitor screens, and equipment whose purpose she could not even guess at. The entire ceiling was devoted to brightly colored signs and geometrical shapes.

"We have a very good staff and patient safety record in this ward," the Charge Nurse went on, "and I don't want you to spoil it. Should you damage your suit and be in danger of drowning, however, mouth-to-mouth resuscitation is not advisable between oxygen- and chlorine-breathers, so you must move quickly to one of the emergency air chambers marked so"—she indicated one of the ceiling designs—"and await rescue. But the accident, or should I say the serious inconvenience, that you must guard against is pollution by patient body wastes. Filtration or replacement of the water volume in a ward this size is a major maintenance operation that would hamper our work and get us talked about in derogatory fashion all over the hospital."

"I understand," Cha Thrat said.

Why had she come to this awful place, she wondered, and could she justify to herself her immediate resignation? In spite of the warnings from O'Mara and Cresk-Sar that she would be starting at the lowest level, this was not work for a Sommaradvan warrior-surgeon. If word of what she was expected to do were to get back to her erstwhile colleagues, she would be forced into the life of a recluse. But these people were not likely to tell her people about it because, to them, such activities were so commonplace as to be unworthy of mention. Perhaps she would be found unsuitable or incompetent and dismissed from the hospital with this demeaning and unpleasant episode secret and her honor intact. But she was dreading what was coming next.

But it was not nearly as bad as she had expected.

"The patients usually know in advance when they need to evacuate," Hredlichli went on, "and will call the nurse with time to spare. Should you be called for this purpose, the equipment you require is stored in the compartment with its door marked like this." A frondlike arm appeared inside its protective envelope, pointing to another distinctively marked panel on the ceiling, then to its distant, brightly lit twin that shone through the green dimness of the ward. It went on, "But don't worry, the patient will know all about the operation of the equipment and will prefer to help itself. Most of them dislike using the thing, you'll find that Chalders embarrass easily, and any who are not immobilized will prefer to use the room marked with that symbol. It is a long, narrow compartment barely large enough to contain one Chalder and is operated by the user. Extraction and filtration of the wastes is automatic, and if anything goes wrong it is a Maintenance problem."

Hredlichli's appendage rose again to point toward the

confusion of shapes at the other end of the ward. "If you need help with a patient, ask Nurse Towan. Most of its time is being spent with a seriously ill patient, so don't distract it unnecessarily. Later today I shall instruct you on the Chalder optimum pulse rate, pressure, and body temperature, and how and where to obtain them. The vital signs are taken and recorded at regular intervals, the frequency depending on the condition of the patient. You will also be shown how to sterilize and dress surgical wounds, which is not a simple job on a water-breather, and in a few days you may be allowed to do it yourself. But first you must get to know your patients."

The appendage was pointing at a doorless opening into the main ward. A sudden paralysis seemed to be affecting all twelve of Cha Thrat's limbs, and she tried desperately to delay any movement by asking questions.

"Nurse Towan," she said. "What species is it?"

"An AMSL," the Charge Nurse replied. "A Creppellian octopoid, and Sector General qualified, so you have nothing to worry about. The patients know that we are being assigned a new-species trainee and are expecting you. Your body configuration is well suited to the water medium, so I suggest that you go in and begin by teaching yourself how to move about the ward."

"Please, a further question," Cha Thrat said desperately. "The AMSL is a water-breather. Why aren't all of the medical attendants here water-breathers? Wouldn't it be simpler if they were Chalders, the same species as their patients?"

"You haven't even met a patient and already you're trying to reorganize the ward!" Hredlichli said, producing another appendage from somewhere and gesticulating with them both. "There are two reasons why we don't do as you suggest. One is that very large patients can be effectively treated by small medics, and Sector

General was designed with precisely that situation in mind. The second is structural. Personnel accommodation and recreation space is at a premium here, and can you imagine how much of it would be taken up by the life-support requirements of, say, a basic medical and nursing staff of one hundred water-breathing Chalders?

"But enough of this," the Charge Nurse said impatiently. "Go into the ward and act as if you know what you're doing. We'll talk later. If I don't go for lunch this instant, they'll find me in a corridor dead from malnutrition..."

It seemed like a very long time before she was able to venture into the green immensity of the ward, and then she swam only as far as a structural support less than five body-lengths from the entrance. The harsh, angular contours of the metal had been visually softened by irregular areas of paint and the attachment of artificial foliage, Cha Thrat saw as she swam around it, no doubt to make it resemble the vegetation of the home world.

Hredlichli had been right; she was able to adapt quickly to movement in water. When she kicked out with her feet and simultaneously swept the four mid-arms downward, she spurted forward and coasted for three body-lengths. When one or two of the mid-arms were held steady and the hands angled, quite delicate directional and positional control was possible. Previously she had never been able to remain under water for more than a few moments, and she was beginning to really enjoy the sensation. She continued to circle the structural member, moving up and down its entire length and examining the artificial vegetation even more closely. There were clusters of what could have been underwater fruit, which glowed with multihued light at her approach, revealing themselves to be a part of the ward lighting system. But the pleasures of discovery were short-lived.

One of the long, dark-green, motionless shadows lying along the floor of the ward had detached itself and was rushing silently toward her. It slowed, took monstrous, terrifying, three-dimensional form and began to circle her slowly as she had been circling the structural support.

The creature was like an enormous, armored fish with a heavy, knife-edged tail, a seemingly haphazard arrangement of stubby fins, and a thick ring of ribbon tentacles projecting from the few gaps in its organic body-armor. The tentacles lay flat along its sides when it was moving forward, but they were long enough to reach beyond the thick, blunt wedge of the head. One tiny, lidless eye watched her as it circled closer.

Suddenly the head divided to reveal a vast pink cavern of a mouth edged with row upon row of enormous white teeth. It drifted closer, so that she could even see the periodic fogging of the water around its gills. The mouth opened even wider.

"Hello, Nurse," it said shyly.

Chapter 5

CHA Thrat was not sure whether the AUGL ward's duty roster had been drawn up by Charge Nurse Hredlichli or a seriously deranged computer overlooked by the Maintenance staff, and she could not ask without calling into question someone's level of mental competence. It was unbalanced, she thought, whether "it" referred to the roster, some anonymous Maintenance entity, or Hredlichli itself. After six days and two and a half nights darting about like an overworked minnow among her outsized Chalders, she had been given two whole days in which she could do whatever she liked—provided that part of the free time was spent at her studies.

The proportion suggested by their noxious Nidian tutor, Cresk-Sar, was ninety-nine percent.

Sector General's corridors held fewer terrors for her now, and she was trying to decide whether to go exploring or continue studying when her door signal sounded.

"Tarsedth?" she called. "Come in."

"I hope that question refers to my purpose in calling," the Kelgian trainee said as it undulated into the room, "and not another expression of doubt regarding my identity. You should know me by *now*!"

Cha Thrat also knew that no reply was often the best reply.

The DBLF came to a halt in front of the viewscreen and went on. "What's *that*, an ELNT lower mandible? You're lucky, Cha Thrat. You've gotten the hang of this physiological classification business a lot faster than the rest of us, or is it just that you study every waking minute? When Cresk-Sar pulled that three-second visual on us and you identified it as a blow-up of an FGLI large metatarsal and phalange before the picture was off the screen—"

"You're right, I was lucky," Cha Thrat broke in. "We had Diagnostician Thornnastor in the ward two days earlier. There was a small misunderstanding, a piece of clumsiness on my part, while we were presenting the patient for examination. For a few moments I had a very close look at a Tralthan large toe while the foot was trying not to step on me."

"And I suppose Hredlichli jumped on you with all five of those squishy things it uses for feet?"

"It told me..." Cha Thrat began, but Tarsedth's mouth and fur had not stopped moving.

"I'm sorry for you," it went on. "That is one tough chlorine-breather. It was Charge Nurse on my PVSJ ward before it applied for other-species duty with the Chalders, and I've been told all about it, including something that happened between it and a PVSJ Senior Physician on Level Fifty-three. I wish I knew what did happen. They tried to explain it to me but who knows what is right, wrong, normal, or utterly scandalous behavior where chlorine-breathers are concerned? Some of the people in this hospital are *strange*."

Cha Thrat stared for a moment at the thirty-limbed, silvery body that sat like a furry question mark in front of the viewscreen. "I agree," she said.

Returning to the original question, Tarsedth said, "Are you in trouble with Hredlichli? About your clumsiness when a Diagnostician was in the ward, I mean? Will it report you to Cresk-Sar?"

"I don't know," Cha Thrat replied. "After we'd finished the evening surgical round, it said that I should take myself out of its sight for the next two days, and no doubt I would enjoy that as much as it would. Did I tell you that it allows me to change some of the surgical dressings now? Under its supervision, of course, and the wounds concerned are almost healed."

"Well," Tarsedth said, "your trouble can't be too serious if it's having you back again. What are you going to do with your two days? Study?"

"Not all the time," she replied. "I want to explore the hospital, the areas where my protective suit will take me,

that is. Cresk-Sar's high-speed tour and lecture sessions
don't give me enough time to stop and ask questions."

The Kelgian dropped another three or four sets of
limbs to the floor, a clear indication that it was about to
leave.

"You'll be living dangerously, Cha Thrat," it said.
"I'm content to learn about this medical madhouse a little at a time; that way I'm less likely to end up as one of
the casualties. But I've been told that the recreation
level is well worth a visit. You could start your explora-
tions from there. Coming?"

"Yes," she said. "There at least the heavies will be
relaxing and at rest, and not charging along the corridors
like mobile disasters waiting to happen to us."

Later, Cha Thrat was to wonder how she could have
been so wrong.

The signs over the entrance read:

RECREATION LEVEL, SPECIES DBDG, DBLF,
DBPK, DCNF, EGCL, ELNT, FGLI, & FROB.
SPECIES GKMN & GLNO AT OWN RISK.

For members of the staff whose written languages
were not represented, the same information was repeated endlessly via translator.

"DCNF," Tarsedth said. "They've got your classification up there already. Probably a routine updating by
Personnel."

"Probably," Cha Thrat said. But she felt very pleased
and, for the first time, important.

After days spent in crowded hospital corridors, her
tiny room, and the even more cramped confines of the
suit she had to wear in the tepid, green depths of the
AUGL ward, the sheer size of the place made her feel
insecure and unsteady. But the spaciousness, the open

sky, and the long distances were apparent rather than real, she soon realized, and the initial shock diminished quickly to become a feeling of pleased surprise.

Trick lighting and some inspired landscaping had given the recreation level its illusion of tremendous spaciousness. The overall effect was of a small tropical beach enclosed on two sides by cliffs and open to a sea that stretched out to a horizon rendered indistinct by heat haze. The sky was blue and cloudless, and the water of the bay was deep blue shading to turquoise where the waves ran onto the bright, golden sand of the beach.

Only the light from the artificial sun, which was too reddish for Cha Thrat's taste, and the alien greenery fringing the beach and cliffs kept it from looking like a tropical bay anywhere on Sommaradva.

But then, space was at a premium in Sector General, she had been told before her first visit to the dining hall, and the people who worked together had to eat together. Now it seemed that they were expected to play together as well.

"Realistic cloud effects are difficult to reproduce," Tarsedth volunteered, "so rather than risk them looking artificial, they don't bother trying. The Maintenance person who suggested I come here told me that. It also said that the best thing about the place was that the gravity was maintained at half Earth-normal, which is close enough to half Kelgia- and Sommaradva-normal. The people who like to rest actively can be more active, and the others find the sand softer to lie on—Watch out!"

Three Tralthans on a total of eighteen massive feet went thundering past them and plowed into the shallows, scattering sand and spray over a wide area. The half-G conditions that allowed the normally slow and ponderous FGLIs to jump about like bipeds also kept the sand they had disturbed airborne for a long time before it settled back to the beach. Some of it had not settled because Cha Thrat was still trying to blink it out of her eyes.

"Over there," Tarsedth said. "We can shelter between the FROB and the two ELNTs. They don't look as if they are very active resters."

But Chat Thrat did not feel like lying still and doing nothing but absorb artificial sunlight. She had too much on her mind, too many questions of the kind that could not be asked without the risk of giving serious offense, and she had found in the past that strenuous physical activity rested the mind—sometimes.

She watched a steep, low-gravity wave roll in and break on the beach. Not all of the turbulence in the bay was artificial—it varied in proportion to the number, size, and enthusiasm of the swimmers. The most favored sport, especially among the heaviest and least stream-lined life-forms, was jumping into the bay from one of the springboards set into the cliff face. The boards, which seemed to her to be dangerously high until she remembered the reduced gravity, could be reached through tunnels concealed within the cliff. One board, the highest of them all, was solidly braced and without flexibility, probably to avoid the risk of an overenthu-siastic diver fracturing its cranium on the artificial sky.

"Would you like to swim?" she asked suddenly. "That is, I mean, if DBLFs can."

"We can, but I won't," the Kelgian said, deepening the sandy trench it had already dug for itself. "It would leave my fur plastered flat and unable to move for the rest of the day. If another DBLF came by I wouldn't be able to talk to it properly. Lie down. Relax."

Cha Thrat folded her two rear legs and gently col-lapsed into a horizontal position, but it must have been obvious even to her other-species friend that she was not relaxed.

"Are you worried about something?" Tarsedth asked, its fur rippling and tufting in concern. "Cresk-Sar? Hredlichli? Your ward?"

Cha Thrat was silent for a moment, wondering how a Sommaradvan warrior-surgeon could explain the problem to a member of a species whose cultural background was completely different, and who might even be a servile. But until she was sure of Tarsedth's exact status, she would consider the Kelgian her professional equal, and speak.

"I do not wish to offend," she said carefully, "but it seems to me that, in spite of the wide-ranging knowledge we are expected to acquire, the strange and varied creatures we care for, and the wonderful devices we use to do it, our work is repetitious, undignified, without personal responsibility, invariably performed under direction, and well, *servile*. We should be doing something more important with our time, or such a large proportion of it, than conveying body wastes from the patients to the disposal facility."

"So that's what's bothering you," Tarsedth said, twisting its conical head in her direction. "A deep, incised wound to the pride."

Cha Thrat did not reply, and it went on. "Before I left Kelgia I was a nursing superintendent responsible for the nursing services on eight wards. Same-species patients, of course, but at least I had come up through nursing. Some of the other trainees, yourself included, were doctors, so I can imagine how they—and you—feel. But the servile condition is temporary. It will be relieved when or if we complete our training to Cresk-Sar's satisfaction. Try not to worry about it. You are learning other-species medicine, if you excuse the expression, from the bottom up.

"Try taking more interest in the other end of the patient," Tarsedth added, "instead of concerning yourself with the plumbing all the time. Talk to them and try to understand how their minds work."

Cha Thrat wondered how she could explain to the Kelgian, who was a member of what seemed to be an advanced but utterly disorganized and classless civilization, that there were things that a warrior-surgeon should and should not do. Even though the medical fraternity on Sommaradva could not have cared less what happened to her, in Sector General she had been forced by circumstances into behavior that was wrong, in both the negative and positive sense, for someone of her professional status. She was acting above and below her level of competence, and it worried her.

"I do talk to them," she said. "One especially, and it says that it likes talking to me. I try not to favor any particular patient, but this one is more distressed than the others. I shouldn't be talking to it as I'm not qualified to treat it, but nobody else can or will do anything for the patient."

Tarsedth's fur rippled with concern. "Is it terminal?"

"I don't know. I don't think so," Cha Thrat replied. "It's been a ward patient for a very long time. Seniors examine it sometimes with advanced trainees present, and Thornnastor spoke to it when the Diagnostician was in the ward with another patient, but not to ask about its condition. I haven't access to its case history, but I'm pretty sure that the medication prescribed for it is palliative rather than curative. It is not neglected or ill treated so much as politely ignored. I'm the only one who will listen to its symptoms, so it talks to me at every opportunity. I shouldn't talk to it, not until I know what's wrong with it, because I'm not qualified."

The movement of Tarsedth's fur settled down to a more even rhythm as it said, "Nonsense! Everybody is qualified to talk, and a bit of verbal sympathy and encouragement can't harm your patient. But if its condition is incurable, your ward water would be teeming with Diagnosticians and Seniors intent on proving otherwise. That's the way things work here; nobody gives up on *anybody*. And your patient's problem will give you something to think about while you do the less attractive jobs. Or don't you want to talk to it?"

"Yes," Cha Thrat said, "I'm very sorry for the great, suffering brute, and I want to help it. But I'm beginning to wonder if it is a ruler, in which case I should not be talking to it."

"Whatever it is, or was, on Chalderescol," Tarsedth said, "has no bearing, or shouldn't have, on its treatment as a patient. What harm can a little nonmedical sympathy and encouragement do either of you? Frankly, I don't see your difficulty."

Patiently Cha Thrat said again, "I'm not qualified."

Tarsedth's fur was moving in a manner that denoted impatience. "I still don't understand you. Talk, don't talk to it. Do whatever you want to do."

"I *have* talked to it," Cha Thrat said, "and that's what worries me— Is something wrong?"

"Can't it leave me alone!" said Tarsedth, its fur tufting into angry spikes. "I'm sure that's Cresk-Sar coming this way, and it's seen our trainee badges. The first question it will ask is why we aren't studying. Can't we ever escape from its infuriating 'I have questions for you' routine?"

The Senior Physician detached itself from a group of two other Nidians and a Melfan who had been moving toward the water's edge and stopped, looking down at them.

"I have questions for both of you," it said inevitably, but unexpectedly went on. "Are you able to relax in this place? Does it enable you to forget all about your work? Your Charge Nurses? Me?"

"How can we forget about you," Tarsedth said, "when you're here, and ready to ask us why we're here?"

The Kelgian's seeming rudeness was unavoidable, Cha Thrat knew, but her reply would have to be more diplomatic.

"The answer to all four questions is, not entirely," she said. "We were relaxing but were discussing problems relating to our work."

"Good," Cresk-Sar said. "I would not want you to forget your work, or me, entirely. Have you a particular problem or question that I can answer for you before I rejoin my friends?"

Tarsedth was burrowing deeper into the artificial sand and pointedly ignoring their tutor who, now that it was off duty, seemed to Cha Thrat to be a much less obnoxious Nidian. Cresk-Sar deserved a polite response, even though the recent topic of discussion, the psychological and emotional problems associated with the removal of other-species body wastes, was not an area in which a Senior Physician would have firsthand experience. Perhaps she could ask a general question that would satisfy both the social requirements of the situation and her own curiosity.

"As trainees," Cha Thrat said, "we are assigned to the less pleasant, nonmedical ward duties, in particular those involving organic wastes. These are an unpleasant but necessary by-product common to all species whose food is ingested, digested, and eliminated. However, there must be wide differences in the chemical composition of other-species wastes. Since the hospital was designed so far as was possible to be a closed ecological system, what becomes of all this material?"

Cresk-Sar seemed to be having difficulty with its breathing for a moment, then it replied, "The system is not completely closed. We do not synthesize all our food or medication and, I am pleased to tell you, there are no intelligent life-forms known to us who can exist on their own or any other species' wastes. As for your question, I don't know the answer, Cha Thrat. Until now the question has never come up."

It turned away quickly and went back to its Melfan and Nidian friends. Shortly afterward the ELNT started to make clicking sounds with its mandibles while the furry DBDGs barked, or perhaps laughed, loudly. Cha Thrat could not find anything humorous in the question. To the contrary, she found the subject actively unpleasant. But the loud, untranslatable noises coming from the group showed no sign of stopping—until they were drowned out by the sharp, insistent, and even louder sounds coming from the public address system.

"Emergency," it blared across the recreation level and from her translator. *"Code Blue, AUGL ward. All named personnel acknowledge on nearest communicator and go immediately to the AUGL ward. Chief Psychologist O'Mara, Charge Nurse Hredlichli, Trainee Cha Thrat. Code Blue. Acknowledge and go at once to—"*

She missed the rest of it because Cresk-Sar had come back and was glaring down at her. It was neither barking nor laughing.

"Move yourself!" it said harshly. "I'll acknowledge the message and go with you. As your tutor I am responsible for your medical misdeeds. Hurry."

As they were leaving the recreation level it went on,

"A Code Blue is an emergency involving extreme danger to both patients and medical staff, the kind of trouble during which untrained personnel are ordered to stay clear. But they have paged you, a trainee, and, of all people, Chief Psychologist O'Mara.

"What have you *done*?"

Chapter 6

CHA Thrat and the Senior Physician arrived at the AUGL ward minutes before O'Mara and Charge Nurse Hredlichli, and joined the other three nurses on duty—two Kelgian DBLFs and a Melfan ELNT—who had abandoned their patients to take shelter in the Nurses' Station.

This normally reprehensible behavior was not being considered as a dereliction of medical duty, the tutor explained, because it was the first time in the hospital's wide experience in staff-patient relations that a Chalder had become violently antisocial.

In the green dimness at the other end of the ward a long, dark shadow drifted slowly from one side-wall to the other, as Cha Thrat had seen many of the mobile, bored, and restless Chalders doing while she had been on duty. Except for a few pieces of decorative greenery detached and drifting untidily between the supports, the ward looked peaceful and normal.

"What about the other patients, Charge Nurse?"

Cresk-Sar asked. As the Senior Physician present it had overall medical responsibility. "Is anyone hurt?"

Hredlichli swam along the line of monitors and said, "Disturbed and frightened, but they have sustained no injuries, nor has their food and medication delivery system been damaged. They've been very lucky."

"Or the patient is being selective in its violence—" O'Mara began, then broke off.

The long shadow at the other end of the ward had foreshortened and was enlarging rapidly as it rushed toward them. Cha Thrat had a glimpse of fins blurred by rapid motion, ribbon tentacles streaming backward, and the serried ranks of gleaming teeth edging the enormous, gaping mouth before it crashed against the transparent wall of the Nurses' Station. The wall bulged inward alarmingly but did not collapse.

It was too large for the doorless entrance, she saw, but it changed position and moved three of its tentacles inside. They were not long enough or strong enough to pull anyone outside to the mouth, although one of the Kelgian nurses had a few anxious moments. Disappointed, the Chalder turned and swam away, with detached vegetation eddying its wake.

O'Mara made a sound that did not translate, then said, "Who is the patient, and why was trainee Cha Thrat called?"

"It is the long-stay patient, AUGL-One Sixteen," the Melfan nurse replied. "Just before it became violent it was calling for the new nurse, Cha Thrat. When I told the patient that the Sommaradvan would be absent for a few days, it stopped communicating and has not spoken to us since, even though its translator is still in position and working. That is why the trainee's name was included when I called in the Code Blue."

"Interesting," the Earth-human said, turning its attention to Cha Thrat. "Why did it want you especially, and why should it start taking the ward apart when you weren't available? Have you established a special relationship with AUGL-One Sixteen?"

Before she could reply, the Nidian said urgently, "Can the psychological ramifications wait, Major? My immediate concern is for the safety of the ward patients and staff. Pathology will give us a fast-acting anesthetic and a dart gun to pacify the patient, and then you can—"

"A dart gun!" one of the Kelgians said, its fur rippling in scorn. "Senior Physician, you are forgetting that your dart has to travel through water, which will slow it down, and then penetrate that organic suit of armor One Sixteen wears! The only sure way of placing the dart effectively would be to shoot it into the soft tissues of the inner mouth. To place it accurately, the person using the gun would have to be very close and might find itself following the dart into the open mouth, with immediately fatal results. I am not volunteering!"

Before Cresk-Sar could reply, Cha Thrat turned to the Senior Physician and said, "If you will explain what exactly it is that I must do, I shall volunteer for this duty."

"You lack the training and experience to—" began the Nidian, and broke off as O'Mara held up its hand for silence.

"Of course you will volunteer," O'Mara said quietly. "But why, Cha Thrat? Are you exceptionally brave? Are you naturally stupid? Do you have an urge to commit suicide? Or are you, perhaps, feeling a measure of responsibility and guilt?"

"Major O'Mara," Hredlichli said firmly, "this is not the time for apportioning responsibility or undertaking deep analysis. What is to be done about Patient One Sixteen? And my other patients?"

"You're right, Charge Nurse," O'Mara said. "I shall

do it my way, by attempting to pacify and reason with One Sixteen. I've spoken to it many times, enough for it to tell me apart from other Earth-humans if I wear this lightweight suit. While I'm working with it I may also need to talk to Cha Thrat, so stay by the communicator, trainee."

"No need, I'll go with you," Cha Thrat said firmly. Silently she began the mental and moral exercises that were supposed to help reconcile her to an untimely ending of her life.

"And I," O'Mara said, making another sound that did not translate, "will be too busy with our demented friend to stop you. Come along, then."

"But it is only a *trainee*, O'Mara!" Cresk-Sar protested. "And in a lightweight suit it might recognize you, all right, as a convenient piece of plastic-wrapped meat. This life-form is omnivorous and until recently they—"

"Cresk-Sar," the Earth-human said, as it swam toward the entrance. "Are you trying to worry me?"

"Oh, very well," the Nidian said. "But I, too, shall do things my way, in case you can't talk yourselves through this problem. Charge Nurse, signal immediately for a four-unit patient transfer team with heavy-duty suits, dart guns, and physical restraints suitable for a fully conscious and uncooperative AUGL . . ."

The tutor was still talking as Cha Thrat swam into the ward behind O'Mara.

For what seemed a very long time they hung silent and motionless in the middle of the ward, watched by an equally still and silent patient from the cover of a patch of torn artificial greenery. O'Mara had told her that they should not do anything that One Sixteen might construe as a threat, that they must therefore appear defenseless before it, and that the first move was up to the patient. Cha Thrat thought that the Earth-Human was probably right, but her whole body was slippery with perspiration, and much warmer than could be explained by the temperature of the green, lukewarm water outside her protective suit. Plainly she was not yet completely reconciled to the ending of her existence.

The voice of the Senior Physician in her suit 'phones made her twitch in every limb.

"The transfer team is here," Cresk-Sar said quietly. "Nothing much is happening at your end. Can I send them in to move the other patients into OR? It will be a tight squeeze in there, but they will be able to receive treatment and be comfortable for a few hours, and you will have One Sixteen all to yourselves."

"Is the treatment urgent?" O'Mara asked softly.

"No," Cha Thrat said, answering the question before Cresk-Sar could relay it to the Charge Nurse. "Just routine observation and recording of vital signs, wound dressing changes, and administration of supportive medication. Nothing really urgent."

"Thank you, Trainee," Hredlichli said in a tone as corrosive as the atmosphere it breathed, then went on. "I have been Charge Nurse here for a short time, Major O'Mara, but I feel that I, too, have the patient's trust. I would like to join you."

"No, to both of you," the Earth-human said firmly. "I don't want our friend to be frightened or unsettled by too many comings and goings within the ward. And Hredlichli, if your protective suit were to rupture, contact with water is instantly lethal to a chlorine-breather, as you very well know. With us oxygen-breathers, we can drown in the stuff if help doesn't reach us in time, but it isn't poisonous or— Uh-oh!"

Patient AUGL-One Sixteen was silent but no longer still. It was rushing at them like a gigantic, organic tor-

pedo, except that torpedoes did not have suddenly opening mouths.

Frantically they swam apart so as to give the attack-
ing Chalder two targets instead of one, the theory being
that while it was disposing of one the other might have
enough time to make it to the safety of the Nurses' Station. But this was planning for a remote contingency, the
Earth-human had insisted. O'Mara would not believe
that AUGL-One Sixteen, who was normally so shy and
timid and amenable, was capable of making a lethal attack on anyone.

On this occasion it was right.

The vast jaws snapped shut just before the Chalder
swept through the gap that had opened between them.
Then the great body curved upward and over them,
dove, and began swimming around them in tight circles.
Turbulence sent them spinning and twisting like leaves at
the center of a whirlpool. Cha Thrat did not know
whether it was circling them in the vertical or horizontal
plane, only that it was so close that she could feel the
compression waves every time the jaws snapped shut,
which was frequently. She had never felt so helpless and
disoriented and frightened in all her life.

"Stop this nonsense, Muromeshomon!" she said
loudly. "We are here to help you. Why are you behaving
like this?"

The Chalder slowed but continued to circle them
closely. It mouth gaped open and it said, "You cannot
help me, you have said that you are not qualified. Nobody here can help me. I do not wish to harm you, or
anyone else, but I am frightened. I am in great pain.
Sometimes I want to hurt everyone. Stay away from me
or I will hurt you . . ."

There was a muffled, underwater clang as its tail
flicked out and struck her air tanks a glancing blow,

sending her spinning again. An Earth-human hand grasped one of her waist limbs, steadying her, and she saw that the patient had returned to its dark corner and was watching them.

"Are you hurt?" O'Mara asked, releasing its grip. "Is your suit all right?"

"Yes," Cha Thrat said, and added, "It left very quickly. I'm sure the blow was accidental."

The Earth-human did not reply for a few moments, then it said, "You called Patient One Sixteen by name. I am aware of its name because the hospital requires this information for possible notification of the next-of-kin, but I would not consider using its name unless there were very exceptional circumstances, and then only with its permission. But somehow you have learned its name and are using it as lightly and thoughtlessly as you would Cresk-Sar's or Hredlichli's, or my name. Cha Thrat, you must never—"

"It told me its name," Cha Thrat broke in. "We exchanged names while we were discussing my observations regarding the inadequacy of its treatment."

"You discussed . . ." O'Mara said incredulously. It made an untranslatable noise and went on. "Tell me what exactly you said to it."

Cha Thrat hesitated. The AUGL had left its dark corner and was moving toward them again, but slowly. It stopped halfway down the ward and hung with its fins and tail still and the ribbon tentacles spread like an undulating, circular fan around it, watching and probably listening to every word they said.

"On second thought, *don't* tell me," O'Mara said angrily. "I'll tell you what I know about the patient first, then you can try to reduce my level of ignorance. That way we will avoid repetition and save time. I don't know how much time it will give us to talk without another interruption. Not a lot, I suspect, so I'll have to speak quickly..."

Patient AUGL-One Sixteen was a long-stay patient whose time in Sector General exceeded that of many of the medical staff. The clinical picture had been and still remained obscure. Several of the hospital's top Diagnosticians had examined it, finding signs of strain in certain areas of the patient's body plating that partly explained its discomfort—a being who was largely exoskeletal, lazy, and something of a glutton could only put on weight from the inside. The generally agreed diagnosis was hypochondria and the condition incurable.

The Chalder had become seriously ill only when there was talk of sending it home, and so the hospital had acquired a permanent patient. It did not mind. Visiting as well as hospital medics and psychologists had given it a going over, and continued to do so, as did the interns and nurses of all the life-forms represented on the staff. It had been probed, pried into, and unmercifully pounded by trainees of varying degrees of gentleness, and it loved every minute of it. The hospital's teaching staff were happy with the arrangement and so was the Chalder.

"Nobody mentions going home to it anymore," O'Mara ended. "Did you?"

"Yes," Cha Thrat said.

O'Mara made another untranslatable noise and she went on quickly. "This explains why the nurses ignored it when other patients needed treatment, and supports my own diagnosis of an unspecified ruler's disease that—"

"Listen, don't speak!" the Earth-human said sharply. The patient seemed to be drifting closer. "My department has tried to get to the root causes of One Sixteen's hypochondria, but I was not required to solve its problem so it remained unsolved. This sounds like an excuse, and it is. But you must understand that Sector General is not and can never be a psychiatric hospital. Can you imagine a place like this where a large proportion of the multispecies patients, the mere sight of which gives sane people nightmares, are physically fit and mentally disturbed? Can you imagine the problems of other-species treatment and restraint? It is difficult enough to be responsible for the mental well-being of the staff without adding disturbed patients, even a harmlessly disturbed patient like One Sixteen, to my load. When a medically ill patient displays signs of mental instability it is kept under close observation, restrained if necessary, and returned to its own people for the appropriate treatment as soon as it is physically well enough to be discharged."

"I understand," Cha Thrat said. "The explanation excuses you."

The Earth-human grew pinker in the face, then said, "Listen carefully, Cha Thrat, this is important. The Chalders are one of the few intelligent species whose personal names are used only between mates, members of the immediate family, or very special friends. Yet you, an other-species stranger, have been told, and have spoken aloud, One Sixteen's personal name. Have you done this in ignorance? Do you realize that this exchange of names means that anything you may have said to it, or any future action you may have promised, is as binding as the most solemn promise given before the highest imaginable physical or metaphysical authority?"

"Do you realize now how serious this is?" O'Mara went on in a tone of quiet urgency. "Why did it tell you its name? What, exactly, was said between you?"

She could not speak for a moment because the patient had moved very close, so close that she could see the individual points of its six rows of teeth. A strangely detached and uncaring portion of her mind wondered what evolutionary imperative had caused the upper three rows to be longer than the lower set. Then the jaw snapped shut with a boney crash that was muffled by the surrounding water, and the caring part of her mind wondered what it would sound like if a limb or her torso were between those teeth.

"Have you fallen asleep?" O'Mara snapped.

"No," she said, wondering why an intelligent being had asked such a stupid question. "We talked because it was lonely and unhappy. The other nurses were busy with a post-op patient and I was not. I told it about Sommaradva and the circumstances that led to me coming here, and some of the things I would be able to do if I qualified for Sector General. It said that I was brave and resourceful, not sick and old and increasingly fearful like itself.

"It said that many times it dreamed of swimming free in the warm ocean of Chalderescol," she went on, "instead of this aseptic, water-filled box with its plastic, inedible vegetation. It could talk about the home world to other AUGL patients, but much of their post-op recovery time was spent under sedation. The medical staff were pleasant to it and would talk, on the rare occasions when they had time to do so. It said that it would never escape from the hospital, that it was too old and frightened and sick."

"Escape?" O'Mara said. "If our permanent patient has begun to regard the hospital as a prison, that is a very healthy sign, psychologically. But go on, what were you saying to it?"

"We spoke of general subjects," she replied. "Our worlds, our work, our past experiences, our friends and families, our opinions—"

"Yes, yes," the Earth-human said impatiently, looking at One Sixteen, who was edging closer. "I'm not interested in the small talk. What did you say that might have brought on this trouble?"

Cha Thrat tried to choose the words that would describe the situation concisely, accurately, and briefly as she replied, "It told me about the space accident and injuries that brought it here originally, and the continuing but irregular episodes of pain that keep it here, and of its deep unhappiness with its existence generally.

"I was uncertain of its exact status on Chalderescol," she went on, "but from the way it had described its work I judged it to be an upper-level warrior, at least, if not a ruler. By that time we had exchanged names, so I decided to tell it that the treatment being provided by the hospital was palliative rather than curative, and it was being treated for the wrong sickness. I said that its malady was not unknown to me and, although I was not qualified to treat the condition, there were wizards on Sommaradva capable of doing so. I suggested, on several occasions, that it was becoming institutionalized and that it might be happier if it returned home."

The patient was very close to them now. Its massive mouth was closed but not still, because there was a regular chewing motion that suggested that the teeth were grinding together. The movement was accompanied by a high-pitched, bubbling moan that was both frightening and strangely pitiful.

"Go on," O'Mara said softly, "but be very careful what you say."

"There is little more to tell," Cha Thrat said. "During our last meeting I told it that I was leaving for a two-day rest period. It would speak only of the wizards, and wanted to know if they could cure its fear as well as the pains. It asked me as a friend to treat it, or send for one of our Sommaradvan brothers who would be able to cure it. I told it that I had some knowledge of the spells of the wizards, but not enough to risk treating it, and that I lacked the status and authority to summon a wizard to the hospital."

"What was the response to that?" O'Mara asked.

"None," Cha Thrat said. "It would not speak to me thereafter."

Abruptly they were looking into the AUGL's open mouth, but it was keeping its uncomfortably short distance as it said, "You were not like the others, who did nothing and promised nothing. You held out the hope of a cure by your wizards, then withdrew it. You cause me pain that is many times worse than that which keeps me here. Go away, Cha Thrat. For your own safety, go away."

The jaws crashed shut and it swept around them and headed for the other end of the ward. They could not see clearly but, judging by the voices coming from the Nurses' Station, it seemed intent on wrecking the place.

"My patients!" Charge Nurse Hredlichli burst out. "My new treatment frames and medication cabinets..."

"According to the monitors," Cresk-Sar broke in, "the patients are still all right, but they've been lucky. I'm sending in the transfer team now to knock out One Sixteen. It will be a bit tricky. Both of you get back here, quickly."

"No, wait," O'Mara said. "We'll try talking to it again. This is not a violent patient and I don't believe that we are in any real danger." On Cha Thrat's frequency it added, "But there is always a first time for being wrong."

For some reason a picture from Cha Thrat's childhood rose suddenly to the surface of her adult mind. She saw again the tiny, many-colored fish that had been her favorite pet, as it circled and butted desperately and hopelessly against the glass walls of its bowl. Beyond those walls, too, lay an environment in which it would quickly asphyxiate and die. But that small fish, like this overlarge one, was not thinking of that.

"When One Sixteen gave you its name," O'Mara said with quiet urgency, "it placed a binding obligation on both of you to help the other in every way possible, as would a life-mate or a member of your family. When you mentioned the possibility of a cure by your Sommarad-van wizards, regardless of the efficacy of such other-species treatment, you were expected to provide the wizard regardless of any effort, cost, or personal danger to yourself."

There were noises of tearing metal and the complain-ing voices of the other AUGLs being transmitted through the green water, and Hredlichli sounded very agitated. O'Mara ignored them and went on. "You must keep faith with it, Cha Thrat, even though your wizards might not be able to help One Sixteen any more than we can. And I realize that you haven't the authority to call in one of your wizards. But if Sector General and the Monitor Corps were to put their combined weight behind you—"

"They wouldn't come to this place," Cha Thrat said. "Wizards are notoriously unstable people, but they are not stupid— It's coming back!"

This time One Sixteen was coming at them more slowly and deliberately, but still too fast for them to swim to safety, nor could the transfer team with their anesthetic darts reach them in time to do any good. There was no sound from the patients in the ward and the beings watching from the Nurses' Station. As the AUGL loomed closer she could see that its eyes had the feral, manic look of a wounded predator, and slowly it was opening its mouth.

"Use its *name*, dammit!" O'Mara said urgently.

"Mu-Muromeshomon," she stammered. "My—my friend, we are here to help you."

The anger in its eyes seemed to dim a little so that they reflected more of its pain. The mouth closed slowly and opened again, but only to speak.

"Friend, you are in great and immediate danger," the AUGL said. "You have spoken my name and told me that the hospital cannot cure me with its medicines and machines, and it no longer tries, and you will not help me even though you have said that a cure is possible. If our positions were reversed I would not act, or refuse to act, as you have done. You are an unequal friend, without honor, and I am disappointed and angry with you. Go away, quickly, and protect your life. I am beyond help."

"No!" Cha Thrat said fiercely. The mouth was opening wider, the eyes were showing a manic gleam once more, and she realized that when the AUGL attacked, she would be its first victim. Desperately she went on. "It is true that I cannot help you. Your sickness does not respond to the healer's herbs or the surgeon's knife, because it is a ruler's disease that requires the spells of a wizard. A Sommaradvan wizard might cure you but, since you are not yourself a Sommaradvan, there is no certainty. Here there is the Earth-human, O'Mara, a wizard with experience of treating rulers of many different life-forms. I would have approached it about your case at once but, being a trainee and unsure of the procedure, I was about to request a meeting for another, an unimportant, reason during which I would have spoken of you in detail . . ."

The AUGL had closed its mouth but was moving its jaws in a way that could be indicating anger or impatience. She went on quickly. "In the hospital I have heard many people speak of O'Mara and his great powers of wizardry—"

"I'm the Chief Psychologist, dammit," O'Mara broke in, "not a wizard. Let's try to be factual about this and not make more promises we can't possibly keep!"

"You are *not* a psychologist!" Cha Thrat said. She was so angry with this Earth-human who would not accept the obvious that for a moment she almost forgot about the threat from One Sixteen. Not for the first time she wondered what obscure and undefined ruler's disease it was that made beings who possessed high intelligence, and The Power in great measure, behave so stupidly at times. Less vehemently, she went on. "On Sommaradva a psychologist is a being, neither servile-healer nor warrior-surgeon, who tries to be a scientist by measuring brain impulses or bodily changes caused by physical and mental stress, or by making detailed observations of behavior. A psychologist tries to impose immutable laws in an area of spells and nightmares and changing realities, and tries to make a science of what has always been an art, an art practiced only by wizards."

They were both watching her, eyes unblinking, motionless. The patient's expression had not changed but the Earth-human's face had gone a much deeper shade of pink.

"A wizard will use or ignore the instruments and tabulations of the psychologist," she continued, "to cast spells that influence the complex, insubstantial structures of the mind. A wizard uses words, silences, minute observation, and intuition to compare and gradually change the sick, internal reality of the patient to the external reality of the world. That is the difference between a psychologist and a wizard."

The Earth-human's face was still unnaturally dark. In a voice that was both quiet and harsh it said, "Thank you for reminding me."

Formally Cha Thrat said, "No thanks are required for that which needs to be done. Please, may I remain here to watch? Before now I have never had the chance to see a wizard at work."

"What," the AUGL asked suddenly, "will the wizard do to me?"

It sounded curious and anxious rather than angry, and for the first time since entering the ward she began to feel safe.

"Nothing," O'Mara said surprisingly. "I shall do nothing at all . . ."

Even on Sommaradva the wizards were full of surprises, unpredictable behavior and words that began by sounding irrelevant, ill chosen, or stupid. What little of the literature that was available to one of the warrior-surgeon level, she had read and reread. So she composed herself and, with great anticipation, watched and listened while the Earth-human wizard did nothing at all.

The spell began very subtly with words, spoken in a manner that was anything but subtle, describing the arrival of AUGL-One Sixteen at the hospital as the commanding officer and sole survivor of its ship. The vessels of water-breathing species, and especially those of the outsize denizens of Chalderescol, were notoriously unwieldy and unsafe, and it had been exonerated of all blame for the accident both by the Monitor Corps investigators and the authorities on Chalderescol—but not by itself. This was realized when the patient's physical injuries had healed and it continued to complain of severe psychosomatic discomfort whenever the subject of returning home was discussed.

Many attempts were made to make the patient realize that it was punishing itself, cutting itself off from its home and friends, for a crime that was very probably imaginary, but without success—it would not consciously admit that it had committed a crime, so telling it that it was not guilty had no effect. A Chalder's most prized possession was its personal integrity, and as an authority that integrity was unassailable. AUGL-One Sixteen was a sensitive, intelligent, and highly qualified being who, outwardly, was a submissive and cooperative patient. But where its particular delusion was concerned it was as susceptible to influence as the orbit of a major planet.

And so Sector General had acquired a permanent patient, an AUGL specimen in perfect health and a continuing and strictly unofficial challenge to its Department of Psychology, because only in the hospital could it be pain-free and relatively happy.

Silently Cha Thrat apologized to the Earth-human for thinking that it had been negligent, and listened in admiration as the spell took positive form.

"And now," O'Mara went on, "due to a combination of circumstances, a significant change has occurred. The talks with transient AUGL patients have made you increasingly homesick. Your anger over your neglect by the medical staff has been growing because, subconsciously, you yourself were beginning to suspect that you were not sick and their attention was unnecessary. And then there was the unwarranted, but for you fortunate, interference by Trainee Cha Thrat, who confirmed your suspicion that you were not being treated as a patient.

"You have much in common with our outspoken

trainee," it continued. "Both of you have reasons, real or imaginary, for not wanting to go home. On Sommaradva as on Chalderescol, personal integrity and public honor are held in high regard. But the trainee is woefully ignorant of the customs of other species and, when you took the unprecedented step of saying your name to a non-Chalder, it disappointed and hurt you grievously by continuing to act toward you as had the other members of the staff. You were driven to react violently but, because of the constraints imposed by your personality type, the violence was directed at inanimate objects.

"But," the Earth-human went on, "the simple act of giving your name to this sympathetic and untutored Sommaradvan, whom you had known only a few days, is the clearest possible indication of how badly you wanted help to get away from the hospital. You *do* still want to go home?"

AUGL-One Sixteen replied with another high-pitched, bubbling sound that did not translate. Its eyes watched only the Earth-human, and the muscles around its closed jaws were no longer clenched into iron rigidity.

"It was a stupid question," O'Mara said. "Of course you want to go home. The trouble is, you are afraid and also want to stay here. A dilemma, obviously. But let me try to solve it by telling you that you are once again a patient here, subject to the hospital regimen and my own special and continuing treatment, and until I pronounce you cured you will *not* go home..."

On the surface the situation had not changed, Cha Thrat thought admiringly. The hospital still retained its permanent AUGL patient, but now there was doubt about the permanency of the arrangement. Now it fully understood its position and had been given a choice, to stay or leave, and its departure date was unspecified so as to relieve its natural fears about leaving. But it was no longer completely satisfied with its life in the hospital, and already the Earth-human wizard was altering its internal reality by gently stressing the rehabilitative aspects of the therapy. Material would be provided by the Monitor Corps on the changes that had occurred on the home world in its absence, which would be useful if it decided to leave and informative should it stay, and there would be regular and frequent visits by O'Mara itself and other persons it would specify.

Oh, yes, she thought as it talked on, this Earth-human wizard was good.

The transfer team and their anesthetic dart guns had long since left the Nurses' Station, which meant that Cresk-Sar and Hredlichli must have decided that the danger from AUGL-One Sixteen had passed. Looking at the passive and distress-free patient who was hanging on O'Mara's every word, she was in entire agreement with them.

". . . And you should now realize," the Earth-human was saying, "that if you want to go, and can convince me that you are able to adapt to home-planet life, I shall with great pleasure and reluctance kick you out. You have been a patient for a very long time and, among many members of the senior staff, our professional concern has developed into the personal variety. But the best thing that a hospital can do for a friend is to send it away, as quickly as possible, cured.

"Do you understand?" O'Mara ended.

For the first time since the Earth-human had begun talking to it, AUGL-One Sixteen turned its attention to Cha Thrat. It said plaintively, "I am feeling much better, I think, but confused and worried by all that I must do. Was that a spell? Is O'Mara a good wizard?"

Cha Thrat tried to control her enthusiasm as she said,

"It is the beginning of a very fine spell, and it is said that a really good wizard makes its patient do all the hard work."

O'Mara made another one of its untranslatable noises and signaled Hredlichli that it was safe for the nurses to return to their patients. As they turned to leave AUGL-One Sixteen, who was once again its friendly and docile self, the Chalder spoke again.

"O'Mara," it said formally, "you may use my name."

When they were again in the air of the lock antechamber and all but Hredlichli had their visors open, the Charge Nurse said angrily, "I don't want that—that interfering *sitsachi* anywhere near me! I know that One Sixteen is going to get better and leave sometime, and I'm glad about that. But just look at the place! Wrecked, it is! I refuse to allow that trainee in my ward. That's final!"

O'Mara looked at the chlorine-breather for a moment, then in the quiet, unemotional tones of a ruler it said, "It is, of course, within your authority to accept or refuse any trainee. But Cha Thrat, whether or not it is accompanied by me, will be granted visiting facilities whenever and as often as the patient itself or myself consider it necessary. I do not foresee a lengthy period of treatment. We are grateful for your cooperation, Charge Nurse, and no doubt you are anxious to return to your duties."

When Hredlichli had gone, Cha Thrat said, "There was no opportunity to speak until now, and I am unsure how my words will be received. On Sommaradva good work is expected of a wizard or any high-level ruler, so that the praise of a subordinate for a superior is unnecessary and insulting. But in this case—"

O'Mara held up a hand for silence. It said, "Anything you say, whether complimentary or otherwise, will have no effect on what is to happen to you, so save your breath.

"You are in serious trouble, Cha Thrat," it went on grimly. "The news of what happened here will soon be all over the hospital. You must understand that to a Charge Nurse the ward is its kingdom, the nursing staff its subjects, and troublemakers, including trainees who exercise too much initiative too soon, are sent into exile, which can, in effect, mean home or to another hospital. I'd be surprised if there is a single Charge Nurse willing to accept you for practical ward training."

The Earth-human paused, giving her a moment to assimilate its words, then went on. "You have two options. Go home, or accept a nonmedical and servile position with Maintenance."

In a more sympathetic tone than she had ever heard it use before, Cresk-Sar said, "You are a most promising and diligent trainee, Cha Thrat. If you were to take such a position you would still be able to visit and talk to One Sixteen, and attend my lectures, and watch the teaching channels during your free time. But without practical ward experience you could not hope to qualify here.

"If you don't resign," the Senior Physician went on, "it may well be that you will discover firsthand the answer to the question you asked me this morning on the recreation level."

Cha Thrat remembered that question very well, and the amusement it had caused among the tutor's friends. She also remembered her initial feelings of shock and shame when her duties as a trainee nurse had been explained to her. Nothing could be more demeaning for a warrior-surgeon than that, she had thought at the time, but she had been wrong.

"I am still ignorant of the laws governing the hospital," she said. "But I realize that I have transgressed them in some fashion and must therefore accept the consequences. I shall not take the easy option."

O'Mara sighed and said, "It is your decision, Cha Thrat."

Before she could reply, the Nidian Senior Physician was talking again. "Putting it into Maintenance would be a criminal waste," the tutor protested. "It is the most promising trainee in its class. If we were to wait until the Hredlichli outcry died down, or until the grapevine is overloaded with another scandal, you might be able to find a ward that would take it for a trial period and—"

"Enough," O'Mara said, visibly relenting. "I don't believe in having second thoughts because the first are usually right. But I'm tired and hungry and I, too, have had enough of your trainee.

"There is such a ward," it went on. "FROB Geriatric, which is chronically understaffed and may be desperate enough to accept Cha Thrat. It is not a ward where I would normally assign a trainee who is not of the patients' own species, but I shall speak to Diagnostician Conway about it at the first opportunity.

"Now go away," it ended sourly, "before I cast a spell consigning both of you to the center of the nearest white dwarf."

As they were heading for the dining hall, Cresk-Sar said, "It's a tough ward and, if anything, the work is even harder than a job in Maintenance. But you can say whatever you like to the patients and nobody will mind. Whatever else happens, you can't get into trouble there."

The Nidian's words were positive and reassuring, but its voice carried undertones of doubt.

Chapter 7

SHE was given two extra days off duty, but whether they were a reward for her help with AUGL-One Sixteen or because it took that long for O'Mara to arrange for her transfer to FROB Geriatric, Cresk-Sar would not say. She paid three lengthy visits to One Sixteen in the AUGL ward, during which her reception was enough to turn its tepid water to ice, but she would not risk returning to the recreation level or exploring the hospital. There was less chance of getting into trouble if she stayed in her room and watched the teaching channels.

Tarsedth pronounced her certifiably insane and wondered why O'Mara had not confirmed this diagnosis.

Two days later she was told to present herself at FROB Geriatric in time for morning duty and to make herself known to the DBLF nurse in charge. Cresk-Sar said that it would not need to introduce her on this occasion because Charge Nurse Segroth, and probably every other being on the hospital staff, would have heard all about her by now. That may have been the reason why, on her meticulously punctual arrival, she was given no opportunity to speak.

"This is a surgical ward," Segroth said briskly, indicating the banks of monitors occupying three walls of the Nurses' Station. "There are seventy Hudlar patients and a nursing staff of thirty-two counting yourself. All the nurses are warm-blooded oxygen-breathers of various species, so you will not need environmental protection other than a gravity compensator and nasal filters. The FROBs are divided into pre- and post-op patients, segregated by a light- and soundproof partition. Until you learn your way around you will not concern yourself, or go anywhere near, a post-op patient."

Before Cha Thrat had time to say that she understood, the Kelgian ran on. "We have an FROB trainee and classmate here who will, I'm sure, be happy to answer any questions you are afraid to ask me."

Silvery fur puckered into irregular waves along its flanks in a way, she had learned from observing Tarsedth, that indicated anger and impatience. It continued. "From what I've heard of you, Nurse, you are the type who will already have studied the available Hudlar material and will be eager to make a contribution. Don't even try. This is a special project of Diagnostician Conway, we are breaking new surgical ground here, so your knowledge is already out of date. Except for those times when you are required by O'Mara for AUGL-One Sixteen, you will do nothing but watch, listen, and occasionally perform a few simple duties at the direction of the more experienced nurses or myself.

"I would not want to be embarrassed," she ended, "by you producing a miracle cure on your first day."

It was easy to pick out her FROB classmate from among the other nurses on duty—they were either Kelgian DBLFs or Melfan ELNTs—and even easier to tell it apart from all the FROB patients. She could scarcely believe that there was such a horrifying difference between a mature and an aged Hudlar.

Her classmate's speaking membrane vibrated quietly on her close approach. It said, "I see you've survived

your first encounter with Segroth. Don't worry about the
Charge Nurse; a Kelgian with authority is even less
charming than one without. If you do exactly as it tells
you, everything will be fine. I'm glad to see a friendly,
familiar face in the ward."

It was an odd thing to say, Cha Thrat thought, because Hudlars did not possess faces as such. But this
one was trying hard to reassure her and she was grateful
for that. It had not, however, called her by name, and
whether the omission was deliberate or due to an over-
sight she did not know. Perhaps the Hudlars and
Chalders had something in common besides great
strength. Until she was sure that their names could be
used without giving offense, they could call each other
"Nurse" or "Hey, you!"

"I'm spraying and sponging-off at the moment," the
Hudlar trainee said. "Would you like to strap on a spare
nutrient tank and follow me around? You can meet some
of our patients."

Without waiting for her reply, it went on. "This one
you won't be able to talk to because its speaking membrane has been muffled so that the sounds it makes will
not distress the other patients and staff. It is in considerable discomfort that does not respond very well to the
pain-killing medication, and, in any case, it is incapable
of coherent speech."

It was immediately obvious that this was not a well
Hudlar. Its six great tentacles, which normally supported
the heavy trunk in an upright position for the whole of its
waking and sleeping life, hung motionless over the sides
of its support cradle like rotted tree trunks. The hard
patches of callus—the knuckles on which it walked
while its digits were curled inward to protect them
against contact with the ground—were discolored, dry,
and cracking. The digits themselves, usually so steady

and precise in their movements, were twitching in continual spasm.

Large areas of its back and flanks were caked with partially absorbed nutrient paint, which would have to be washed off before the next meal could be sprayed on. As she watched, a milky perspiration was forming on its underside and dripping into the suction pan under its cradle.

"What's wrong with it?" Cha Thrat asked. "Can it, is it being cured?"

"Old age," the nurse said harshly. In a more controlled and clinical tone it went on. "We Hudlars are an energy-hungry species with a greatly elevated metabolic rate. With advancing age it is the food absorption and waste elimination mechanisms, both of which are normally under voluntary control, that are first to suffer progressive degeneration. Would you respray this area as soon as I've washed off the dried food, please?"

"Of course," Cha Thrat said.

"This in turn causes a severe impairment in the circulation to the limbs," the Hudlar went on, "leading to increasing deterioration in the associated nerve and muscle systems. The eventual result is general paralysis, necrosis of the limb extremities, and termination."

It used the sponge briskly and moved clear to enable Cha Thrat to apply fresh nutrient, but when it resumed speaking its voice had lost some of its former clinical calm.

"The most serious problem for the Hudlar geriatric patient," it said, "is that the brain, which requires a relatively small proportion of the available energy, remains organically unimpaired by the degenerative process until a few moments after its double heart has ceased to function. Therein lies the real tragedy. Rare indeed is the Hudlar mind that can remain stable inside a body which is disintegrating painfully all around it. You can understand why this ward, which has been recently extended for the Conway Project, is the closest that the hospital comes to providing treatment for psychologically disturbed patients.

"At least," it added, forcing a lighter tone as they moved to the next patient, "that was so until you started analyzing your AUGL-One Sixteen."

"Please don't remind me of that," Cha Thrat said.

There was another thick, cylindrical muffler encasing the next patient's speaking membrane, but either the sounds the Hudlar was making were too loud for it or the equipment was faulty. Much of what it was saying, which was clearly the product of advanced dementia and great pain, was picked up by her translator.

"I have questions," Cha Thrat said suddenly. "By implication they may be offensive to you, and perhaps critical of Hudlar philosophical values and professional ethics. On Sommaradva the situation within the medical profession may be different. I do not wish to risk insulting you."

"Ask," the other nurse said. "I shall accept your apology, if required, in advance."

"Earlier I asked if these patients could be cured," she said carefully, "and you have not yet replied. Are they incurable? And if so, why were they not advised to self-terminate before their condition reached this stage?"

For several minutes the Hudlar continued to sponge stale nutrient from the second patient's back without speaking, then it said, "You surprise but do not offend me, Nurse. I cannot myself criticize Sommaradvan medical practice because, until we joined the Federation a few generations ago, curative medicine and surgery were unknown on my world. But do I understand correctly that you urge your incurable patients to self-terminate?"

"Not exactly," Cha Thrat replied. "If a servile-healer or warrior-surgeon or a wizard will not take personal responsibility for curing a patient, the patient will not be cured. It is given all the facts of the situation, simply, accurately, and without the kindly but misguided lying and false encouragement that seem to be so prevalent among the nursing staff here. There is no attempt to exert influence in either direction; the decision is left entirely to the patient."

While she was speaking the other had stopped working. It said, "Nurse, you must never discuss a patient's case with it in this fashion, regardless of your feelings about our medical white lies. You would be in very serious trouble if you did."

"I won't," Cha Thrat said. "At least not until, or unless, the hospital once again gives me the position and responsibilities of a surgeon."

"Not even then," the Hudlar said worriedly.

"I don't understand," she said. "If I accept total responsibility for a patient's cure—"

"So you were a surgeon back home," the other nurse broke in, obviously wanting to avoid an argument. "I, too, am hoping to take home a surgical qualification."

Cha Thrat did not want an argument, either. She said, "How many years will that take?"

"Two, if I'm lucky," the Hudlar replied. "I don't intend going for the full other-species surgical qualification, just basic nursing and the FROB surgical course, taken concurrently. I joined the new Conway Project, so I'll be needed at home as soon as I can possibly make it.

"And to answer your earlier question," it added. "Believe it or not, Nurse, the condition of the majority of these patients will be alleviated if not cured. They will be able to lead long and useful lives that will be pain-free, mentally and, within limits, physically active."

"I'm impressed," Cha Thrat said, trying to keep the incredulity she felt from showing in her voice. "What is the Conway Project?"

"Rather than listen to my incomplete and inaccurate description," the Hudlar replied, "it would be better for you to learn about the project from Conway itself. It is the hospital's Diagnostician-in-Charge of Surgery, and it will be lecturing and demonstrating its new FROB major operative techniques here this afternoon.

"I shall be required to observe the operation," it went on. "But we will need surgeons so badly and in such large numbers that you would only have to express an interest in the project, not actually join it, to be invited to attend. It would be reassuring to have someone beside me who is almost as ignorant as I am."

"Other-species surgery," Cha Thrat said, "is my principal interest. But I've only just arrived in the ward. Would the Charge Nurse release me from duty so soon?"

"Of course," the FROB said as they were moving to the next patient. "Just so long as you do nothing to antagonize it."

"I won't," she said, then added, "at least, not deliberately."

There was no muffler around the third patient's speaking membrane, and a few minutes before their arrival it had been having an animated conversation about its grandchildren with a patient across the ward. Cha Thrat spoke the ritual greeting used by the healers on Sommaradva and, it seemed, by every medic in the hospital.

"How are you feeling today?"

"Well, thank you, Nurse," the patient replied, as she knew it would.

Plainly the being was anything but well. Although it was mentally alert and the degenerative process had not yet advanced to the stage where the pain-killing medication had no effect, the mere sight of the surface condition of the body and tentacles made her itch. But, like so many of the other patients she had treated, this one would not dream of suggesting that her ability was somehow lacking by saying that it was *not* well.

"When you've absorbed some more food," she said while her partner was busy with its sponge, "you will feel even better."

Fractionally better, she added silently.

"I haven't seen you before, Nurse," the patient went on. "You're new, aren't you? I think you have a most interesting and visually pleasing shape."

"The last time that was said to me," Cha Thrat said as she turned on the spray, "it was by an overardent young Sommaradvan of the opposite sex."

Untranslatable sounds came from the patient's speaking membrane and the great, disease-wasted body began twitching in its cradle. Then it said, "Your sexual integrity is quite safe with me, Nurse. Regrettably, I am too old and infirm for it to be otherwise."

A Sommaradvan memory came back to her, of seriously wounded and immobilized warrior-patients of her own species trying to flirt with her during surgical rounds, and she did not know whether to laugh or cry.

"Thank you," she said. "But I may need further reassurance in this matter when you become convalescent..."

It was the same with the other patients. The Hudlar nurse said very little while the patients and Cha Thrat did all the talking. She was new to the ward, a member of a species from a world about which they knew nothing, and a subject, therefore, of the most intense but polite curiosity. They did not want to discuss themselves or their distressing physical conditions, they wanted to talk about Cha Thrat and Sommaradva, and she was pleased to satisfy their curiosity—at least about the more pleasant aspects of her life there.

The constant talking helped her to forget her growing fatigue and the fact that, in spite of the gravity compensators reducing the weight of the heavy nutrient tank to zero, the harness straps were making a painful and possibly permanent impression on her upper thorax. Then suddenly there were only three patients left to sponge and feed, and Segroth had materialized behind them.

"If you work as well as you talk, Cha Thrat," the Charge Nurse said, "I shall have no complaints." To the Hudlar, it added, "How is it doing, Nurse?"

"It assists me very well, Charge Nurse," the FROB trainee replied, "and without complaint. It is pleasant and at ease with the patients."

"Good, good," Segroth said, its fur rippling in approval. "But Cha Thrat belongs to another one of those species that require food at least three times a day if a pleasant disposition is to be maintained, and the midday meal is overdue. Would you like to finish the rest of the patients by yourself, Nurse?"

"Of course," the Hudlar said as Segroth was turning away.

"Charge Nurse," Cha Thrat said quickly. "I realize that I've only just arrived, but could I have permission to attend the—"

"The Conway lecture," Segroth finished for her. "Naturally, you'll find any excuse to escape the hard work of the ward. But perhaps I do you an injustice. Judging by the conversations I have overheard on the sound sensors, you have displayed good control of your feelings while talking with the patients and, considering your surgical background, the practical aspects of the lecture should not worry you. However, if any part of the demonstration distresses you, leave at once and as unobtrusively as possible.

"Permission would normally be refused a newly joined trainee like yourself," it ended, "but if you can make it to the dining hall and back inside the hour, you may attend."

"Thank you," Cha Thrat said to the Kelgian's already departing back. Quickly she began loosening the nutrient tank harness.

"Before you go, Nurse," the Hudlar trainee said, "would you mind using some of that stuff on me? I'm starving!"

Cha Thrat was among the first to arrive and stood— Hudlars did not use chairs, so the FROB lecture theater did not provide them—as close as possible to the operating cradle while she watched the place fill up. There was a scattering of Melfan ELNTs, Kelgian DBLFs, and Tralthan FGLIs among those present, but the majority were Hudlars in various stages of training. She was hemmed in by FROBs, so much so that she did not think that she would be able to leave even if she should want to, and she assumed—she still could not tell them apart —that the one standing closest to her was her partner of the morning.

From the conversations going on around her it was obvious that Diagnostician Conway was regarded as a very important being indeed, a medical near-deity in whose mind resided, by means of a powerful spell and the instrumentation of O'Mara, the knowledge, memories, and instincts of many other-species personalities. Having seen the hapless condition of the FROB ward's pre-op patients, she was looking forward with growing anticipation to seeing it perform.

In appearance Conway was not at all impressive. It was an Earth-human DBDG, slightly above average in height, with head fur that was a darker gray than the wizard O'Mara's.

It spoke with the quiet certainty of a great ruler, and began the lecture without preamble.

"For any of you who may not be completely informed regarding the Hudlar Project, and who may be concerned with the ethical position, let me assure you that the patient on which we will be operating today, its fellows in the FROB ward, and all the other geriatric and pre-geriatric cases waiting in great distress on the home world, are all candidates for elective surgery.

"The number of cases is so great—a significant proportion of the planetary population, in fact—that we cannot possibly treat them in Sector General . . ."

As the Earth-human Diagnostician talked on, Cha Thrat became increasingly disheartened by the sheer magnitude of the problem. A planet that contained, at any given time, many millions of beings in the same horrifying condition as the patients she had been recently attending was an idea that her mind did not want to face. But it became clear that Conway had faced it and was working toward an eventual solution—by training large numbers of the medically untutored Hudlars, assisted by other-species volunteers, to help themselves.

Initially, Sector General would provide basic tuition in FROB physiology, pre- and postoperative nursing care, and training in just one simple surgical procedure. The successful candidates, unless they displayed such an unusually high aptitude that they were offered positions on the staff, would return home to establish their own training organizations. Within three generations there would be enough own-species specialist surgeons to make this dreadful and hitherto unavoidable scourge of the Hudlars a thing of the past.

The sheer scale and what appeared to be the utter,

criminal irresponsibility of the project shocked and sickened Cha Thrat. Conway was not training surgeons, it was turning out vast numbers of conscienceless, organic machines! She had been surprised when the Hudlar trainee had mentioned the time required for qualification, and it was possible that the hospital's tutors would be able to provide the necessary practical training during that short period. But what about the long-term indoctrination, the courses of mental and physical exercises that would prepare the candidates for the acceptance of responsibility and pain, and the long, presurgery novitiate? As the Diagnostician talked on, there was no mention of these things.

"This is incredible!" Cha Thrat said suddenly.

Softly the Hudlar beside her said, "Yes, indeed. But be quiet, Nurse, and listen."

"The degree and extent of the suffering among aging FROBs is impossible to imagine or describe," the Earthhuman was saying. "If the majority of the other races in the Federation were faced with the same problem, there would be one simple, if completely unsatisfactory, answer for the individuals concerned. But the Hudlars, unfortunately or otherwise, are philosophically incapable of self-termination.

"Would you bring in Patient FROB-Eleven Thirty-two, please."

A mobile operating frame driven by a Kelgian nurse glided to a stop in front of the Diagnostician. It held the patient—one of the Hudlars she had sprayed that morning—already prepared for surgery.

"The condition of Eleven Thirty-two," the Earthhuman went on, "is too far advanced for surgical intervention to reverse the degenerative processes completely. However, today's procedure will ensure that the remainder of the patient's life will be virtually pain-free, which, in turn, means that it will be mentally alert, and, it will be able to lead a useful if not very active life. With Hudlars who elect for surgery before the onset of the condition, and there are few members in the age groups concerned who do not so elect, the results are immeasurably better.

"Before we begin," it continued, unclipping the deep scanner, "I would like to discuss the physiological reasons behind the distressing clinical picture we see before us..."

What miracle of irresponsible and illegal surgery, Cha Thrat wondered sickly, *could make Eleven Thirty-two well again?*

But her curiosity was outweighed by a growing fear. She did not know whether or not she could bear to hear the answers that this terrible Earth-person would give, and still retain her sanity.

"In common with the majority of the life-forms known to us," the Diagnostician continued, "the primary cause of the degenerative process known as aging is caused by increasing loss of efficiency in the major organs and an associated circulatory failure.

"With the FROB life-form," it went on, "the irreversible loss of function and the abnormal degree of calcification and fissuring in the extremities is aggravated by the demand for nutrient, which is no longer available.

"From your FROB physiology lectures," it continued, "you know that a healthy adult of the species possesses an extremely high metabolic rate that requires a virtually continuous supply of nutrient, which is metabolized, via the absorption mechanism, to supply major organs such as the two hearts, the absorption organs themselves, the womb when the entity is in gravid female mode, and, of course, the limbs. These six immensely strong limbs form the most energy-hungry system of the body, and demand close to eighty percent of the total nutrient metabolized.

"If this excessive demand is removed from the energy equation," the Diagnostician said slowly and emphatically, "the nutrient supply to less-demanding systems is automatically increased to optimum."

There was no longer any doubt in Cha Thrat's mind regarding the surgical intentions of the Earth-human, but still she was trying to convince herself that the situation was not quite as bad as it seemed. With quiet urgency she asked, "Do this life-form's limbs regenerate?"

"That is a stupid question," the Hudlar beside her said. "No, if such were the case, the limb musculature and circulation would not have degenerated to their present state in the first place. Please be quiet, Nurse, and listen."

"I meant the Earth-human's limbs," Cha Thrat said insistently, "not the patient's."

"No," the Hudlar impatiently said. When she tried to ask other questions, it ignored her.

Conway was saying, "The major problem encountered while performing deep surgery on any life-form evolved for heavy gravity and high atmospheric pressure conditions is, of course, internal organ displacement and decompression damage. But with this type of operation there is no real problem. The bleeding is controlled with clamps, and the procedure is simple enough for any of you advanced trainees to perform it under supervision.

"In fact," the Diagnostician added, showing its teeth suddenly, "I shall not even lay a cutter on this patient. The responsibility for the operation will be collectively yours."

A quiet, polite uproar greeted the Earth-human's

words and the trainees surged closer to the barrier, imprisoning Cha Thrat within a barricade of metal-hard Hudlar bodies and tentacles. So many conversations were going on at once that several times her translator was overloaded, but from what she did hear it seemed that they were all in favor of this utterly shameful act of professional cowardice, and stupidly eager rather than afraid to take surgical responsibility.

She had never in her wildest and most fearful imaginings expected anything like this, nor thought to prepare herself for such a vicious and demoralizing attack on her ethical code. Suddenly she wanted away from this nightmare with its group of demented and immoral Hudlars. But they were all too busy flapping their speaking membranes at each other to hear her.

"Quiet, please," Diagnostician Conway said, and there was silence. "I don't believe in springing surprises, pleasant or otherwise, but sooner or later you Hudlars will be performing multiple amputations like this on your home world hour after hour, day after day, and I feel that you should get used to the idea sooner rather than later."

It paused to look at a white card it was holding in one hand, then said, "Trainee FROB-Seventy-three, you will begin."

Cha Thrat had an almost overwhelming urge to shout and scream that she wanted out and far away from this hellish demonstration. But Conway, a Diagnostician and one of the hospital's high rulers, had commanded silence, and the discipline of a lifetime could not be broken—even though she was far from Sommaradva. She pushed silently against the wall of Hudlar bodies enclosing her on three sides, but her attempts to pass through were ignored if they were even noticed. Everyone's eyes were focused exclusively on the operating cradle and patient FROB-Eleven Thirty-two and, in spite of her attempts to look elsewhere, hers were turned in the same direction.

It was obvious from the start that Seventy-three's problem was psychological rather than surgical, and caused by the close proximity of one of the hospital's foremost Diagnosticians watching every move it made. But Conway was being both tactful and reassuring during its spoken commentary on the operation. Whenever the trainee seemed hesitant, it managed to include the necessary advice and directions without making the recipient feel stupid and even more unsettled.

There was something of the wizard in this Diagnostician, Cha Thrat thought, but that in no way excused its unprofessional behavior.

"The Number Three cutter is used for the initial incision and for removing the underlying layers of muscle," Conway was saying, "but some of us prefer the finer Number Five for the venous and arterial work, since the smoother edges of the incisions make suturing much easier as well as aiding subsequent healing.

"The nerve bundles," it went on, "are given extra length and covered with inert metal caps, and are positioned just beneath the surface of the stump. This facilitates the nerve impulse augmentors that will later control the prosthetics..."

"What," Cha Thrat wondered aloud, "are prosthetics?"

"Artificial limbs," the Hudlar beside her said. "Watch and listen; you can ask questions afterward."

There was plenty to see but less to hear because Trainee FROB-Seventy-three was working much faster and no longer seemed to be in need of the Diagnostician's covert directions. Not only could Cha Thrat look directly at the operative field, but the internal scanner picture was also being projected onto a large screen above and behind the patient, so that she could watch the careful, precise movements of the instruments within the limb.

Then suddenly there was no limb—it had fallen stiffly, like the diseased brnch of a tree, into a container on the floor—and she had her first view of a stump. Desperately she fought the urge to be physically sick.

"The large flap of tegument is folded over the stub limb," Conway was saying, "and is attached by staples that dissolve when the healing process is complete. Because of the elevated internal pressure of this life-form and the extreme resistance of the tegument to puncturing by needle, normal suturing is useless and it is advisable, in fact, to err on the generous side where the staples are concerned."

There had been unsavory rumors of cases like this on Sommaradva, traumatic amputation of limbs during a major industrial or transportation accident, after which the casualty had survived, or insisted on surviving. The wounds had been discreetly tidied up, usually by young, nonresponsible and as yet unqualified warrior-surgeons or even, if nobody else was available, by an amenable servile-healer. But even when the warriors concerned had sustained the wounds as a result of an act of bravery, the matter was hushed up and forgotten as quickly as possible.

The casualties went into voluntary exile. They would never dream of revealing their disabilities or deformities to the public gaze, nor would they have been allowed to do so. On Sommaradva they had too much respect for their bodies. And for people to parade around with mechanical devices replacing their limbs was abhorrent and unthinkable.

"Thank you, Seventy-three, that was well done," the Earth-human said, glancing once again at its white card. "Trainee Sixty-one, would you like to show us what you can do?"

Abhorrent and repulsive though it was, Cha Thrat could not take her eyes from the operating cradle while the new FROB demonstrated its surgical prowess. The depth and positioning of every incision and instrument was burned into her memory as if she were watching some horrid but fascinating perversion. Sixty-one was followed by two other advanced trainees, and patient FROB-Eleven Thirty-two was left with only two of its six limbs remaining in place.

"There is still a fair degree of mobility in one of the forelimbs," Conway said, "and, considering the advanced age and reduced mental adaptability, I feel that it should be left intact for psychological as well as physiological reasons. It may well be that the increased blood and available nutrient supply due to the absence of the other limbs will partially improve the muscle condition and circulation in this one. As you can see, the other forelimb has degenerated virtually to the point of necrosis and must be removed.

"Trainee Cha Thrat," it added, "will perform the amputation."

Suddenly they were all looking at her, and for a moment Cha Thrat had the ridiculous feeling that she was in the center of a three-dimensional picture, frozen in this nightmare for all eternity. But the real nightmare lay a few minutes in the future, when she would be forced into a major professional decision.

Her partner from the ward vibrated its speaking membrane quietly. "This is a great professional compliment, Nurse."

Before she could reply, the Diagnostician was speaking again, to everyone.

It said, "Cha Thrat is a native of a newly discovered world, Sommaradva, where it was a qualified surgeon. It has prior experience of other-species surgery on an Earth-human DBDG, a life-form that it had encountered for the first time only a few hours earlier. In spite of this, the work was skillfully done, Senior Physician Edanelt tells me, and undoubtedly saved the entity's limb and probably its life. And now it can further increase its other-species surgical experience with a much less difficult procedure on an FROB."

Encouragingly it ended, "Come forward, Cha Thrat. Don't be afraid. If anything should go wrong, I will be here to help."

There was a great, cold fear inside her mixed with the helpless anger of having to face the ultimate challenge without adequate spiritual preparation. But the Diagnostician's concluding words, suggesting that her natural fear might somehow keep her from doing the work, filled her with righteous anger. It was a hospital ruler and, no matter how misguided and irresponsibile its orders to her had seemed, they would be obeyed—that was the law. And no Sommaradvan of the warrior class would show fear before anyone, and that included a group of other-species strangers. But still she hesitated.

Impatiently the Earth-human said, "Are you capable of performing this operation?"

"Yes," she said.

Had it asked her if she *wanted* to perform the operation, Cha Thrat thought sadly as she moved toward the cradle, the answer would have been different. Then, with the incredibly sharp FROB Number Three cutter in her hand, she tried again.

"What," she asked quickly, "is my precise responsibility in this case?"

The Earth-human took a deep breath and let it out slowly, then said, "You are responsible for the surgical removal of the patient's left forelimb."

"Is it possible to save this limb?" she asked hesitantly. "Can the circulation be improved, perhaps by surgical enlargement of the blood vessels, or by—"

"No," said Conway firmly. "Please begin."

She made the initial incisions and proceeded exactly as the others had done, without further hesitation or need of prompting by the Diagnostician. Knowing what was to happen, she suppressed her fear and steadfastly refused to worry about or feel the pain until the moment it would engulf her. She was utterly determined now to show this strange, highly advanced but seemingly nonresponsible medic how a truly dedicated warrior-surgeon of Sommaradva was expected to behave.

As she was inserting the last few staples into the flap covering the stump, the Diagnostician said warmly, "That was fast, precise, and quite exemplary work, Cha Thrat. I am particularly impressed by— What are you *doing*?"

She thought that her intentions were obvious as soon as she lifted the Number Three cutter. Sommaradvan DCNFs did not possess forelimbs as such but, she thought proudly, the removal of a left-side medial limb would satisfy the professional requirements of the situation. One quick, neat slice was enough, then she looked at it lying in the container among the Hudlar limbs and gripped the stump tightly to control the bleeding.

Her last conscious memory of the episode was of

Diagnostician Conway shouting above the general uproar into the communicator.

"FROB lecture theater on the double," it was saying urgently. "One DCNF, a traumatic amputation, self-inflicted. Ready the OR on Level Forty-three, dammit, and assemble a microsurgery team!"

Chapter 8

SHE could not be sure about the time required for her post-op recuperation, only that there had been lengthy periods of unconsciousness and a great many visits from Chief Psychologist O'Mara and Diagnosticians Thornnastor and Conway. The DBLF nurse assigned to her made caustic comments about the special attention she was receiving from the hospital's hierarchy, the quantity of food she was moving for a supposedly sick patient, and about a newly arrived Nidian trainee whose furry little head had been turned by Cresk-Sar of all people. But when she tried to discuss her own case it was obvious from the Kelgian nurse's agitated fur that that was a forbidden subject.

It did not matter because, by accident or design, the medication she was receiving had the effect of making her feel as if her mind was some kind of dirigible airship, moving at her direction but detached and floating free of all mundane problems. It was, she realized, a very comfortable but suggestible state.

During one of its later visits, O'Mara had suggested that, regardless of her reasons for acting as she had, she had discharged her particularly strict professional obligations, so that no further action was required on her part. The limb had been completely severed and removed from the torso. The fact that Conway and Thornnastor had together performed some very fancy microsurgery to reattach it, with no loss of function or feeling, was a piece of good fortune that she should accept gratefully and without guilt.

It had taken a long time to convince the wizard that she had already arrived at the same conclusion, and that she was grateful, not only for her good fortune, but to Diagnosticians Conway and Thornnastor for giving her back the limb. The only part of the incident that continued to puzzle her, she had told O'Mara, was the adverse reaction of everyone to the noble and praiseworthy thing she had done.

O'Mara had seemed to relax then, and it had proceeded with a long, devious spell that involved subjects which Cha Thrat had considered too personal and sensitive to be discussed with a fellow Sommaradvan, much less a stranger. Perhaps it was the medication that reduced her feelings of shock and outrage, and made the suggestions of the wizard seem worthy of consideration rather than outright rejection.

One of its suggestions had been that, when viewed nonsubjectively, the action she had taken had been neither noble nor praiseworthy, but a little bit silly. By the end of that visit she almost agreed with it, and suddenly she was allowed visitors.

Tarsedth and the Hudlar trainee were the first callers. The Kelgian came bustling forward to ask how she was feeling and to examine her scars, while the FROB remained standing in silence just inside the entrance. Cha

Thrat wondered if there was anything bothering it, forgetting for the moment that her medication frequently caused her to vocalize her thoughts.

"Nothing," said Tarsedth. "Just ignore the big softie. When I arrived it was outside the door, don't know for how long, afraid that the mere sight of another Hudlar would give you some kind of emotional relapse. In spite of all that muscle, Hudlars are sensitive souls. According to what O'Mara told Cresk-Sar, you are unlikely to do anything sudden or melodramatic. You are neither mentally unbalanced nor emotionally disturbed. Its exact words were that you were normally crazy but not certifiably mad, which is the condition of quite a few people who work in this place."

It turned suddenly to regard the FROB, then went on. "Come closer! It is in bed, with a limb and most of its body immobilized, it has been blasted into low orbit with tranquilizers, and it isn't likely to bite you!"

The Hudlar came forward and said shyly, "We all, everyone who was there, wish you well. That includes Patient Eleven Thirty-two, who is pain-free now and making good progress. And Charge Nurse Segroth whose good wishes were, ah, more perfunctory. Will you recover the full use of the limb?"

"Don't be stupid," Tarsedth broke in. "With two Diagnosticians on the case it doesn't dare not make a complete recovery." To Cha Thrat it went on. "But so much has been happening to you recently that I can't keep up. Is it true that you ticked off the Chief Psychologist in front of everybody in the Chalder ward, called it some kind of witch-doctor, and reminded it of its professional duty toward Patient AUGL-One Sixteen? According to the stories going around—"

"It wasn't quite as bad as that," Cha Thrat said.

"It never is," the DBLF said, its fur subsiding in disappointment. "But the business during the FROB demonstration, now. You can't deny or diminish what happened there."

"Perhaps," the Hudlar quietly said, "it would rather not talk about that."

"Why not?" Tarsedth asked. "Everyone else is talking about it."

Cha Thrat was silent for a moment as she looked up at the head and shoulders of the Kelgian projecting like a silver-furred cone over one side of her bed and the enormous body of the Hudlar looming over the other. She tried to make her unnaturally fuzzy mind concentrate on what she wanted to say.

"I would prefer to talk about all the lectures I've missed," she said finally. "Was there anything especially interesting or important? And would you ask Cresk-Sar if I could have a remote control for the viewscreen, so I can tune in to the teaching channels? Tell it that I have nothing to do here and I would like to continue with my studies as soon as possible."

"Friend," Tarsedth said, its fur rising into angry spikes, "I think you would be wasting your time."

For the first time she wished that her Kelgian classmate was capable of something less than complete honesty. She had been expecting to hear something like this, but the bad news could have been broken more gently.

"What our forthright friend should have told you," the Hudlar said, "is that we inquired about your exact status from Senior Physician Cresk-Sar, who would not give us a firm answer. It said that you were guilty not so much of contravening hospital rules but of breaking rules that nobody had dreamed of writing. The decision on what to do with you has been referred up, it said, and you could expect a visit from O'Mara quite soon.

"When asked if we could bring you lecture material," it ended apologetically, "Cresk-Sar said no."

It did not make any difference how it was broken, she thought after they had gone, the news was equally bad. But the sudden, raucous sound of her bedside communicator kept her from dwelling for too long on her troubles.

It was Patient AUGL-One Sixteen who, with Charge Nurse Hredlichi's cooperation, was shouting into one of the Nurses' Station communicators from the entrance to the Chalder ward. It began by apologizing for the physiological and environmental problems that kept it from visiting her in person, then told her how much it was missing her visits—the Earth-human wizard O'Mara, it said, lacked her sympathetic manner and charm—and it hoped she was recovering with no physical or mental distress.

"Everything is fine," she lied. It was not a good thing to burden a patient with its medic's troubles, even when the medic was temporarily a patient. "How are you?"

"Very well, thank you," the Chalder replied, sounding enthusiastic in spite of the fact that its words were reaching her through two communicators, a translator, and a considerable quantity of water. "O'Mara says that I can leave and rejoin my family very soon, and can start contacting the space administration on Chalder about my old job. I'm still young for a Chalder, you know, and I do really feel well."

"I'm very happy for you, One Sixteen," Cha Thrat said, deliberately omitting its name because others might be listening who were not entitled to use it. She was surprised by the strength of her feelings toward the creature.

"I've heard the nurses talking," the Chalder went on, "and it seems like you are in serious trouble. I hope all goes well for you, but if not, and you have to leave the hospital . . . Well, you are so far from Sommaradva out here that if you felt like seeing another world on your way home, my people would be pleased to have you for as long as you liked to stay. We're pretty well advanced on Chalderescol and your food synthesis and life-support would be no problem.

"It's a beautiful world," it added, "much, much nicer than the Chalder ward . . ."

When the Chalder eventually broke contact, she settled back into the pillows, feeling tired but not depressed or unhappy, thinking about the ocean world of Chalderescol. Before joining the AUGL ward she had studied the library tape on that world with the idea of being able to talk about home to the patients, so she was not completely unfamiliar with the planet. The thought of living there was exciting, and she knew that, as an off-planet person entitled to call Muromeshomon by name, its family and friends would make her welcome however long or short her stay. But thoughts like that were uncomfortable because they presupposed that she would be leaving the hospital.

Instead she wondered how the normally shy and gentle Chalder had been able to prevail upon the acid-tongued Hredlichli to use the Nurses' Station communicator as it had done. Could it have forced cooperation by threatening to wreck the place again? Or, more likely, had the Chalder's call to her been supported, perhaps even suggested, by O'Mara?

That, too, was an uncomfortable thought, but it did not keep her awake. The continuing spell of the Earth-human wizard or the medication it had prescribed, or both, were still having their insidious effect.

During the days that followed she was visited singly and, where physiological considerations permitted, in small groups by her classmates. Cresk-Sar came twice but, like all the other visitors, the tutor would not talk about medical matters at all. Then one day O'Mara and Diagnostician Conway arrived together and would discuss nothing else.

"Good morning, Cha Thrat, how are you feeling?" the Diagnostician began, as she knew it would.

"Very well, thank you," she replied, as it knew she would. After that she was subjected to the most meticulously thorough physical examination she had ever experienced.

"You've probably realized by now that all of this wasn't strictly necessary," Conway said as it replaced the sheet that had been covering her body. "However, it was my first opportunity to have a really close look at the DCNF physiological classification as a whole, as opposed to one of the limbs. Thank you, it was interesting and most instructive.

"But now that you are completely recovered," it went on, with a quick glance toward O'Mara, "and will require only a course of exercises before you would be fit for duty, what are we going to do with you?"

She suspected that it was a rhetorical question, but she badly wanted to reply to it. Anxiously she said, "There have been mistakes, misunderstandings. They will not occur again. I would like to remain in the hospital and continue my training."

"*No!*" Conway said sharply. In a quieter voice it went on. "You are a fine surgeon, Cha Thrat—potentially a great one. Losing you would be a shameful waste of talent. But keeping you on the medical staff, with your peculiar ideas of what constitutes ethical behavior, is out of the question. There isn't a ward in the hospital that would accept you for practical training now. Segroth took you only because O'Mara and I requested it.

"I like to make my surgery lectures as interesting and

exciting as possible for the trainees," Conway added, "but there are limits, dammit!"

Before either of them could say the words that would send her from the hospital, Cha Thrat said quickly, "What if something could be done that would guarantee my future good behavior? One of my early lectures was on the Educator tape system of teaching alien physiology and medicine that, in effect, gives the recipient an other-species viewpoint. If I could be given such a tape, one with a more acceptable, to you, code of professional behavior, then I would be sure to stay out of trouble."

She waited anxiously, but the two Earth-humans were looking at each other in silence, ignoring her.

Without the Educator or physiology tape system, she had learned, a multispecies hospital like Sector General could not have existed. No single brain, regardless of species, could hold the enormous quantity of physiological knowledge required to successfully treat the variety of patients the hospital received. But complete physiological data on any patient's species was available by means of an Educator tape, which was simply the brain record of some great medical mind belonging to the same or a similar species as the patient to be treated.

A being taking such a tape had to share its mind with a completely alien personality. Subjectively, that was exactly how it felt; all of the memories and experiences and personality traits of the being who had donated the tape were impressed on the receiving mind, not just selected pieces of medical data. An Educator tape could not be edited and the degree of confusion, emotional disorientation, and personality dislocation caused to a recipient could not be adequately described even by the Senior Physicians and Diagnosticians who experienced it.

The Diagnosticians were the hospital's highest medical rulers, beings whose minds were both adaptable and stable enough to retain permanently up to ten physiology tapes at one time. To their data-crammed minds was given the job of original research into xenological medicine and the treatment of new diseases in newly discovered life-forms.

But Cha Thrat was not interested in subjecting herself voluntarily, as had the Diagnosticians, to a multiplicity of alien ideas and influences. She had heard it said among the staff that any person sane enough to be a Diagnostician had to be mad, and she could well believe it. Her idea represented a much less drastic solution to the problem.

"If I had an Earth-human, a Kelgian, even a Nidian personality sharing my mind," she persisted, "I would understand why the things I sometimes do are considered wrong, and would be able to avoid doing them. The other-species material would be used for interpersonal behavioral guidance only. As a trainee I would not try to use its medical or surgical knowledge on my patients without permission."

The Diagnostician was suddenly overcome by an attack of coughing. When it recovered it said, "Thank you, Cha Thrat. I'm sure the patients would thank you, too. But it's impossible to... O'Mara, this is your field. You answer it."

The Chief Psychologist moved close to the bedside and looked down at her. It said, "Hospital regulations do not allow me to do as you ask, nor would I do so if I could. Even though you are an unusually strong and stubborn personality, you would find it very difficult to control the other occupant of your mind. It *isn't* an alien entity fighting for control, but because the type of leading medical specialist who donates the tapes is frequently a very strong-minded and aggressive person used to getting its own way, it would feel as if it is taking control. The ensuing purely subjective conflict could give rise to episodes of pain, skin eruptions, and more troublesome organic malfunctionings. All have a psychosomatic basis, of course, but they will hurt you just as much as the real thing. The risk of permanent mental damage is great and, until a trainee has learned to understand the external personalities of the beings around it, it would not receive one of their Educator tapes.

"In your case there is an additional reason," O'Mara added. "You are a female."

Sommaradvan prejudices, she thought furiously, *even here in Sector General!* and made a sound that at home would have resulted in an immediate and probably violent breakdown in communication. Fortunately, the sound did not translate.

"The conclusion you have just jumped to is wrong," O'Mara went on. "It is simply that the females of all the two-sexed species yet discovered have evolved with certain peculiarities, as opposed to abnormalities, of mind. One of them is a deeply rooted, sex-based fastidiousness and aversion toward anything or anyone entering or trying to possess their minds. The only exception is in the situation when life-mating has taken place, where, in many species, the processes of physical and mental sharing and the feelings of possession complement each other. But I can't imagine you falling in love with an other-species mind impression."

"Do male entities," Cha Thrat asked, both satisfied and intrigued by the explanation, "receive mind recordings from other-species females, then? Could *I* be given a female tape?"

"There is only one recorded instance of that..." O'Mara began.

"Let's not go into that," Conway broke in, its face becoming a darker shade of pink. "I'm sorry, Cha Thrat, you cannot be given an Educator tape, now or ever. O'Mara has explained why, just as he has explained the political circumstances of your arrival here and the delicate state of the cultural contact on Sommaradva that would be jeopardized if we simply dismissed you from the hospital. Wouldn't it be better for all concerned if you left of your own free will?"

Cha Thrat was silent for a moment, her eyes turned toward the limb that she had thought would be lost forever, trying to find the right words. Then she said, "You don't owe me anything for my work on ship ruler Chiang. I have already explained, during my first meeting with the Chief Psychologist, that the delay in attending to its injuries was caused by my not wanting to lose a limb because if, as a result of my decision to perform the operation it lost a limb, then so would I. As a warrior-surgeon I cannot escape a responsibility willingly accepted.

"And now," she went on, "if I were to leave the hospital as you suggest, it would not be of my own free will. I cannot do, or leave undone, something that I know to be wrong."

The Diagnostician was also looking at the replaced limb. "I believe you," it said.

O'Mara exhaled slowly and half turned to leave. It said, "I'm very sorry I didn't pick up on that 'losing a limb' remark you made at our first meeting; it would have saved us all a lot of trouble. Against my better judgment I relented after the AUGL-One Sixteen business, but the bloody drama during the FROB demonstration was too much. The remainder of your stay here will not be very pleasant because, in spite of the earlier recommendations you've had from Diagnostician Conway and myself, nobody wants you anywhere near their patients.

"Let's face it, Cha Thrat," it ended as both Earthhumans moved toward the door, "you're in the doghouse."

She heard them talking with a third person in the corridor, but the words were too muffled for translation. Then the door opened and another Earth-human entered. It was wearing the dark-green uniform of the Monitor Corps and looked familiar.

Cheerfully it said, "I've been waiting outside in case they couldn't talk you into leaving, and O'Mara was pretty sure they wouldn't. I'm Timmins, in case you don't remember me. We have to have a long talk.

"And before you ask," it went on, "the doghouse, so far as you're concerned, is the Maintenance Department."

Chapter 9

IT was obvious from the beginning that Lieutenant Timmins did not consider its job to be either servile or menial, and it was not long before the Lieutenant had her beginning to feel the same way. It wasn't just the Earth-human's quiet enthusiasm for its job, there was also the portable viewer and set of study tapes it had left at her bedside that convinced her that this was work for warriors—although not, of course, for warrior-surgeons. The wide-ranging and complex problems of providing technical and environmental support for the sixty-odd— some of them very odd indeed—life-forms comprising the hospital's patients and staff made her earlier medical and physiological studies seem easy by comparison.

Her last formal contact with the training program was when Cresk-Sar arrived, carried out a brief but thorough examination, and, subject to the findings of the eye specialist, Doctor Yeppha, who would be visiting her shortly, pronounced her physically fit to begin the new duties. She asked if there would be any objection to her continuing to view the medical teaching channels in her free time, and the Senior Physician told her that she could watch whatever she pleased in her spare time, but it was unlikely that she would ever be able to put any of the medical knowledge gained into practice.

It ended by saying that while it was relieved that she was no longer the Training Department's responsibility, it was sorry to lose her and that it joined her erstwhile colleagues in wishing her success and personal satisfaction in the new work she had chosen.

Doctor Yeppha was a new life-form to her experience, a small, tripedal, fragile being that she classified as DRVJ. From the furry dome of its head there sprouted, singly and in small clusters, at least twenty eyes. She wondered whether the overabundance of visual sensors had any bearing on its choice of specialty, but thought it better not to ask.

"Good morning, Cha Thrat," it said, taking a tape from the pouch at its waist and pushing it into the viewer. "This is a visual acuity test designed primarily to check for color blindness. We don't care if you have muscles like a Hudlar or a Cinrusskin, there are machines to do the really heavy work, but you have to be able to see. Not only that, you must be able to clearly identify colors and the subtle shades and dilution of color brought about by changes in the intensity of the ambient lighting. What do you see there?"

"A circle made up of red spots," Cha Thrat replied, "enclosing a star of green and blue spots."

"Good," Yeppha said. "I am making this sound much simpler than it really is, but you will learn the complexities in time. The service bays and interconnecting tunnels are filled with cable looms and plumbing all of which is color coded. This enables the maintenance people to tell at a glance which are power cables and which the less dangerous communication lines, or which pipes carry oxygen, chlorine, methane, or organic effluvia. The danger of contamination of wards by other-species atmospheres is always present, and such an environmental catastrophe should not be allowed to occur because some partially sighted nincompoop has connected up the wrong set of pipes. What do you see now?"

And so it went on, with Yeppha putting designs in subtly graduated colors on the screen and Cha Thrat telling it what she saw or did not see. Finally the DRVJ turned off the viewer and replaced the tape in its pouch.

"You don't have as many eyes as I do," it said, "but they all work. There is no bar, therefore, to you joining the Maintenance Department. My sincere commiserations. Good luck!"

The first three days were to be devoted exclusively to unsupervised lessons in internal navigation. Timmins explained that whenever or wherever an emergency occurred, or even if a minor fault was reported, the maintenance people were expected to be at the site of the trouble with minimum delay. Because they would normally be carrying tools or replacement parts with them on a self-powered trolley, they were forbidden the use of the main hospital corridors, except in the direst of emergencies—staff and patient traffic there was congested enough as it was without risking a vehicular thrombosis. She was therefore expected to find her way from A to B, with diversions through H, P, and W, without leaving the service bays and tunnels or asking directions of anyone she might meet.

Neither was she allowed to make an illegal check on her position by emerging into the main corridor system to go to lunch.

"Wearing the lightweight protective envelope will probably be unnecessary," Timmins said as he lifted the grating in the floor just outside her room, "but maintenance people always wear them in case they have to pass through an area where there may be a nonurgent seepage of own-species toxic gas. You have sensors to warn you of the presence of all toxic contaminants, including radiation, a lamp in case one of the tunnels has a lighting failure, a map with your route clearly shown, a distress beacon in case you become hopelessly lost or some other personal emergency occurs, and, if I may say so, more than enough food to keep you alive for a week much less a day!

"Don't worry and don't try to hurry, Cha Thrat," it went on. "Look on this as a long, leisurely walk through unexplored territory, with frequent breaks for a picnic. I'll see you outside Access Hatch Twelve in Corridor Seven on Level One Twenty in fifteen hours, or less."

It laughed suddenly and added, "Or possibly more."

The service tunnels were very well lit, but low and narrow—at least so far as the Sommaradvan life-form was concerned—with alcoves set at frequent intervals along their length. The alcoves were puzzling in that they were empty of cable runs, pipes, or any form of mechanisms, but she discovered their purpose when a Kelgian driving a powered trolley came charging along the tunnel toward her and yelled, "Move aside, stupid!"

Apart from that encounter she seemed to have the tunnel to herself, and she was able to move much more easily than she had ever been able to do in the main corridor whose floor was now above her head. Through the ventilator grilles she could clearly hear the sounds of thumping and tapping and slithering of other-species ambulatory appendages overhead, and the indescribable babble of growling, hissing, gobbling, and cheeping conversation that accompanied it.

She moved forward steadily, careful not to be surprised by another fast-moving vehicle as she consulted her map, and occasionally stopped to dictate notes describing the size, diameter, and color codings on the protective casings of the mechanisms and connecting pipes and cable runs that covered the tunnel walls and roof. The notes, Timmins had told her, would enable it to check her progress during the test, as well as give her an important check on her general location.

The power and communication lines would look the same anywhere in the hospital, but most of the plumbing here bore the color codings for water and the atmospheric mixture favored by the warm-blooded, oxygen-breathing life-forms that made up more than half of the Federation's member species. Under the levels where they breathed chlorine, methane, or super-heated steam the colors would be much different and so would be her protective clothing.

A mechanism that did not appear to be working caught her attention. Through its transparent cover she could see a group of unlit indicators and a serial number that probably meant something to the entities who had built the thing, but to nobody else who was not familiar with their written language. She located and pressed the plate of the audible label and switched on her translator.

"I am a standby pump on the drinking water supply line to the DBLF ward Eighty-three diet kitchen," it announced. "Functioning is automatic when required, currently inoperative. The hinged inspection panel is opened by inserting your general-purpose key into the slot marked with a red circle and turning right through ninety degrees. For component repair or replacement consult Maintenance Instructions Tape Three, Section One Twenty. Don't forget to close the panel again before you leave.

"I am a standby pump..." it was beginning again when she took her hand away, silencing it.

At first she had been worried by the thought of traveling continuously along the low, narrow service tunnels, even though O'Mara had assured Timmins that her psych profile was free of any tendency toward claustrophobia. All of the tunnels were brightly lit and, she had been told, they remained so even if they were unoccupied for long periods. On Sommaradva this would have been considered a criminal waste of power. But in Sector General the additional demand on the main reactor for continuous lighting was negligible, and was more than outweighed by the maintenance problem that would have been posed if fallible on-off switches had been installed at every tunnel intersection.

Gradually her route took her away from the corridors and the alien cacophony of the people using them, and she felt more completely and utterly alone than she had believed it possible to feel.

The absence of outside sounds made the subdued

humming and clicking of the power and pumping systems around her appear to grow louder and more threatening, and she took to pressing the audible labels at random, just to hear another voice—even though it was simply a machine identifying itself and its often mystifying purpose.

Occasionally she found herself thanking the machine for the information.

The color codings had begun to change from the oxygen-nitrogen and water markings to those for chlorine and the corrosive liquid that the Illensan PVSJ metabolism used as a working fluid, and the corridors were shorter with many more twists and turns. Before her confusion could grow into panic, she decided to make herself as comfortable as possible in an alcove, substantially reduce the quantity of food she was carrying, and think.

According to her map she was passing from the PVSJ section downward through one of the synthesizer facilities that produced the food required by the chlorine-breathers and into the section devoted to the supply of the AUGL water-breathers. That explained the seemingly contradictory markings and the square-sectioned conduits that made hissing, rumbling noises as the solid, prepackaged PVSJ food was being moved pneumatically along them. However, a large corner of the AUGL section had been converted to a PVSJ operating room and post-op observation ward, and this was joined to the main chlorine section by an ascending spiral corridor containing moving ramps for the rapid transfer of staff and patients, since the PVSJs were not physiologically suited to the use of stairs. The twists and turns of the service tunnel were necessary to get around these topologically complex obstructions. But if she got safely past this complicated interpenetration of the water- and chlorine-breathing sections, the journey should be much simpler.

There was no shortage of vocal company. Warning labels, which spoke whether she pressed them or not, advised her to check constantly for cross-species contamination.

Provision had been made to take food without unsealing her protective suit, but her sensors showed the area clear of toxic material in dangerous quantities, so she opened her visor. The smell was an indescribable combination of every sharp, acrid, heavy, unpleasant, and even pleasant smell that she had ever encountered but, fortunately, only in trace quantities. She ate her food, quickly closed the visor, and moved on with increased confidence.

Three long, straight sections of corridor later she realized that her confidence had been misplaced.

According to her estimates of the distances and directions she had traveled, Cha Thrat should be somewhere between the Hudlar and Tralthan levels. The tunnel walls should have been carrying the thick, heavily insulated power cables for the FROBs' artificial gravity grids and at least one distinctively marked pipe to supply their nutrient sprayers, as well as the air, water, and return waste conduits required by the warm-blooded, oxygen-breathing FGLIs. But the cable runs bore color combinations that should not have been there, and the only atmosphere line visible was the small-diameterpipe supplying air to the tunnel itself. Irritated with herself, she pressed the nearest audible label.

"I am an automatic self-monitoring control unit for synthesizer process One Twelve B," it said importantly. "Press blue stud and access panel will move aside. Warning. Only the container and audible label are reusable. If faulty, components must be replaced and not repaired. Not to be opened by MSVK, LSVO, or other species with low radiation tolerance unless special protective measures are taken."

She had no desire to open the cabinet, even though her radiation monitor was indicating that the area was safe for her particular life-form. At the next alcove she had another look at her map and list of color codings.

Somehow she had wandered into one of the sections that were inhabited only by automatic machinery. The map indicated fifteen such areas within the main hospital complex, and none of them was anywhere near her planned route. Plainly she had taken a wrong turning, perhaps a series of wrong turnings, soon after leaving the spiral tunnel connecting the PVSJ ward with its new operating room.

She moved on again, watching the tunnel walls and roof in the hope that the next change in the color codings would give her a clue to where she might be. She also cursed her own stupidity aloud and touched every label she passed, but soon decided that both activities were nonproductive. It was a wise decision because, at the next tunnel intersection, she heard distant voices.

Timmins had told her not to speak to anyone or to enter any of the public corridors. But, she reasoned, if she was already hopelessly off-course then there was nothing to stop her taking the side tunnel and moving toward the sound. Perhaps by listening at one of the corridor ventilating grilles she might overhear a conversation that would give her a clue to her present whereabouts.

The thought made Cha Thrat feel ashamed but, compared with some of the things she had been forced to think about recently, it was a small, personal dishonor that she thought she could live with.

There were lengthy breaks in the conversation. At first the voices were too quiet and distant for her translator to catch what was being said, and when she came closer the people concerned were indulging in one of their lengthy silences. The result was that when she came to the next intersection, she saw them before there was another chance to overhear them.

They were a Kelgian DBLF and an Earth-human DBDG, dressed in Maintenance coveralls with the additional insignia of Monitor Corps rank. There were tools and dismantled sections of piping on the floor between them and, after glancing up at her briefly, they went on talking to each other.

"I wondered what was coming at us along the corridor," the Kelgian said, "and making more noise than a drunken Tralthan. It must be the new DCNF we were told about, on its first day underground. We mustn't talk to it, not that I'd want to, anyway. Strange-looking creature, isn't it?"

"I wouldn't dream of talking to it, or vice versa," the DBDG replied. "Pass me the Number Eleven gripper and hold your end steady. Do you think it knows where it's going?"

The Kelgian's conical head turned briefly in the direction Cha Thrat was headed, and it said, "Not unless it was feeling that the tunnel walls were closing in on it, and it wanted to treat threatened claustrophobia with a jolt of agoraphobia by walking on the outer hull. This is no job for a Corps senior non-com shortly, if what the Major says is true, to be promoted Lieutenant."

"This is no job for anybody, so don't worry about it," the Earth-human said. It turned to look pointedly along the corridor to the left. "On the other hand, it could be contemplating a visit to the VTXM section. Stupid in a lightweight suit, of course, but maintenance trainees have to be stupid or they'd try for some other job."

The Kelgian made an angry sound that did not translate, then said, "Why is it that nowhere in the vast immensity of explored space have we discovered yet a single life-form whose body wastes smell nice?"

"My furry friend," the Earth-human said, "I think you may have touched upon one of the great philosophical truths. And on the subject of inexplicable phenomena, how could a Melfan Size Three dilator get into their waste-disposal system and travel through four levels before it gummed up the works down here?"

She could see the Kelgian's fur rippling under its coveralls as it said, "Do you think that DCNF is stupid? Is it going to stand there watching us all day? Is it intending to follow us home?"

"From what I've heard about Sommaradvans," the DBDG replied, still not looking directly at her, "I'd say it wasn't so much stupid as a bit slow-witted."

"Definitely slow-witted," the Kelgian agreed.

But Cha Thrat had already realized that, cloaked though they were by statements that were derogatory and personally insulting, the overheard conversation had contained three accurate points of reference which would easily enable her to establish her position and return to the planned route. She regarded the two maintenance people for a moment, sorry that she was forbidden to speak to them as they were to her. Quickly she made the formal sign of thanks between equals, then turned away to move in the only direction the two beings had *not* discussed.

"I think," the Kelgian said, "it made a rude gesture with its forward medial limb."

"In its place," the Earth-human replied, "I'd have done the same."

During the remainder of that interminable journey she double-checked every change of direction and kept watch for any unexpected alterations in color codings on the way to Level One Twenty, and paused only once to make another large dent in her food store. When she opened Access Hatch Twelve and climbed into Corridor Seven, Timmins was already there.

"Well done, Cha Thrat, you made it," the Earth-human said, showing its teeth. "Next time I'd better make the trip a little longer, and a lot more complicated. After that I'll let you help out with a few simple jobs. You may as well start earning your keep."

Feeling pleased and a little confused, she said, "I thought I arrived early. Have I kept you waiting long?"

Timmins shook its head. "Your distress beacon was for your own personal reassurance in case you felt lost or frightened. It was part of the test. But we keep permanent tracers on our people at all times, so I was aware of every move you made. Devious, aren't I? But you passed very close to a maintenance team at one stage. I hope you didn't ask them for directions. You know the rule."

Cha Thrat wondered if there was any rule in Sector General so inflexible that it could not be bent out of shape, and she hoped that the outer signs of her embarrassment could not be read by a member of another species.

"No," she replied truthfully, "we didn't speak to each other."

Chapter 10

IN the event, she was not given a job until Timmins had shown her the full range and complexity of the work that, one day, she might be capable of taking on. It was obvious that the Earth-human was quietly but intensely proud of its Maintenance Department and, with good reason, was showing off while trying to instill a little of its own pride in her. True, much of the work was servile, but there were aspects of it that called for the qualities of a warrior or even a minor ruler. Unlike the rigid stratification of labor practiced on Sommaradva, however, in the Maintenance Department advancement toward the higher levels was encouraged.

Timmins was doing an awful lot of encouraging, and seemed to be spending an unusually large proportion of its time showing her around.

"With respect," she said after one particularly interesting tour of the low-temperature methane levels, "your rank and obvious ability suggest that you have more important uses for your time than spending it with me, your most recent and, I suspect, most technically ignorant maintenance trainee. Why am I given this special treatment?"

Timmins laughed quietly and said, "You mustn't think that I'm neglecting more important work to be with you,

Cha Thrat. If I'm needed I can be contacted without delay. But that is unlikely to happen because my subordinates try very hard to make me feel redundant.

"You should find the next section particularly interesting," it went on. "It is the VTXM ward, which, strange as it may seem, forms part of the main reactor. You know from your medical lectures that the Telfi are a gestalt life-form who live by the direct absorption of hard radiation, so that all patient examination and treatment is by remote-controlled sensors and manipulators. To be assigned to maintenance in this area you would need special training in—"

"Special training," Cha Thrat broke in, beginning to lose her patience, "means special treatment. I have already asked this question. Am I being given special treatment?"

"Yes," the Earth-human said sharply. It waited while a refrigerated vehicle containing one of the frigid-blooded SNLU methane-breathers rolled past, then went on. "Of course you are being given special treatment."

"Why?"

Timmins did not reply.

"Why do you not answer this simple question?" she persisted.

"Because," the Earth-human said, its face deepening in color, "your question does not have a simple answer, and I'm not sure if I am the right person to give it to you, since I might also give offense, cause you mental pain, insult you, or make you angry."

Cha Thrat walked in silence for a moment, then said, "I think that your consideration for my feelings makes you the right person. And a subordinate who has acted wrongly may indeed feel mental pain or anger or intense self-dislike but surely, if the superior speaks justly, no offense can be taken nor insult given."

The Earth-human shook its head in a gesture, she had learned, that could mean either negation or puzzlement. It said, "There are times, Cha Thrat, when you make me feel like the subordinate. But what the hell, I'll try to answer. You are being accorded special treatment because of the wrong we did to you and the mental discomfort we have caused, and there are several important people who feel obligated to do something about it."

"But surely," she said incredulously, "I am the one who has behaved wrongly."

"That you have," Timmins said, "but as a direct result of us wronging you first. The Monitor Corps are responsible for allowing, no, *encouraging* you to come here in the first place, and waiving the entry requirements. The wrongdoing that followed this combination of misguided gratitude for saving Chiang's life and sheer political opportunism was the inevitable result."

"But I wanted to come," Cha Thrat protested, "and I still want to stay."

"To punish yourself for recent misdeeds?" Timmins asked quietly. "I've been trying to convince you that we are originally to blame for those."

"I am not mentally or morally warped," she replied, trying to control her anger at what, on her home world, would have been a grave insult. "I accept just punishment, but I would not seek to inflict it on myself. There are some very disquieting and unpleasant aspects to life here, but in no level of Sommaradvan society could I be subject to such a variety and intensity of experience. That is why I would like to stay."

The Earth-human was silent for a moment, then it said, "Conway, O'Mara, and Cresk-Sar among others, even Hredlichli, were sure that your reasons for wanting to stay here were positive rather than negative and that there was little chance of my getting you to agree to a return home..."

It broke off as Cha Thrat stopped dead in the corridor.

Angrily she said, "Have you been discussing with all these people my deeds and misdeeds, my competence or incompetence, perhaps my future prospects, without inviting me to be present?"

"Move, you're causing a traffic problem," Timmins said. "And there is no reason for anger. Since that business during the Hudlar demo there isn't a single being in the hospital who has *not* talked about your deeds, misdeeds, competence, or lack thereof, and your highly questionable future prospects in the hospital. Having you present at all those discussions was not possible. But if you want to know what was said about you in great and interminable detail—the serious discussions, that is, as opposed to mere hospital gossip—I believe O'Mara has added the recordings to your psych file and might play them back to you on request. Or again, he might not.

"Alternatively," it went on when they were moving again, "you may wish me to give you a brief summary of these discussions, inaccurate in that the excess verbiage and the more impolite and colorful phraseology will be deleted."

"That," Cha Thrat said, "is what I wish."

"Very well," it replied. "Let me begin by saying that the Monitor Corps personnel and all of the senior medical staff members involved are responsible for this situation. During the initial interview with O'Mara you mentioned that the lengthy delay in your decision to treat Chiang was that you did not want to lose a limb. O'Mara assumed, wrongly, that you were referring only to Chiang's limb, and he thinks that in an other-species interview he should have been more alert to the exact meaning of the words spoken, and that he is primarily responsible for your self-amputation.

"Conway feels responsible," it went on, "because he ordered you to perform the Hudlar limb removal without knowing anything about your very strict code of professional ethics. Cresk-Sar thinks it should have questioned you more closely on the same subject. Both of them believe that you would make a fine other-species surgeon if you could be deconditioned and reeducated. And Hredlichli blames itself for ignoring the special friendship that developed between you and AUGL-One Sixteen. And, of course, the Monitor Corps, which is originally responsible for the problem, suggested a solution that would give the minimum displeasure to everyone."

"By transferring me to Maintenance," she finished for it.

"That was never a serious suggestion," the Earthhuman said, "because we couldn't believe that you would accept it. No, we wanted to send you home."

A small part of her mind was moving her body forward and around the heavier or more senior staff members, while the rest of it felt angry and bitterly disappointed in the life-form beside her that she had begun to think of as a friend.

"Naturally," Timmins went on, "we tried to take your feelings into account. You were interested in meeting and working with off-planet life-forms, so we would give you a cultural liaison position, as an advisor on Sommaradvan affairs, on our base there. Or on *Descartes*, our largest specialized other-species contact vessel, which will be orbiting your world until another new intelligent species is discovered somewhere. Your position would be one of considerable responsibility, and could not be influenced in any way by the people who dislike you on Sommaradva.

"Naturally, nothing could be guaranteed at this stage," it continued. "But subject to your satisfactory performance with us you would be allowed to choose between a permanent position with the Corps' Sommaradva establishment as an interspecies cultural advisor or as a member of the contact team on *Descartes*. We tried to do what we thought was best for you, friend, and everyone else."

"You did," Cha Thrat said, feeling her anger and disappointment melting away. "Thank you."

"We thought it was a reasonable compromise," Timmins said. "But O'Mara said no. He insisted that you be given a maintenance job here in the hospital and have the Corps induction procedures attended to as quickly as possible."

"Why?"

"I don't know why," it replied. "Who knows how a Chief Psychologist's mind works?"

"Why," she repeated, "must I join your Monitor Corps?"

"Oh, that," Timmins said. "Purely for administrative convenience. The supply and maintenance of Sector General is our responsibility, and anyone who is not a patient or on the medical staff is automatically a member of the Monitor Corps. The personnel computer has to know your name, rank, and number so as to be able to pay your salary and so we can tell you what to do.

"Theoretically," it added.

"I have never disobeyed the lawful order of a superior..." Cha Thrat began, when it held up its hand again.

"A Corps joke, don't worry about it," Timmins said. "The point I'm trying to make is that our Chief Psychologist bears the administrative rank of major, but it is difficult to define the limits of his authority in this place, because he orders full Colonels and Diagnosticians around, and not always politely. Your own rank of junior technician, Environmental Maintenance, Grade Two, which became effective as soon as we received O'Mara's instructions, will not give you as much leeway."

"Please," she said urgently, "this is a serious matter. It is my understanding that the Monitor Corps is an organization of warriors. It has been many generations on Sommaradva since our warrior-level citizens fought together in battle. Peace and present-day technology offer danger enough. As a warrior-surgeon I am required to heal wounds, not inflict them."

"Seriously," the Earth-human said, "I think your information on the Corps came chiefly from the entertainment channels. Space battles and hand-to-hand combat are an extremely rare occurrence, and the library tapes will give you a much truer, and more boring, description of what we do and why we do it. Study the material. You'll find that there will be no conflict of loyalty between your duties to the Corps, your home world, or your ethical standards.

"We've arrived," it added briskly, pointing at the sign on the heavy door before them. "From here on we'll need heavy radiation armor. Oh, you've another question?"

"It's about my salary,"she said hesitantly.

Timmins laughed and said, "I do so hate these altruistic types who consider money unimportant. The pay at your present rank isn't large. Personnel will be able to tell you the equivalent in Sommaradvan currency, but then there isn't much to spend it on here. You can always save it and your leave allowance and travel. Perhaps visit your AUGL friend on Chalderescol sometime, or go to—"

"There would be enough money for an interstellar trip like that?" she broke in.

The Earth-human went into a paroxym of coughing, recovered, then said, "There would *not* be enough money to pay for an interstellar trip. However, because of the isolated position of Sector General, free Corps transport is available for physiologically suitable hospital personnel to travel to their home planets or, with a bit of fiddling, to the planet of your choice. The money could be spent there, enjoying yourself. Now will you please get into that armor?"

Cha Thrat did not move and the Earth-human watched her without speaking.

Finally she said, "I am being given special treatment, shown areas where I am not qualified to work and mechanisms that I can't hope to use for a very long time. No doubt this is being done as an incentive, to show me what is possible for me to achieve in the future. I understand and appreciate the thinking behind this, but I would much prefer to stop sightseeing and do some simple, and useful, work."

"Well, good for you!" Timmins said, showing its teeth approvingly. "We can't look directly at the Telfi anyway, so we aren't missing much. Suppose you begin by learning to drive a delivery sled. A small one, at first, so that an accident will damage you more than the hospital structure. And you'll have to really master your internal geography, and be able to navigate accurately and at speed through the service tunnel network. It seems to be a law of nature that when a ward or diet kitchen has to be resupplied, the requisition is always urgent and usually arrives late.

"We'll head for the internal transport hangar now," it ended, "unless you have another question?"

She had, but thought it better to wait until they were moving again before asking it.

"What about the damage to the AUGL ward for which

I was indirectly responsible?" she said. "Will the cost be deducted from my salary?"

Timmins showed its teeth again and said, "I'd say that it would take about three years to pay for the damage caused by your AUGL friend. But when the damage was done you were one of the medical trainee crazies, not a serious and responsible member of the Maintenance Department, so don't worry about it."

She did not worry about it because, for the rest of the day, there were far more important things to worry about—principally the control and guidance of the uncontrollable and misguided, multiply accursed heap of machinery called an antigravity sled.

In operation the vehicle rode a repulsion cushion so that there was no contact with the deck, and changes in direction were effected by lowering friction pads, angling the thrusters, or, for fine control, leaning sideways. If emergency braking was necessary, the power was switched off. This caused the vehicle to drop to the deck and grind noisily to a halt. But this maneuver was discouraged because it made the driver very unpopular with the service crew who had to realign the repulsor grids.

By the end of the day her vehicle had slipped and spun all over the transport hangar floor, hit every collapsible marker that she was supposed to steer around, and generally displayed a high level of noncooperation. Timmins gave her a packet of study tapes, told her to look over them before next morning, and said that her driving was pretty good for a beginner.

Three days later she began to believe it.

"I drove a sled with a trailer attached, both fully loaded, from Level Eighteen to Thirty-three," she told Tarsedth, when her one-time classmate visited her for the customary evening gossip. "I did it using only the service tunnels, and without hitting anything or anybody."

"Should I be impressed?" the Kelgian asked.

"A little," Cha Thrat said, feeling more than a little deflated. "What's been happening to you?"

"Cresk-Sar transferred to me LSVO Surgical," Tarsedth said, its fur rippling in an unreadable mixture of emotions. "It said I was ready to broaden my other-species nursing experience, and working with a light-gravity life-form would improve my delicacy of touch. And anyway, it said, Charge Nurse Lentilatsar, the rotten, chlorine-breathing slimy slob, was not entirely happy with the way I exercised my initiative. What tape is that? It looks massively uninteresting."

"To the contrary," Cha Thrat said, touching the pause stud. The screen showed a picture of a group of Monitor Corps officers meeting the great Earth-human MacEwan and the equally legendary Orligian Grawlya-Ki, the true founders, it was said, of Sector General hospital. "It's the history, organization, and present activities of the Monitor Corps. I find it very interesting, but ethically confusing. For example, why must a peace-keeping force be so heavily armed?"

"Because, stupid, it couldn't if it wasn't," Tarsedth said. It went on quickly. "But on the subject of the Monitor Corps I'm an expert. A lot of Kelgians join these days, and I was going to try for a position as Surgeon-Lieutenant, a ship's medic, that is, and might still do it if I don't qualify here.

"Of course," it went on enthusiastically, "there are other, nonmilitary, openings..."

As the Galactic Federation's executive and law-enforcement arm, the Monitor Corps was essentially a police force on an interstellar scale, but during the first century since it had come into existence it had become much more. Originally, when the Federation had comprised a rather unstable alliance of only four inhabited systems—Nidia, Orligia, Traltha, and Earth—its personnel had been exclusively Earth-human. But those Earth-humans were responsible for discovering other inhabited systems, and more and more intelligent lifeforms, and for establishing friendly contact with them.

The result was that the Federation now numbered among its citizens close on seventy different species—the figure was constantly being revised upward—and the peace-keeping function had taken second place to that of the Survey, Exploration, and Other-species Communications activities. The people with the heavy weaponry did not mind because a police force, unlike an army, feels at its most effective when there is nothing for it to do but keep in training by carving up the odd mineral-rich asteroid for the mining people, or clearing and leveling large tracts of virgin land on a newly discovered world in preparation for the landing of colonists.

The last time a Monitor Corps police action had been indistinguishable from an act of war had been nearly two decades ago, when they had defended Sector General itself from the badly misguided Etlans, who had since become law-abiding citizens of the Federation. A few of them had even joined the Corps.

"Nowadays membership is open to any species," Tarsedth continued, "although for physiological reasons, life-support and accommodation problems on board the smaller ships, most of the space-going personnel are warm-blooded oxygen-breathers.

"Like I said," the Kelgian went on, undulating forward and restarting the tape, "there are lots of interesting openings for restless, adventurous, home-hating types like us. You could do worse than join."

"I have joined," Cha Thrat said. "But driving a gravity sled isn't exactly adventurous."

Tarsedth's fur spiked in surprise, then settled down again as it said, "Of course you have. Stupid of me, I'd forgotten that all nonmedical staff are automatically coopted into the Monitor Corps. And I've seen how you people drive. Adventurous verging on the suicidal best describes it. But you made a good decision. Congratulations."

The decision had been made for her, Cha Thrat thought wryly, but that did not mean that it was necessarily a wrong decision. They had settled back to watch the remainder of the Monitor Corps history tape when Tarsedth's fur became agitated again.

"I'm worried about you and the Corps people, Cha Thrat," the Kelgian said suddenly. "They can be a bit stuffy about some things, easy-going about others. Just study and work hard. And think carefully before you do anything that will get you kicked out."

Chapter 11

TIME slipped past and Cha Thrat felt that she was making no progress at all, until one day she realized that she was performing as routine tasks that only a little earlier would have been impossible. Much of the work was servile but, strangely, she was becoming increasingly interested in it and felt proud when she did it well.

Sometimes the morning assignments contained unpleasant surprises.

"Today you will begin moving power cells and other consumables to the ambulance ship *Rhabwar*," Timmins said, consulting its worksheet. "But there is a small job I want you to do first—new vegetable decoration for the AUGL ward. Study the attachment instructions before you go so that the medics will think you know what you're doing . . . Is there a problem, Cha Thrat?"

There were other and more senior technicians in her section—three Kelgians, an Ian, and an Orligian—waiting for the day's assignments. She doubted her ability to take over one of their jobs, and hers was probably too elementary for the Lieutenant to consider swapping assignments, but she had to try.

Perhaps the Earth-human would accord her some of the earlier special treatment that, for some reason, had been completely absent since she had been put to work.

"There is a problem," Cha Thrat said quietly. The note of pleading in her voice was probably lost in the process of translation, she thought as she went on. "As you know, I am not well liked by Charge Nurse Hredlichli, and my presence in the AUGL ward is likely to cause, at very least, verbal unpleasantness. The bad feeling for which I am largely responsible may fade in time, but right now I think that it would be better to send someone else."

Timmins regarded her silently for a moment, then it smiled and said, "Right now, Cha Thrat, I wouldn't want to send anyone else to the AUGL ward. Don't worry about it.

"Krachlan," it went on briskly. "You are for Level Eighty-three, another fault reported in the power converter at Station Fourteen B. We may have to replace the unit . . ."

All the way to the Chalder level, Cha Thrat seethed quietly as she wondered how such a stupid, insensitive, cross-species miscegenation as Timmins had risen to its high rank and responsibilities without sustaining mortal injury at the hands, claws, or tentacles of a subordinate. By the time she reached the AUGL ward and entered inconspicuously by the service tunnel lock, she had calmed sufficiently to remember a few, a very few, of Timmins's good qualities.

She was relieved when nobody came near her as she went to work. All of the patients and nursing staff seemed to be congregated at the other end of the ward and dimly, through the clouded green water, she could see the distinctive coveralls of a transfer team member. Plainly something of great interest was happening back there, which meant that with luck she would be able to complete her work undisturbed and unnoticed.

Seemingly it was not to be her lucky day.

"It's you again," said the familiar, acid-tongued voice of Hredlichli, who had approached silently from behind her. "How long will it take for you to finish hanging that vile stuff?"

"Most of the morning, Charge Nurse," Cha Thrat replied politely.

She did not want to get into an argument with the chlorine-breather, and it seemed as if one were about to start. She wondered if it was possible to forestall it by doing all the talking herself on a subject that Hredlichli could not argue about, the improved comfort of its patients.

"The reason for it taking so long to install, Charge Nurse," she said quickly, "is that this vegetation isn't the usual plastic reproduction. I've been told that it has just arrived from Chalderescol, that it is a native underwater plant-form, very hardy and requiring the minimum of attention, and that it releases a pleasant, waterborne aroma that is said to be psychologically beneficial to the recuperating patient.

"Maintenance will periodically check its growth and general health," she went on before the chlorine-breather could respond, "and supply the nutrient material. But the patients could be given the job of caring for it, as something interesting to do to relieve their boredom, and to leave the nurses free to attend—"

"Cha Thrat," Hredlichli broke in sharply, "are you telling me how I should run my ward?"

"No," she replied, wishing not for the first time that her mouth did not run so far ahead of her mind. "I apologize, Charge Nurse. I no longer have responsibility for any aspect of patient care, and I did not wish to imply that I did. While I am here I shall not even talk to a patient."

Hredlichli made an untranslatable sound, then said, "You'll talk to one patient, at least. That is why I asked Timmins to send you here today. Your friend, AUGL-One Sixteen, is going home, and I thought you might want to wish it well—everybody else in the ward seems to be doing so. Leave that disgusting mess you're working on and finish it later."

Cha Thrat could not speak for a moment. Since the transfer to Maintenance she had lost contact with her Chalder friend, and knew only that it was still on the hospital's list of patients under treatment. The most she had hoped for today, and it had been a pretty forlorn hope, was that Hredlichli would allow her a few words with the patient while she was working. But this was completely unexpected.

"Thank you, Charge Nurse," she said finally. "This is most considerate of you."

The chlorine-breather made another untranslatable

noise. It said, "Since I was appointed Charge Nurse here I've been agitating to have this antiquated underwater dungeon redecorated, reequipped, and converted into something resembling a proper ward. Thanks to you that is now being done, and once I recovered from the initial trauma of having my ward wrecked, I decided that I owed you one.

"Even so," it added, "I shall not suffer terminal mental anguish if I don't see you again after today."

AUGL-One Sixteen had already been inserted into its transfer tank and only the hatch above its head remained to be sealed, after which it would be moved through the lock in the outer hull and across to the waiting Chalder ship. A group comprised of well-wishing nurses, visibly impatient transfer team members, and the Earth-human O'Mara hung around the opening like a shoal of ungainly fish, but the loud, bubbling sounds from the tank's water-purifying equipment made it difficult to hear what was being said. As she approached, the Chief Psychologist waved the others back.

"Keep it short, Cha Thrat, the team is behind schedule," O'Mara said, turning away and leaving her alone with the ex-patient.

For what seemed a long time she looked at the one enormous eye and the great teeth in the part of its head visible through the open seal, and the words she wanted to speak would not come. Finally she said, "That looks like a very small tank, are you comfortable in there?"

"Quite comfortable, Cha Thrat," the Chalder replied. "Actually, it isn't much smaller than my accommodation on the ship. But that constriction will be temporary, soon I'll have a planetary ocean to swim in.

"And before you ask," the AUGL went on, "I am feeling fine, really well, in fact, so you don't have to go poking about in this pain-free and disgustingly healthy body checking my vital signs."

"I don't ask questions like that anymore," Cha Thrat said, wishing suddenly that she could laugh like Earth-humans to hide the fact that she did not feel like laughing. "I'm in Maintenance now, so my instruments are much larger and would be very much more uncomfortable."

"O'Mara told me about that," the Chalder said. "Is the work interesting?"

Neither of them, Cha Thrat felt sure, were saying the things they wanted to say.

"Very interesting," she replied. "I'm learning a lot about the inner workings of this place, and the Monitor Corps pays me, not very much, for doing it. When I've saved enough to take some leave on Chalderescol, I'll go and see how everything is with you."

"If you visited me, Cha Thrat," the AUGL broke in, "you would not be allowed to spend any of your hard-earned Monitor currency on Chalderescol. As you are a name-user and off-world member of my family, they would be deeply insulted, and would probably have you for lunch, if you tried."

"In that case," Cha Thrat said happily, "I shall probably visit you quite soon."

"If you don't swim clear, Technician," said an Earth-human in Transfer Team coveralls who had appeared beside her, "we'll seal you in the tank now, and you can damn well travel there with your friend!"

"Muromeshomon," she said quietly as the seal was closing, "may you fare well."

When she turned to go back to the unplanted vegetation, Cha Thrat's mind was concentrated on her Chalder friend to such an extent that she did not think of the impropriety of what she, a mere second-grade technician, said to the Earth-human Monitor Corps Major as she passed it.

"My congratulations, Chief Psychologist," she said gratefully, "on a most successfull spell."

O'Mara responded by opening its mouth, but not even an untranslatable sound came out.

The three days that followed were spent on the *Rhabwar* resupply job, bringing crew consumables and time-expired equipment to the largely Earth-human maintenance people charged with bringing the ambulance ship to peak operating efficiency, and occasionally assisting with the installation of some of the simpler items. On its next trip *Rhabwar* would be carrying Diagnostician Conway, a former leader of its medical team, and the present crew did not want it to find any cause for complaint.

On the fourth day, Timmins asked Cha Thrat to wait while the other assignments were given out.

"You seem to be very interested in our special ambulance ship," the Lieutenant said when they were alone. "I'm told that you've been climbing all over and through it, and mostly when it's empty and you are supposed to be off-duty. Is this so?"

"Yes, sir," Cha Thrat said enthusiastically. "It is a complex and beautifully functional vessel, judging by what I've heard and seen, and it is almost a miniature version of the hospital itself. The casualty treatment and other-species environmental arrangements are especially..." She broke off, to add warily, "I would not try to test or use any of this equipment without permission."

"I should hope not!" the Lieutenant said. "All right, then. I have another job for you, on *Rhabwar*, if you think you can do it. Come with me."

It was a small compartment that had been converted

from a post-op recovery room, and it still retained its direct access to the ELNT Operating Theater. The ceiling had been lowered, which indicated that the occupant-to-be either crawled or did not stand very tall, and the plumbing and power supply lines, revealed by the incomplete wall paneling, bore the color codings for a warm-blooded oxygen-breather with normal gravity and atmospheric pressure requirements.

The wall panels that were in place had been finished to resemble rough planking with a strangely textured grain which resembled a mineral rather than wood. There was an untidy heap of decorative vegetation on the floor waiting to be hung, and beside it a large picture of a landscape that could have been taken in any forested lakeland on Sommaradva, if it had not been for subtle differences in the tree formations.

The framework and padding of a small, low-level bed was placed against the wall facing the entrance. But the most noticeable feature of the room, after she had blundered painfully against it, was the transparent wall that divided it in two. At one end of the wall there was a large door, outlined in red for visibility, and a smaller, central opening that contained remote handling and examination equipment capable of reaching across to the bed.

"This room is being prepared for a very special patient," Timmins said. "It is a Gogleskan, physiological classification FOKT, who is a personal friend of Diagnostician Conway. The patient, indeed its whole species, has serious problems about which you can brief yourself when you have more time. It is a gravid female nearing full term. There are psychological factors that require that it receives constant reassurance, and Conway is clearing his present workload during the next few weeks so that he will be free to travel to Goglesk, pick up the

patient, and return with it to Sector General in plenty of
time before the event takes place."

"I understand," Cha Thrat said.

"What I want you to do," Timmins went on, "is to set
up a smaller and simpler version of this accommodation
on *Rhabwar*'s casualty deck. You will draw the components from Stores and be given full assembly instructions. The work is slightly above your present technical
level, but there is ample time for someone else to complete the job if you can't do it. Do you want to try?"

"Oh, yes," she said.

"Good," the Earth-human said. "Look closely at this
place. Pay special attention to the attachment fittings of
the transparent wall. Don't worry too much about the
remote-controlled manipulators because the ship has its
own. The patient restraints will have to be tested, but
only under the supervision of one of the medical team
who will be visiting you from time to time.

"Unlike this compartment," it went on, "your casualty deck facility will be in use only during the trip from
Goglesk to the hospital, so the wall covering will be a
plastic film, painted to represent the wood paneling here
and applied to the ship's inner plating and bulkheads.
This saves on installation time and, anyway, Captain
Fletcher would not approve of us boring unnecessary
holes in his ship. When you think you understand what
you will be doing, collect the material from Stores and
take it to the ship. I'll see you there before you go off-
duty..."

"Why the transparent wall and remote handling
equipment?" Cha Thrat asked quickly, as the Lieutenant
turned to go. "An FOKT classification doesn't sound
like a particularly large or dangerous life-form."

"...To answer any questions not covered by your information tape," it ended firmly. "Enjoy yourself."

The days that followed were not particularly enjoyable except in retrospect. The tri-di drawings and assembly instructions gave her a permanent headache during the first day and night but, from then on, Timmins's visits to check on progress became less and less frequent. There were three visits from Charge Nurse Naydrad, the Kelgian member of the medical team who, Tarsedth informed her, was an expert in heavy rescue techniques.

Cha Thrat was polite without being subservient and Naydrad, in the manner of all Kelgians, was consistently rude. But it did not find fault with her work, and it answered any questions that it did not consider either irrelevant or stupid.

"I do not fully understand the reason for the transparent division in this compartment," she said during one of its visits. "The Lieutenant tells me it is for psychological reasons, so that the patient will feel protected. But surely it would feel more protected by an opaque wall and a small window. Is the FOKT in need of a wizard as well as an obstetrician?"

"A *wizard*?" said the Kelgian in surprise, then it went on. "Of course, you must be the ex-medical trainee they're all talking about who thinks O'Mara is a witch-doctor. Personally, I think you're right. But it isn't just the patient, Khone, who needs a wizard, it's the whole planetary population of Goglesk. Khone is a volunteer, a test case and a very brave or stupid FOKT."

"I still don't understand," Cha Thrat said. "Could you explain, please?"

"No," Naydrad replied. "I don't have the time to explain all the ramifications of the case, especially to a maintenance technician who has a morbid curiosity but no direct concern, or who feels lonely and wants to talk instead of work. Be glad you have no responsibility, this is a very tricky one.

"Anyway," it went on, pointing toward the viewer and reference shelves at the other side of the compartment, "our copy of the case-history tape runs for over two hours, if you're that interested. Just don't take it off the ship."

She continued working, in spite of a constant temptation to break off for a quick look at the FOKT tape, until the maintenance engineer who had been checking Control poked its Earth-human head into the casualty deck.

"Time for lunch," it said. "I'm going to the dining hall. Coming?"

"No, thank you," she replied. "There's something I have to do here."

"This is the second time in three days you've missed lunch," the Earth-human said. "Do Sommaradvans have some kind of crazy work ethic? Aren't you hungry, or is it just an understandable aversion to hospital food?"

"No, yes very, and sometimes," Cha Thrat said.

"I've a pack of sandwiches," it said. "Guaranteed nutritious, nontoxic to all oxy-breathers and if you don't look too closely at what's inside, you should be able to make them stay down. Interested?"

"Very much," Cha Thrat replied gratefully, thinking that now she would be able to satisfy her complaining stomach and spend the whole lunch period watching the FOKT tape.

The muted but insistent sound of the emergency siren brought her mind back from Goglesk and its peculiar problems to the realization that she had spent much longer than the stipulated lunch period watching the tape, and that the empty ship was rapidly filling with people.

She saw three Earth-humans in Monitor Corps green

go past the casualty deck entrance, heading toward Control, and a few minutes later the lumpy green ball that was Danalta rolled onto the casualty deck. It was closely followed by an Earth-human, wearing whites with Pathology Department insignia, who had to be the DBDG female, Murchison; then Naydrad and Prilicla entered, the Kelgian undulating rapidly along the deck and the insectile Cinrusskin empath using the ceiling. The Charge Nurse went straight to the viewer, which was still running the FOKT tape, and switched it off as two more Earth-humans came in.

One of them was Timmins and the other, judging by the uniform insignia and its air of authority, was the ship's ruler, Major Fletcher. It was the Lieutenant who spoke first.

"How long will it take you to finish here?" it said.

"The rest of today," Cha Thrat replied promptly, "and most of the night."

Fletcher shook its head.

"I could bring in more people, sir," Timmins said. "They would have to be briefed on the job, which would waste some time. But I'm sure I could shorten that to four, perhaps three hours."

The ship ruler shook its head again.

"There is only one alternative," the Lieutenant said.

For the first time Fletcher looked directly at Cha Thrat. It said, "The Lieutenant tells me that you are capable of completing and testing this facility yourself. Are you?"

"Yes," Cha Thrat said.

"Have you any objections to doing so during a three-day trip to Goglesk?"

"No," she said firmly.

The Earth-human looked up at Prilicla, the leader of the ship's medical team, not needing to speak.

"I feel no strong objections from my colleagues to this being accompanying us, friend Fletcher," the empath said, "since this is an emergency."

"In that case," Fletcher said as it turned to go, "we leave in fifteen minutes."

Timmins looked as if it wanted to say something, a word of caution, perhaps, or advice, or reassurance. Instead it held up a loosely clenched fist with the opposable thumb projecting vertically from it in a gesture she had not seen it make before, and then it, too, was gone. Cha Thrat heard the sound of its feet on the metal floor of the ship's boarding tube and, in spite of the four widely different life-forms closely surrounding her, suddenly she felt all alone.

"Don't worry, Cha Thrat," Prilicla said, the musical trills and clicks of its native speech backing the translated words. "You are among friends."

"There's a problem," Naydrad said. "No acceleration furniture to suit that stupid shape of yours. Lie down on a casualty litter and I'll strap you in."

Chapter 12

THE FOKT facility was completed and thoroughly tested, first by Naydrad and then, on the orders of Major Fletcher, by *Rhabwar*'s engineer officer, Lieutenant Chen. That, apart from brief meetings on the way to or from the combination dining area and recreation deck, was her only direct contact with any of the ship's officers.

It was not that they tried to discourage such contact between the officer-ruler level and a being of the lowest technical rank, or that they deliberately tried to make her feel inferior. They did neither. But all Monitor Corps personnel who passed the very high technical and academic requirements for service on interstellar ships were automatically considered, at least to the status-conscious mind of a Sommaradvan, to be as close to ruler status as made no difference. Without meaning to give offense they kept slipping into a highly technical and esoteric language of their own, and they made her feel very uncomfortable.

In any case she felt more at home with the civilian medics than with the beings who, apart from a few small but significant badges on their collars, wore the same uniform as she did. As well, it was impossible to be in the same company as Prilicla without feeling very comfortable indeed. So she made herself as inconspicuous as her physiology would permit, reminded herself constantly that she now belonged to the maintenance rather than the medical fraternity, and tried very hard not to join in while the others were discussing the mission.

Goglesk had been a borderline case so far as the Cultural Contact people were concerned. Full contact with a technologically backward culture could be dangerous because, when the Monitor Corps ships dropped out of their skies, they could never be sure whether they were giving the natives evidence of a future technological goal at which they could aim or a destructive inferiority complex. But the Gogleskans, in spite of their backwardness in the physical sciences and the devastating racial psychosis that forced them to remain so, were psychologically stable, at least as individuals, and their planet had not known war for many thousands of years.

The easiest course would have been for the Corps to withdraw and leave the Gogleskan culture to continue as it had been doing since the dawn of its history, and write their problem off as insoluble. Instead they had made one of their very few compromises by setting up a small base for the purposes of observation, investigation, and limited contact.

Progress for any intelligent species depended on increasing levels of cooperation among its individuals and family or tribal groups. On Goglesk, however, any attempt at close cooperation brought drastically reduced intelligence, a mindless urge to destruction, and serious physical injury in its wake, so that the Gogleskans had been forced into becoming a race of individualists who had close physical contact only during the brief reproductive period or while caring for the very young.

The problem had come about as the result of a solution forced on them in presapient times. They had been a food source for every predator infesting their oceans, but they, too, had evolved natural weapons of offense and defense—stings that paralyzed or killed the smaller life-forms and long cranial tendrils that gave them the faculty of telepathy by contact. When threatened by large predators they had linked bodies and minds together to the size required to neutralize any attacker with their combined stings.

There was fossil evidence on Goglesk of a titanic struggle for survival between them and a gigantic and particularly ferocius species of ocean predator, a battle that had raged for many, many thousands of years. The FOKTs had won in the end, and had evolved into intelligent land-dwellers, but they had paid a terrible price.

In order to sting to death one of those giant predators,

physical and telepathic link-ups of hundreds of individual FOKTs had been required. A great many of them had perished, been torn apart or eaten during every such encounter, and the consequent and oft-repeated death agonies of the slain had been shared telepathically by every single member of the groups. In an attempt to reduce their suffering, the effects of the group telepathy had been diluted by the generation of a mindless urge to destroy indiscriminately everything within reach. But even so, the mental scars inflicted during their prehistory had not healed.

Once heard, the audible signal emitted by Gogleskans in distress that triggered the process could not be ignored at either the conscious or unconscious levels, because that call to join represented only one thing—the threat of ultimate danger. And even in present times, when such threats were imaginary or insignificant, it made no difference. A joining led inevitably to the mindless destruction of everything in their immediate vicinity—housing, vehicles, mechanisms, books, or art objects—that they had been able to build or accomplish as individuals.

That was why the present-day Gogleskans would not allow, except on very rare occasions, anyone to touch or come close to them or even address them in anything but the most impersonal terms, while they fought helplessly and, until Conway's recent visit to the planet, hopelessly against the conditioning imposed on them by evolution.

It was plain to Cha Thrat that the only subjects that the medical team wanted to discuss were the Gogleskan problems in general and Khone in particular, and they talked about them endlessly and without arriving anywhere except back to where they had started. Several times she had wanted to make suggestions or ask questions, but found that if she kept quiet and waited patiently, a form of behavior that had always been foreign

to her nature, the ideas and the questions were suggested
and answered by one of the others.

Usually it was Naydrad who asked such questions,
although much less politely than Cha Thrat would have
done.

"Conway should be here," the Kelgian said, fur ruf-
fling in disapproval. "It made a promise to the patient.
There should be no excuses."

The yellow-pink face of Pathologist Murchison deepened in color. On the ceiling Prilicla's iridescent wings
were quivering in response to the emotional radiation
being generated below, but neither the empath nor the
female Earth-human spoke.

"It is my understanding," Danalta said suddenly,
moving the eye it had extruded to regard the Kelgian,
"that Conway was successful in breaching the conditioning of just one Gogleskan, by an accidental, dangerous,
and unprecedented joining of minds. For this reason the
Diagnostician is the only other-species being who has
any chance of approaching the patient closely, much less
of touching it before or during the birth. Even though the
call came much earlier than expected, there must be
many others in the hospital who are capable and willing
to take over the Diagnostician's workload for the few
days necessary for the trip.

"I, too, think that Conway should have come with
us," the shape-changer ended. "Khone is its friend, and
it promised to do so."

While Danalta was speaking, Murchison's face had
retained the deep-pink coloration except for patches of
whiteness around its lips, and it was obvious from Prilicla's trembling that the Pathologist's emotional radiation
was anything but pleasant for an empath.

"I agree with you," Murchison said in a tone that suggested otherwise, "that nobody, not even the Diagnosti-

cian-in-Charge of Surgery, is indispensable. And I'm not defending him simply because he happens to be my lifemate. He can call for assistance from quite a few of the Senior Physicians who are capable of performing the work. But not quickly, not while surgery is actually in progress. And the briefings for his operating schedule would have taken time, two hours at least. The Goglesk call had the Most Urgent prefix. We had to leave at once, without him."

Danalta did not reply, but Naydrad's fur made discontented waves as the Kelgian said, "Is this the only excuse Conway gave you for breaking its promise to the patient? If so, it is unsatisfactory. We have all had experience with emergencies arising that necessitated people doing other people's work, without notice or detailed briefings. There is a lack of consideration being shown for its patient—"

"Which one?" Murchison asked angrily. "Khone or the being presently under his knife? And an emergency, in case you've forgotten, occurs spontaneously or because a situation is out of control. It should not be caused deliberately simply because someone feels honorbound to be somewhere else.

"In any case," it went on, "he was in surgery and did not have time to say more than a few words, which were that we should leave at once without him, and not worry about it."

"Then it is you who is making excuses for your lifemate's misbehavior..." Naydrad began when Prilicla, speaking for the first time, interrupted it.

"Please," it said gently, "I feel our friend Cha Thrat wanting to say something."

As a Senior Physician and leader of *Rhabwar*'s medical team it would have been quite in order for Prilicla to tell them that their continued bickering was causing it

discomfort, and that they should shut their speaking orifices forthwith. But she also knew that the little empath
would never dream of doing any such thing, because the
resultant feelings of embarrassment and guilt over the
pain they had caused their inoffensive, well-loved, and
emotion-sensitive team leader would have rendered it
even more uncomfortable.

It was therefore in Prilicla's own selfish interests to
give orders indirectly so as to minimize the generation of
unpleasant feelings around it. If it felt her wanting to
speak, it was probable that it could also feel that she,
too, was wanting to reduce the current unpleasantness.

They were all staring at her, and Prilicla had ceased
trembling. Plainly the emotion of curiosity was much
less distressing than that which had gone before.

"I, too," Cha Thrat said, "have studied the Goglesk
tape, and in particular the material on Khone—"

"Surely this is no concern of yours," Danalta broke
in. "You are a maintenance person."

"A most inquisitive maintenance person," Naydrad
said. "Let it speak."

"A maintenance person," she replied angrily, "should
be inquisitive about the being for whose accommodation
she is responsible!" Then she saw Prilicla begin to tremble again, and controlled her feelings as she went on. "It
seems to me that you may be concerning yourselves
needlessly. Diagnostician Conway did not speak to Pathologist Murchison as if it felt unduly concerned. What
exactly did the message from Goglesk say about the condition of the patient?"

"Nothing," Murchison said. "We know nothing of the
clinical picture. It isn't possible to send a lengthy message from a small, low-powered base like Goglesk. A lot
of energy is needed to punch a signal through hyperspace
so that—"

"Thank you," Cha Thrat said politely. "The technical problems were covered in one of my maintenance lectures. What did the message say?"

Murchison's face had deepened in color again as it said, "The exact wording was 'Attention, Conway, Sector General. Most Urgent. Khone requires ambulance ship soonest possible. Wainright, Goglesk Base.'"

For a moment Cha Thrat was silent, ordering her thoughts, then she said, "I am assuming that Healer Khone and its other-species friend have been keeping themselves informed regarding each other's progress. Probably they have been exchanging lengthier, more detailed and perhaps personal messages carried aboard the Monitor Corps courier vessels operating in this sector, which would avoid the obvious disadvantages of information transmitted through hyperspace."

Naydrad's fur was indicating that it was about to interrupt. She went on quickly. "From my study of the Gogleskan material, I am also assuming that Khone is, within the limits imposed by its conditioning, an unusually thoughtful and considerate being who would be unwilling to inconvenience its friends unnecessarily. Even if Conway had not mentioned the subject directly, Khone would already have learned from its sharing of the Earth-human's mind the full extent of the duties, responsibilities, and workload carried by a Diagnostician. And Conway, naturally, would be equally well informed about Khone's mind and its probable reaction to that knowledge.

"As the being who wished to be responsible for this patient," she continued, "the hyperspace signal was for Conway's attention. But it urgently requested an ambulance ship, not the presence of the Diagnostician.

"Conway knew why this was so," Cha Thrat went on, "because it also knew as much about Gogleskan pregnancies as Khone itself did, so it might be that the literal wording of the signal released Conway from the promise. Knowing that its patient required nothing more than fast transport to the hospital, the Diagnostician was not overly concerned, and it told you not to be concerned, either, by its absence.

"It may well be," she ended, "that the recent criticism of Diagnostician Conway's seemingly unethical behavior was without basis."

Naydrad turned toward Murchison and made the closest thing to an apology that a Kelgian could make as it said, "Cha Thrat is probably right, and I am stupid."

"Undoubtedly right," Danalta joined in. "I'm sorry, Pathologist. If I was in Earth-human form right now, my face would be red."

Murchison did not reply but continued to stare at Cha Thrat. The Pathologist's face had returned to its normal coloration, but otherwise displayed no expression that she could read. Prilicla drifted toward her until she could feel the slight, regular down-draft from its wings.

"Cha Thrat," the Cinrusskin said quietly, "I have a strong feeling that you have made a new friend . . ."

It broke off as the casualty deck's speaker came to life with the overamplified voice of Fletcher.

"Senior Physician, Control here." it said. "Hyperspace Jump complete and we are estimating the Goglesk orbiting maneuver in three hours, two minutes. The lander is powered up and ready to go, so you can transfer your medical gear as soon as convenient.

"We are in normal-space radio contact with Lieutenant Wainright," it went on, "who wants to talk to you about your patient, Khone."

"Thank you, Captain," Prilicla replied. "We want to talk about Khone as well. Please relay friend Wainright's message to the casualty deck here and to the lander bay when we move out. We can work as we talk."

"Will do," Fletcher said. "Relay complete. You are through to Senior Physician Prilicla, Lieutenant. Go ahead."

In spite of the distortion caused by the translation into Sommaradvan, Cha Thrat could detect the deep anxiety in Wainright's voice. She listened carefully with only part of her mind on the job of helping Naydrad load medical equipment onto the litter.

"I'm sorry, Doctor," it said, "the original arrangements for the pickup on our landing area will have to be scrapped. Khone isn't able to travel, and sending transport manned by off-planet people to collect it from its town will be tricky. At a time like this the natives are particularly, well, twitchy, and the arrival of visually horrifying alien monsters to carry it and its unborn child away could cause a joining and—"

"Friend Wainright," Prilicla interrupted gently, "what is the condition of the patient?"

"I don't know, Doctor," the Lieutenant replied. "When we met three days ago it told me that Junior would arrive very soon and would I please send for the ambulance ship. It also said that it had to make arrangements to have its patients cared for, and that it would come to the base shortly before the lander was due. Then a few hours ago a message was relayed verbally to the base saying that it could not move from its house, but the bearer of the message could not tell me whether the cause was illness or injury. Also, it asked if you had another power pack for the scanner Conway left with it. Khone has been impressing its patients with that particular marvel of Federation medical science and the energy cell is flat, which would explain why Khone was unable to give us any clinical information on its own present condition."

"I'm sure you are right, friend Wainright," Prilicla said. "However, the patient's sudden loss of mobility indicates a possibly serious condition that may be deteriorating. Can you suggest a method of getting it into the lander, quickly and with minimum risk to itself and its friends?"

"Frankly, no, Doctor," Wainright said. "This is going to be a maximum-risk job from the word go. If it was a member of any other species we know of, I could load it onto my flyer and bring it to you within a few minutes. But no Gogleskan, not even Healer Khone, could sit that close to an off-planet creature without emitting a distress call, and you know what would happen then."

"We do," Prilicla said, trembling at the thought of the widespread, self-inflicted property damage to the town and the mental anguish of the inhabitants that would ensue.

The Lieutenant went on. "Your best bet would be to ignore the base and land as close as possible to Khone's house, in a small clearing between it and the shore of an inland lake. I'll circle the area in a flyer and guide you down. Maybe we can devise something on the spot. You'll need some special remote handling devices to move it out, but I can help you with the external dimensions of Khone's house and doorways..."

While Cha Thrat helped the rest of the medical team move equipment into the lander, Wainright and the empath continued to wrestle with the problem. But it was obvious that they had no clear answers and were, instead, trying to provide for all eventualities.

"Cha Thrat," Prilicla said, breaking off its conversation with the base commander. "As a nonmember of the crew I cannot give you orders, but we'll need as many extra hands down there as we can assemble. You are particularly well equipped with manipulatory appendages, as well as an understanding of the devices used to move and temporarily accommodate the patient, and I feel in you a willingness to accompany us."

"Your feeling is correct," Cha Thrat said, knowing that the intensity of excitement and gratitude the other's words had generated made verbal thanks unnecessary.

"If we load any more gadgetry into the lander," Naydrad said, "there won't be enough space for the patient, much less a hulking great Sommaradvan."

But there was enough space inside the lander to take all of them, especially when those not wearing gravity compensators, which was everyone but Prilicla, were further compressed by the lander's savage deceleration. Lieutenant Dodds, *Rhabwar*'s astrogation officer and the lander's pilot, had been told that speed had priority over a comfortable ride, and it obeyed that particular order with enthusiasm. So fast and uncomfortable was the descent that Cha Thrat saw nothing of Goglesk until she stepped onto its surface.

For a few moments she thought that she was back on Sommaradva, standing in a grassy clearing beside the shore of a great inland lake and with the tree-shrouded outlines of a small, servile township in the middle distance. But the ground beneath her feet was not that of her home planet, and the grass, wildflowers, and all the vegetation around her were subtly different in color, odor, and leaf structure from their counterparts on Sommaradva. Even the distant trees, although looking incredibly similar to some of the lowland varieties at home, were the products of a completely different evolutionary background.

Sector General had seemed strange and shocking to

her at first, but it had been a fabrication of metal, a gigantic artificial house. *This* was a different world!

"Is your species afflicted with sudden and inexplicable bouts of paralysis?" Naydrad asked. "Stop wasting time and bring out the litter."

She was guiding the powered litter down the unloading ramp when Wainright's flyer landed and rolled to a stop close beside them. The five Earth-humans who manned the Goglesk base jumped out. Four of them scattered quickly and began running toward the town, testing their translation and public address equipment as they went, while the Lieutenant came toward the lander.

"If you have anything to do that involves two or more of you working closely together," it said quickly, "do it now while the flyer is hiding you from view of the town. And when you move out, remain at least five meters apart. If these people see you moving closer together than that, or making actual bodily contact by touching limbs, it won't precipitate a joining, but it will cause them to feel deeply shocked and intensely uncomfortable. You must also—"

"Thank you, friend Wainright," Prilicla said gently. "We cannot be reminded too often to be careful."

The Lieutenant's features deepened in color, and it did not speak again until, walking i a well-separated line abreast, they were approaching the outskirts of the town.

"It doesn't look like much to us," Wainright said softly, the feelings behind its words making Prilicla tremble, "but they had to fight very hard every day of their lives to achieve it, and I think they're losing."

The town occupied a wide crescent of grass and stony outcroppings enclosing a small, natural harbor. There were several jetties projecting into deep water, and most of the craft tied up alongside had thin, high funnels and

paddle wheels as well as sails. One of the boats, clearly
the legacy of a past joining, was smoke-blackened and
sunk at its moorings. Hugging the water's edge was a
widely separated line of three- and four-story buildings,
made of wood, stone, and dried clay. Ascending ramps
running around all four walls gave access to the upper
levels, so that from certain angles the buildings resembled thin pyramids.

These, according to the Goglesk tape, were the
town's manufacturing and food-processing facilities, and
she thought that the smell of Gogleskan raw fish was just
as unpleasant as that of their Sommaradvan counterparts. Perhaps that was the reason why the private
dwellings, whose roofs and main structural supports
were provided by the trees around the edge of the clearing, were so far away from the harbor.

As they moved over the top of a small hill, Wainright
pointed out a low, partially roofed structure with a
stream running under it. From their elevated position
they could see into the maze of corridors and tiny rooms
that was the town's hospital and Khone's adjoining
dwelling.

The Lieutenant began speaking quietly into its suit
mike, and she could hear the words of warning and reassurance being relayed at full volume from the speakers
carried by the four Earth-humans who had preceded
them.

"Please do not be afraid," it was saying. "Despite the
strange and frightening appearance of the beings you are
seeing, they will not harm you. We are here to collect
Healer Khone, at its own request, for treatment in our
hospital. While we are transferring Khone to our vehicle
we may have to come very close to the healer, and this
may accidentally cause a call for joining to go out. A
joining must not be allowed to happen, and so we urge

everyone to move away from your homes, deep into the forest or far from the shore, so that a distress signal will not reach you. As an additional safeguard, we will place around the healer's home devices that will make a loud and continuous sound. This sound will be as unpleasant to you as it is to us, but it will merge with and change the sound of any nearby distress signal so that it will no longer be a call for joining."

Wainright looked toward Prilicla and when the empath signaled its approval, it changed to the personal suit frequency and went on. "Record and rerun that, please, until I either amend the message or tell you to stop."

"Will they believe all that?" Naydrad called suddenly from its position along the line. "Do they really trust us off-planet monsters?"

The Lieutenant moved several paces down the hill before replying. "They trust the Monitor Corps because we have been able to help them in various ways. Khone trusts Conway for obvious reasons and as their trusted healer, it has been able to convince the townspeople that Conway's horrifying friends are also worthy of trust. The trouble is, Gogleskans are a race of loners who don't always do as they're told.

"Some of them," it went on, "could have good reasons for not wanting to leave their homes. Illness or infirmity, young children to be cared for, or for reasons that seem good only to a Gogleskan. That's why we have to use the sound distorters."

Naydrad seemed satisfied but Cha Thrat was not. Out of consideration for Prilicla, who would suffer everyone else's feelings of anxiety as well as her own, she remained silent.

Like everyone else in Maintenance, she knew about those distorters. Suggested and designed by Ees-Tawn, the department's head of Unique Technology, in response to one of Conway's long-term Gogleskan requirements, the devices were still in the prototype stage. If successful they would go into mass production until they were in every Gogleskan home, factory, and seagoing vessel. It was not expected that the devices would eliminate joinings entirely, but with sensitive audio detectors coupled to automatic actuators, it was hoped that the link-ups that did occur would be limited to a few persons. That would mean that a joining's destructive potential would be negligible, shorter in duration, and psychologically less damaging to the beings concerned.

Under laboratory conditions the distorters were effective against several FOKT distress call recordings provided by Conway, but the device had yet to be tested on Goglesk itself.

The stink of fish worsened, and the sound of the monitors broadcasting the Lieutenant's message grew louder as they neared the hospital. Apart from a few glimpses she had of the Earth-humans moving between the houses at the edge of the clearing, there were no signs of life in the town.

"Stop sending now," Wainright briskly said. "Anyone who hasn't acted on the message by now doesn't intend to. Harmon, take up the flyer and give me an aerial view of this area. The rest of you place the distorters around the hospital, then stand by. Cha Thrat, Naydrad, ready with the litter?"

Quickly, Cha Thrat positioned the vehicle close to the entrance of Khone's dwelling, ran out the rear ramp, and opened the canopy in readiness to receive the patient. They could not risk touching Khone within sight of other Gogleskans and were hoping that the little healer would come out and board the vehicle itself. In case it did not, Naydrad would send in its remote-controlled probe to find out why.

Because they would make conversation difficult—
and so far nothing had happened that could cause any
Gogleskan to emit a distress call—the distorters remained silent.

"Friend Khone," Prilicla said, and the waves of sympathy, reassurance, and friendship emanating from it
were almost palpable. "We have come to help you.
Please come out."

They waited for what seemed like a very long time,
but there was neither sight nor sound of Khone.

"Naydrad . . ." Wainright began.

"I'm doing it," the Kelgian snapped.

The tiny vehicle, bristling with sound, vision, and
biosensors as well as a comprehensive array of handling
devices, rolled across the uneven surface and into
Khone's front entrance, pushing aside the curtain of
woven vegetable fibers that hung there. The view all
around it was projected onto the litter's repeater screen.

Cha Thrat thought that the probe itself, to someone
who did not know its purpose, was a frightening object.
Then she reminded herself that Diagnostician Conway,
and through it Khone, knew all about such mechanisms.

The probe revealed nothing but a deserted house.

"Perhaps friend Khone required special medication
from the hospital and went to get it," Prilicla said worriedly. "But I cannot feel its emotional radiation, which
means that it is either far from here or unconscious. If
the latter, then it may require urgent attention, so we
cannot afford to waste time by searching every room and
passageway in the hospital with the probe. It will be
quicker if I search for it myself."

Its iridescent wings were beating slowly, already
moving it forward when it went on. "Move well back,
please, so that your conscious feelings will not obscure
the fainter, unconscious radiation of the patient."

"Wait!" the Lieutenant said urgently. "If you find it, and it awakens suddenly to see you hovering above it . . ."

"You are correct, friend Wainright," Prilicla said. "It might be frightened into sending out a distress call. Use your distorters."

Cha Thrat quickly moved back with the medical team beyond the range of maximum sensitivity for the Cinrusskin's empathic faculty, and they adjusted their headsets to deaden external sounds while enabling them to communicate with each other. As a screaming, moaning, whistling cacophony erupted from the distorter positions around the hospital, Cha Thrat wondered about the depth of unconsciousness of their patient. The noise was enough to wake the dead.

It was more than enough to rouse Khone.

Chapter 13

"I feel it!" Prilicla called, excitement causing its hovering flight to become wildly unstable. "Friend Naydrad, send in the probe. The patient is directly beneath me, but I don't want to risk frightening it by a sudden, close approach. Quickly, it is very weak and in pain."

Now that it had an accurate fix on Khone's position, Naydrad quickly guided the probe to the room occupied by the Gogleskan. Prilicla rejoined the others around the litter's repeater screen where the sensor data was already being displayed.

The pictures showed the interior of one of the hospital's tiny examination rooms with the figure of Khone lying against the low wall that separated the healer and patient during treatment. A small table contained a variety of very long-handled, highly polished wooden implements that appeared to be probes, dilators, and spatulas for the nonsurgical investigation of body orifices, some jars of local medication, and, incongruously, the lifeless x-ray scanner left by Conway. A few of the instruments had fallen to the floor, and it seemed likely that Khone had been examining a patient on the other side of the wall when the healer had collapsed. It was also probable that the patient concerned had originated the last message received by Wainright.

"I am Prilicla, friend Khone," the empath said via the probe's communicator. "Do not be afraid..."

Wainright made an untranslatable sound to remind Prilicla that, apart from the initial words of identification, Gogleskans did not address each other as persons and became mentally distressed if anyone tried to do so.

"This device will not cause pain or harm," Prilicla continued more impersonally. "Its purpose is to lift the patient, very gently, and convey it to a position where expert attention is available. It is beginning to do so now."

On the repeater screen Cha Thrat saw the probe extend two wide, flat plates and slide them between the floor and Khone's recumbent body.

"Stop!"

The two voices, Khone's through the communicator and Prilicla's in response to the Gogleskan's blast of emotional radiation, sounded as one. The empath's fragile body was shaking as if caught in a high wind.

"I'm sorry, friend Khone..." it began, then remembering, went on. "Sincere apologies are tendered for the severe discomfort caused to the patient. Even greater gentleness will be striven for in future. But is the patient-healer able to furnish information on the exact position of, and possible reasons for, the pain?"

"Yes and no," Khone said weakly. Its pain had diminished because Prilicla was no longer trembling. It went on. "The pain is located in the area of the birth canal. There is loss of function and diminished sensation in the lower limbs, and the upper limbs and the medial area are similarly but less markedly affected. The cardiac action is accelerated and respiration is difficult. It is thought that the birth process had begun and was interrupted, but the reason is unknown because the scanner has not worked for some time and it is doubted if the patient's digits retain sufficient dexterity to change the power cell."

"The probe mounts its own scanner," Prilicla said reassuringly, "and its visual and clinical findings will be transmitted to the healers out here. It will also change the power cell in the other scanner so that the patient will be able to aid the healers outside with its own Gogleskan observations and experience."

The empath began trembling again, but Cha Thrat had the feeling that the shaking was due to its personal concern for Khone rather than a return of the other's pain.

"The scanner is being deployed now," Prilicla went on. "It will approach closely but will not touch the patient."

"Thanks are expressed," Khone said.

As she watched the increasingly detailed scan of Khone's pelvic area, Cha Thrat grew more and more angry over her ignorance of Gogleskan physiology. And it made little difference that the degree of ignorance of

Prilicla, Murchison, and Naydrad was only slightly less than her own. The one person with the ability to help Khone now was many light-years away in Sector General, and there was a strong probability that even the presence of the Diagnostician Conway would not have resolved this problem.

"The healer-patient can see for itself," Prilicla said gently, "that the fetus is large and is improperly presented to the birth canal. It is also pressing against the major nerve bundles and impeding the blood supply to the muscles in the area, making it impossible for the fetus to be expelled in its present position.

"Would the healer-patient agree," the empath went on, "that the birth cannot proceed without immediate surgical intervention?"

"No!" Khone said vehemently, forgetting to be impersonal. "You must not touch me!"

"But we're your..." Prilicla began. It hesitated for an instant, then went on. "Only friends wishing to help the patient are here. The psychological difficulties are understood. If necessary the probe can be instructed to administer sedative medication so that the patient will be unconscious and unaware of being touched while the operation is in progress."

"No," Khone said again. "The patient must be conscious during and for a short period following the birth. There are things that the parent must do for the newborn. Can your mechanism be instructed to perform the operation? The patient would be less frightened by the touch of a machine than that of an off-world monster."

Prilicla trembled again with the emotional effort needed to make a negative reply. It said, "Regrettably not. The remote-controlled manipulators are not sufficiently accurate or responsive for such a delicate procedure. If an observation might be made, the patient is in a severely weakened state and may shortly become unconscious without the assistance of medication."

Khone was silent for a moment, then with a note of desperation in its voice the Gogleskan said, "It is consciously realized that the off-world healers feel friendship and deep concern for the patient. But subconsciously, on the darker, unthinking levels of the mind, the close approach of one of these visually horrifying creatures would represent an immediate and deadly threat to the life of the patient, which would inevitably lead to a call for joining."

"The call would not be heard," Prilicla said, and explained the purpose of the sound distorters. But Khone's reply set the empath trembling again.

"A call for joining," it said, "presupposes a condition of extreme mental distress that is followed by a massive and uncontrolled expenditure of physical energy. The effect on the patient and fetus could lead to termination."

Quickly Prilicla said, "Time is short and the clinical condition is deteriorating rapidly. Risks must be taken. The probe mechanism can be made to provide two-way vision, and pictures of the off-world friends will be sent. Will the patient choose from among them the least frightening being, who will then try to assist it?"

While the litter's vision pickup swung to cover each of them in turn, Khone was saying "The Earth-humans are familiar and trusted, as are the Cinrusskin and Kelgian seen during the earlier visit to Goglesk, but all of them would arouse blind, instinctive terror if they approached closely. The other two beings are unfamiliar, both to the recollection of the patient or in the memories of the Earth-human Conway. Are they healers?"

There was a note of relief in the empath's voice as it replied, "Both are recent arrivals at the hospital and were unknown to Conway at the time of its first visit.

The small, globular being is Danalta, an entity capable of taking any required physical form including, if desirable, that of a Gogleskan, or of extruding any limbs or sensory organs necessary for the repair or alleviation of an organic malfunction. It will work under the Senior Physician's direction and is an ideal choice for—"

"*A shape-changer!*" Khone broke it. "Apologies are tendered to this entity, whose nonphysical qualities are doubtless admirable, but the thought of such a being is terrifying, and its close approach in the guise of one of my people would be unbearably repugnant. No!

"The tall creature," it added, "would be much less disturbing."

"The tall being," said Prilicla apologetically, "is a hospital maintenance technician."

"And previously," Cha Thrat added quietly, "a warrior-surgeon of Sommaradva, with other-species experience."

The empath was trembling again, and this time because of the storm of mixed feelings being generated by the other members of the medical team.

"Apologies are tendered," Prilicla said hastily. "A short delay is necessary. This matter requires discussion."

"For clinical reasons," Khone replied, "the patient-healer hopes that the delay will be very short."

It was Pathologist Murchison who spoke first. It said, "Your other-species experience is limited to an Earth-human DBDG and a Hudlar FROB, both involving simple, external surgery to a limb. Neither of them or, for that matter, your own DCNF classification, bears any resemblance to a Gogleskan FOKT. After that Hudlar limb-for-a-limb business, I'm surprised you want to take the responsibility."

"If this goes wrong," Naydrad joined in, its fur

twitching with concern, "if the patient or newborn terminate, I don't know what piece of medical melodrama you will pull in atonement. Better keep out of this."

"I don't know why," Danalta said, in a tone that suggested that its feelings were hurt, "it prefers an ungainly, stiff-boned life-form like Cha Thrat to me."

"The reason," Khone said, making them realize that they had forgotten to switch off the probe's communicator, "is degrading and probably insulting to the being concerned, but it should be mentioned in case the Sommaradvan finds it necessary to withdraw its offer."

Khone went on. "There are physical, psychological, and perhaps ridiculous reasons why this being might closely approach, but not touch except with long-handled instruments, the patient."

There were few visual similarities between the FOKT and DCNF classifications, Khone explained, except in the eyes of very young Gogleskans who tried to make models of their parents. But the mass of hair covering the ovoid body, the four short, splayed-out legs, the digital clusters, and the four long, cranial stings, were beyond their sculptoring skill. Instead they produced lumpy, conical shapes made from mud and grass, into which they stuck twigs that were not always straight or of uniform thickness. The results, on a much smaller scale, had a distinct resemblance to the body configuration of a Sommaradvan.

These crudely fashioned models were fabricated during the years preceding the change from childhood to maturity, when the young adult's stings became a threat to its parent's life, and they were kept and treasured by both parent and offspring as reminders of the only times in their lives when they could feel in safety the warmth and closeness of extended contact with another of their kind.

It was a memory that, in their later and incredibly lonely adult lives, helped keep them sane.

Murchison was the first to react after Khone finished speaking. The Pathologist looked at Cha Thrat and said incredulously, "I think it is telling us that you look like an oversized Gogleskan equivalent of an Earth teddy bear!"

Wainright gave a nervous laugh, and the others did not react. Probably they were as ignorant about teddy bears as Cha Thrat was. However, if the creature resembled her in many ways, it could not be entirely unbeautiful.

"The Sommaradvan is willing to assist," Cha Thrat said, "and offense has not been taken."

"And neither," Prilicla said, turning its eyes toward her, "will responsibility be taken."

The musical trills and clickings that were the Cinrusskin's native speech changed in pitch, and for the first time in Cha Thrat's experience the little empath's translated words carried the firmness and authority of a ruler as it went on. "Unless the Sommaradvan can give an unqualified assurance that there is no possibility of a recurrence of the Hudlar amputation, the Sommaradvan will not be allowed to assist.

"The healer-maintenance technician is being used for one reason only," it continued, "because the close proximity of the more experienced healers is contraindicated for this patient. It will consider itself simply as an organic probe whose mind, sensors, and digits are under the direction of the Senior Physician, who accepts sole responsibility for treatment and subsequent fate of the patient. Is this clearly understood?"

The idea of sharing or, in this instance, completely relegating responsibility for her actions to another person was repugnant to a warrior-surgeon, even though she could understand the reasons for it. But stronger than her feeling of shame was the sudden, warm upsurge of gratitude and pride at once again being called to work as a healer.

"It is understood," she said.

Silently the empath indicated that it was changing from the probe frequency, so as not to be verbally hampered by having to use the listening Gogleskan's impersonal mode of speech.

"Thank you, Cha Thrat," it said quickly. "Use my Cinrusskin instruments, they are best suited to your upper digits and I would feel more comfortable directing you in their use. Fit the protective devices before trying to do anything else; you could not help the patient if you were to be paralyzed by its stings. When you are with Khone, make no sudden movements that might frighten it without first explaining the reason for them. I shall be monitoring friend Khone's emotional radiation from here, and will warn you if any action causes a sudden increase of fear. But you are well aware of the situation, Cha Thrat. Please hurry."

Naydrad had her carrier pack already filled and waiting. She added the replacement power cell for Khone's scanner and began climbing from the top of the litter on to the hospital roof.

"Good luck," Murchison said. Naydrad ruffled its fur and the others made untranslatable noises.

The roof sagged alarmingly under Cha Thrat's weight, and one of her forefeet went right through the flimsy structure, but it was a much quicker route than crawling through a maze of low-ceilinged corridors. She dropped into the uncovered passageway leading to Khone's room, crouched awkwardly onto two knees and three of her medial limbs, and, with Prilicla warning the patient of her arrival, moved only her head and shoulders through the entrance. For the first time she was able to study a Gogleskan FOKT at close quarters.

"The intention," Cha Thrat said carefully, "is not to touch the patient directly."

"Gratitude is expressed," Khone replied in a voice that was barely audible above the sound of the distorters.

The mass of unruly hair and spikes that covered the erect, ovoid body were less irregular in color and position than the probe pictures had suggested. The body hair had mobility, although not to the extent as that possessed by the Kelgians, and lying motionless amid the multicolored cranial fur were a number of long, pale tendrils that were used only during a joining to link the member minds of the group. Four small, vertical orifices, two for breathing and speaking and two for food ingestion, encircled its waist.

The spikes covering the body were highly flexible, grouped together into digital clusters, and were capable of fine manipulation, and the lower body was encircled by a thick apron of muscle, under which the four short legs could be withdrawn when the being wished to rest.

Now it lay on its side, a position from which even a fully fit and active Gogleskan would have difficulty in recovering.

Quietly Cha Thrat said, "Instruct the probe to bring the scanner here. When the power cell has been replaced, return it to within easy reach of the patient, then move the machine aside."

To Khone she went on. "Unlike the visiting healers, the patient has been unaware of its own condition and an immediate self-examination is requested. Since the patient is also a healer with extensive knowledge of its own life processes, any comments or suggestions it cares to make would be helped to the off-planet colleagues."

Prilicla's voice came from her earpiece but not the probe's speaker, which meant that the empath wanted to talk to her alone. It said, "That was well spoken, Cha Thrat. No patient, no matter how ill or injured, wants to feel completely useless and dependent. Otherwise well-intentioned healers sometimes forget that."

That was one of the first lessons she had learned at the medical school on Sommaradva. Another, which had obviously been learned by Prilicla, was that junior medics facing a new and difficult job benefited from encouragement."

"The patient," Khone said suddenly, "is unable to guide the scanner."

There was nothing in the Cinrusskin's instrument pack long enough to reach Khone from Cha Thrat's present position. Impersonally she asked, "Is it permitted to use the Gogleskan instruments?"

"Of course," Khone said.

On the side table there was a set of long, expanding tongs, made from highly polished wood and with hinges of a soft, reddish metal, used for bringing instruments or dressings to bear on the otherwise untouchable Gogleskan patients. Lying beside them was a thin, conical object that had been fashioned crudely from dried clay, with short twigs and straw stuck all over it. She had mistaken it at first for a piece of decorative or aromatic vegetation. Now that she knew what it was, Cha Thrat thought that its resemblance to the aesthetically pleasing Sommaradvan body shape was close only in the eyes of a very sick Gogleskan.

Awkwardly at first, she used the tongs to lift the scanner from the limp grasp of Khone's digits and moved it over the abdominal area. While the patient was concentrating on the screen, she edged further into the room and closer to the patient. The unnatural position of her bent forelegs and spine, and the fact that virtually her entire body weight was being supported on medial limbs normally used only for manipulation, was threatening to send the associated muscles into spasm. To ease them she rocked very slowly from side to side, moving a little closer each time.

"The Sommaradvan healer is larger than was expected," Khone said suddenly, looking up from the scanner. It did not take Prilicla to tell her that the Gogleskan was very frightened.

Cha Thrat held herself motionless for a moment, then said, "The Sommaradvan healer, despite its size, will no more harm the patient than the sculptured likeness lying on the floor. The patient must surely know this."

"The patient knows this," Khone agreed, with a distinct trace of anger in its voice. "But has the Sommaradvan healer ever suffered nightmares, in which it is haunted, and hunted, by dark and fearful creatures of the undermind intent on its destruction? And instead of fleeing in unreasoning fear, has it ever tried to stop in the midst of such a nightmare, and think through or around its terror, and turned to face these dreadful phantasms, and tried to look upon them as friends?"

Ashamed, Cha Thrat said, "Apologies are tendered, and admiration for the patient-healer who is trying to do, who is doing, that which the stupid and insensitive Sommaradvan healer would find impossible."

Prilicla's voice sounded in her earpiece. "You have irritated friend Khone, Cha Thrat, but its fear has receded a little."

She took the opportunity of moving closer and said, "It is realized that the patient-healer's intentions toward the Sommaradvan are friendly, and any harm that might befall it would be the result of a purely instinctive reaction or accident. Both eventualities can be avoided by rendering the stings harmless..."

Khone's emotional reaction to that suggestion had both Prilicla and Cha Thrat badly worried, but time was running out for this patient and, if anything was going to be done for it, there was no real alternative to capping those stings. The little Gogleskan knew that as well as they did. It was being asked to surrender its only remaining weapon.

Cha Thrat dared not move a muscle other than her larynx, and that one was being seriously overworked as she tried to convince Khone's unconscious as well as its already half-convinced conscious mind that, in a truly civilized society, weapons were unnecessary. She told it that she, too, was a female, although she had yet to produce an offspring. She spoke of her most personal feelings, many of them petty rather than praiseworthy, about her past life and career on Sommaradva and in Sector General, and of the things she had done wrong in both places.

The team members waiting impatiently by the litter must be wondering if she had contracted a ruler's disease and had lost contact with the reality of the situation, but there was no time to stop and explain. Somehow she had to get through to the Gogleskan's dark undermind and convince it that psychologically she was leaving herself as open and defenseless by what she was telling it as Khone was by relinquishing its only natural weapons.

She could hear Naydrad's voice, which was being picked up by the Cinrusskin's headset, demanding to know whether Khone was a psychiatrist as well as a healer, and if so, the stupid Sommaradvan had picked the wrong time to lie on its couch! Prilicla did not speak and she went on talking unhurriedly to the patient whose voice, like the rest of it, seemed to be paralyzed by fear.

Suddenly there was a response.

"The Sommaradvan has problems," Khone said. "But if intelligent beings did not occasionally do stupid things, there would be no progress at all."

Cha Thrat was unsure whether the Gogleskan's words represented some deep, philosophical truth or were merely the product of a mind clouded by pain and confusion. She said, "The problems of the healer-patient are much more urgent."

"There is agreement," Khone said. "Very well, the stings may be covered. But the patient must be touched only by the machine."

Cha Thrat sighed. It had been too much to hope that a few highly personal revelations would demolish the conditioning of millennia. Without moving any closer, she held the scanner in position with the long tongs and used the rear medial limb to open her pack so that the probe's manipulators, which were being guided with great precision by Naydrad, could extract the sting covers.

Those covers had been designed to contain the needle-pointed stings and absorb their venom. Once in position, they released an adhesive that would ensure that they remained so until Khone reached Sector General. This property of the covers had not been mentioned to the patient. But with the distorters making it impossible for any call for joining to be heard by the other townspeople and its stings rendered impotent, the Gogleskan would be unable to avoid direct physical contact with one of the frightful off-worlders.

Considering the rapidly worsening clinical picture, the sooner that happened the better.

But Khone was not stupid and probably it had already realized what was to happen, which would explain its growing agitation as two, then three of the four sting covers were placed in position. Now it was moving its head weakly from side to side, deliberately avoiding the last cover. Quickly Cha Thrat tried to give it something else to think about.

"As can be clearly observed in the scanner and bio-sensor displays," she said impersonally, "the fetus is being presented laterally to the birth canal and is immobilized in this position. It has exerted pressure on important blood vessels and nerve connections to the parent's mid- and lower body, which has resulted in loss of muscle function and sensation and, unless relieved, will lead to necrosis in the areas concerned. The umbilical is also being increasingly compressed as the involuntary muscles continue trying to expel the fetus. The fetal heartbeat is weak, rapid, and irregular, and the vital signs of the parent are not good, either. Has the patient-healer any suggestion or comments on this case?"

Khone did not reply.

Only Prilicla would know how much Cha Thrat's coldly impersonal tone belied her true feelings toward the incredibly brave little creature who lay like a tumbled haystack so close to her, but still too far away in the non-material distances of the mind for her to be able to help it. Yet they were alike in so many ways, she thought. Both had taken risks that no other members of their species were willing to take—she had treated an off-world life-form she had never seen before, and Khone had volunteered itself for treatment by off-worlders. But of the two, Khone was the braver and its risks the greater.

"Is this condition rare or common among gravid females," she asked quietly, "and what is the normal procedure in such cases?"

The other's voice was so weak that the reply was barely audible as it said, "The condition is not rare. Normal procedure in such cases is to administer massive doses of medication that enables the patient and fetus to terminate with minimum discomfort."

Cha Thrat could think of nothing to say or do.

In the stillness of Khone's room she became increasingly aware of the external noises: the constant whistling and hissing of the distorters; and coming to her through the empath's communicator, the voice of Naydrad complaining about the difficulty of capping the stings of a patient who would not cooperate; and more quietly, Murchison, Danalta, and Prilicla itself as they suggested and quickly discarded a number of wildly differing procedures.

"The medical team's voices are unclear," Cha Thrat said anxiously. "Has anything been decided? What are the immediate instructions?"

Suddenly the voices became loud and very clear indeed, because they were coming from the probe's speaker as well as her own earpiece. Naydrad, its attention concentrated on the probe's remote-controlled manipulators as it tried to fit the last sting cover, must have decided that she wanted more volume and reacted to her statement without thinking.

The conversation was completely unguarded.

Prilicla was speaking, quietly and reassuringly, and clearly unaware that its words were reaching Khone as well as herself, Cha Thrat realized. The intense and conflicting emotional radiation emanating from the other team members grouped so closely around it was keeping the empath from detecting her own sudden burst of surprise and fear.

"Cha Thrat," it said, "there has been some argument, which has since been resolved in your favor, regarding who should perform the operation. Friend Khone's need is urgent, its condition has deteriorated to the stage

where the risk of moving it out for surgery is unaccept-
able, and your only option is to—"

"No!" she said urgently. "Please stop *talking*!"

"Do not be distressed, Cha Thrat," the empath continued, mistaking the reason for the objection. "Your
professional competence is not in doubt, and Pathologist
Murchison and myself have studied Conway's notes on
the FOKT life-form, as have you, and we will guide you
at every stage of the procedure and take complete responsibility throughout.

"Immediate surgical intervention is required to relieve
this condition," it went on. "As soon as the last sting is
capped, you will use a Number Eight scalpel to enlarge
the birth opening with an incision from the pelvis up to
the— What is happening?"

There was no need to tell it what was happening because in the time taken to ask the question it already
knew the answer. Khone, faced with the imminent prospect of a major surgical attack, had reacted instinctively
by emitting the call for joining and was trying to sting to
death the only strange, and therefore threatening, being
within reach. With its legs virtually paralyzed, Khone
was twisting violently from side to side and using its digital clusters to pull itself toward Cha Thrat.

The remaining uncapped sting, long, yellow, and with
tiny drops of venom already oozing from its point, was
swaying and jerking closer. Frantically Cha Thrat pushed
backward with the forefeet and medial limbs, launching
herself toward the Gogleskan and grasping the base of
the sting with three of her upper hands.

"Stop it!" she shouted above the noise of the call.
Forgetting to be impersonal, she went on. "Stop moving
or you'll injure yourself and the young one. I'm a friend,
I want to help you. Naydrad, cap it! Cap it quickly!"

"Hold it still, then," the Kelgian snapped back,

swinging the probe's manipulator arm above Khone's jerking head. "Hold it very still."

But that was not easy to do. Her upper, neck-level arms and digits had been evolved for more precise and delicate operations and lacked the heavy musculature of the medial limbs, and using them meant that Khone's head and her own were almost touching. She strained desperately to tighten her ridiculously weak grip on the sting, sending waves of pain into her neck and upper thorax. She knew that if those fingers slipped the sting would immediately be plunged into the top of her head.

The medical team would probably get to her quickly enough to save her life, but not those of Khone and the fetus, which was their only reason for being here. She was wondering how Murchison, the Diagnostician's life-mate; and Prilicla, its long-term friend; and Cha Thrat herself would face Conway with the news of Khone's death when Naydrad shouted, "Got it!"

The last sting was covered. She could relax for a mo-ment. But not Khone, who was still jerking and writhing on the floor and stabbing ineffectually at her with all four of its capped stings. Close up, the sound of its distress call was like a gale whistling and howling through a ruined building.

"At least the distorters are working," Wainright said, and added warningly, "but hurry it up, they won't last much longer."

She ignored the Earth-human and grasped tufts of the Gogleskan's hair in her upper and medial hands, trying vainly to hold it motionless. Pleadingly she said, "Stop moving. You're wasting what little strength you've got. You'll die and the baby will die. Please stop moving. I'm not an enemy, I'm your *friend*!"

The call for joining was still howling out with un-diminished volume, making her wonder how such a small creature could make so great a noise, but its physical movements were becoming noticeably less violent. Was it a symptom of sheer physical weakness, or was she getting through to the Gogleskan? Then she saw that the long, pale tendrils on its head were uncurling from the concealing hair and were standing out straight. Two of them fell slowly to lie along the top of her own head, and suddenly Cha Thrat wanted to scream.

Being Khone's friend was much, much worse than being its enemy.

Chapter 14

THERE was fear as she had never known it before—the sudden, overriding, and senseless fear of everything and everyone that was not joined tightly to her for the group defense; and a terrible, blind fury that diminished the fear; and the memories and expectation of pains past, present, and to come. And with those fearful memories there came a dreadful and confused nightmare of all the frightful and painful things that had ever happened to her—on Sommaradva and Goglesk and in Sector General. Many elements of the nightmare were utterly strange to her; the feeling of terror at the sight of Prilicla, which was ridiculous, and the sense of loss at the departure of the male Gogleskan who had fathered the child within her. But now there was no fear of the outsized, off-world animated doll who was trying to help her.

Even with the confusion of fear, pain, and alien experiences dulling her capacity to think, the conclusion was inescapable. Khone had invaded her mind.

Now she *knew* what it was like to be a Gogleskan; at a time like this the choice was simple. Friends joined and enemies—everyone and everything that was not part of the group—were attacked and destroyed. She wanted to break everything in the room, the furniture, instruments, decorations, and then tear down the flimsy walls, and she wanted to drag Khone around with her to help her do it. Desperately she tried to control the blind and utterly alien fury that was building up in her.

Amid the storm of Gogleskan impressions a tiny part of her own mind surfaced for a moment, observing that the tight grip she retained on Khone's fur must have fooled its subconscious into believing that she had joined with it, and was therefore a friend worthy of mind-sharing.

I am Cha Thrat, she told herself fiercely, *once a Sommaradvan warrior-surgeon and now a trainee maintenance technician of Sector General. I am not Khone of Goglesk and I am not here to join and destroy...*

But this was a joining, and memories of a larger, more destructive joining came crowding into her mind.

She seemed to be standing on top of a land vehicle stopped on high ground overlooking the town, watching the joining as it happened. The Earth-human Wainright was beside her, warning her that the Gogleskans were dangerously close, that they should leave, that there was nothing she could do and, for some strange reason, while it was saying these things it sometimes called "Doctor" but more often "sir." She felt very bad because she knew that the joining had been her fault, that it had happened because she had tried to help, and had touched, an industrial accident casualty. Below her she could clearly see Khone attaching itself to the other Gogleskans without being able to understand the reason, and at the same time she *was* Khone and knew the reason.

With individual Gogleskans hurrying to join it from nearby buildings, moored ships, and surrounding tree dwellings, the group-entity became a great, mobile, stinging carpet that crawled around large buildings and engulfed small ones as if it did not know or care what it was doing. In its wake it left a trail of smashed equipment, vehicles, dead animals, and a capsized ship. The group-entity moved inland to continue its self-destructive defense against an enemy out of prehistory.

In spite of the terrible fear of that nonexistent enemy in Khone's mind, which was now her mind, Cha Thrat tried to make herself think logically about what had happened to her. She thought of the wizard O'Mara and how it had said that Educator tapes would never be for her, and remembered the reasons it had given. Now she knew what it was like to have a completely alien entity occupying her mind, and she wondered if her sanity would be affected. Perhaps the fact that Khone, like herself, was a female might make a difference.

But there was a growing realization that it was not only Khone's mind and memories that she had to contend with. The memory and viewpoint from the top of the land vehicle was not from the Gogleskan's mind, nor her own. There were memories of the ambulance ship and the exploits of its medical team that were definitely not her own, and some vivid and—to her—fearful and wonderful recollections of events in Sector General that were totally outside her experience. Had O'Mara been right? Were factual recollections and insane fantasies intermingling, and she was no longer sane?

But she did not think she was insane. Madness was supposed to be an escape from a too-painful reality to a condition that was more bearable. There was too much pain here and the memories or fantasies were too painfully sharp. And one of them was of Lieutenant Wainright standing beside her, its head on a level with hers, and calling her "sir."

With a sudden shiver of fear and wonder she realized what was happening. She was sharing Khone's mind, and Khone had earlier shared it with someone else.

Conway!

For some time Cha Thrat had been aware of Prilicla's voice in her earpiece, but the words were just sounds without meaning to her already overloaded mind. Then she felt its warmth and sympathy and reassurance all around her, and the pain and confusion receded a little so that the meaning came through.

"Cha Thrat, my friend," the empath was saying, "please respond. You have been holding onto the patient's fur for the past few minutes, not doing anything and not answering us. I am on the roof directly above you, and your emotional radiation distresses me. Please, what is wrong? Have you been stung?"

"N-no," she replied shakily, "there is no physical damage. I feel badly confused and frightened, and the patient is—"

"I can read your feelings, Cha Thrat," Prilicla said gently, "but not the reason for them. There is nothing to be ashamed of, you've already done more than could be reasonably expected of you, and it was unfair of us to let you volunteer for this operation in the first place. We are in danger of losing the patient. Please withdraw and let me perform the surgery—"

"No," Cha Thrat said, feeling Khone's body twitch in her hands. The long, silvery tendrils that were the organic conductors for the uniquely Gogleskan form of telepathy-by-wire were still lying across her head, and anything Cha Thrat felt or heard or thought was immediately available to Khone, who did not like the idea of an alien monster operating on it, for reasons that were both personal and medical. Cha Thrat added, "Please give me a moment. I'm beginning to regain control of my mind."

"You are," Prilicla said, "but hurry."

Incredibly, it was her mind-partner who was doing most to aid the process. In common with the rest of its long-suffering and nightmare-ridden species, it had learned how to control and compartmentalize its thinking, feelings, and natural urges so that the enforced loneliness necessary to avoid a joining was not only bearable but, at times, happy. And now the Conway-memories of Sector General and some of its monstrous patients were surging into the forefront of her mind.

Be selective, Khone was telling her. *Use only what is useful.*

All the memories and experience of a Sommaradvan warrior-surgeon, a Gogleskan healer, and half an Earth-human lifetime spent in Sector General were hers, and with that vast quantity of other-species medical and physiological expertise available she could not believe that, even at this late stage, the Khone case was hopeless. Then from somewhere in that vast and incredibly varied store of knowledge, the glimmerings of an idea began to take shape.

"I no longer feel that surgical intervention is the answer," she said firmly, "even as a last resort. It is unlikely that the patient would survive."

"Who the blazes does it think it is?" Murchison said angrily. "Who's in charge of this op, anyway? Prilicla, pin its ears back!"

Cha Thrat could have answered both questions, but

did not. She knew that her words and tone had been wrong for someone in her lowly position—she sounded much too self-assured and authoritative. But there was no time for either long explanations or pretensions of humility, and it would be better if the true explanation was never given. With any luck Pathologist Murchison would believe, and go on believing, that Cha Thrat was a self-opinionated maintenance technician and one-time trainee nurse with delusions of grandeur and, for the time being at least, the team leader was leaving her ears unpinned.

"Explain," Prilicla said.

Quickly Cha Thrat reviewed the current clinical picture, gravely worsened now by the extreme debilitation that, even in a healthy Gogleskan, followed a joining. When she said that Khone lacked the strength and physical resources to withstand major surgery—it would have to be a cesarean procedure rather than a simple enlargement of the birth opening—she spoke with absolute certainty because she had the patient-healer's viewpoint of the case as well as her own. But she did not mention that, saying instead that Khone's emotional radiation would confirm her observations.

"It does," the empath said.

She went on quickly. "The FOKT classification is one of the few life-forms capable of resting in the upright position, although they can also lie down. Since their ancestors emerged from the oceans, their bodies and internal organs have been acted on by vertical G forces, as are those of the Hudlars and Tralthans and Rhenithi. I am reminded of a case in Tralthan Maternity a few years ago that was broadly similar to this one and required—"

"You didn't learn *that* from Cresk-Sar," Murchison broke in suddenly. "Trainee nurses aren't told about the near-failures, at least not in first year."

"I liked to study odd cases outside the syllabus," Cha Thrat lied smoothly, "and I still do, when I'm not engrossed in a maintenance manual."

Her emotional radiation would tell the Cinrusskin that she was lying, but it could only guess at what she was lying about. All it said was "Describe your procedure."

"Before I do," she went on quickly, "please remove the canopy from the litter and reposition the gravity grids to act laterally in opposite directions. Set the body restraints to the size and weight of the patient under anything up to an alternating plus and minus three Gs. Move the probe into the passageway, so I can step from it onto the roof. Hurry, please. I'm bringing out the patient now and will explain on the way..."

Cradling the barely conscious Khone in two medial arms and with all of her free hands gripping its fur tightly to make it feel that it was still joined to a friend, she climbed awkwardly onto the roof and sidled back the way she had come. Prilicla hovered anxiously above her all the way, Naydrad complained bitterly that its litter would never be the same again, and Murchison reminded it that they had a maintenance technician, or something, with them.

She continued to grip the Gogleskan's fur while Naydrad expertly fitted the restraints and Murchison attached an oxygen supply to all breathing orifices. With her head touching Khone's and the long, silvery tendrils still making contact, she checked that the other had a clear view of the scanner display, which she in her present awkward position did not, then braced herself and gave the signal to begin.

Cha Thrat felt her head and upper limbs being pulled sideways as Naydrad fed power to the gravity grid positioned above the patient's head. It was difficult to keep her balance because her lower body and legs were outside the influence of the artificial gravity field. But so far as Khone was concerned, it was tied upside-down to the litter under double, increasing to treble and Gogleskan standard gravity pull.

"Heart rate irregular," Prilicla reported quietly. "Blood pressure increasing in the upper body and head, respiration labored, minor displacement of thoracic organs, but the fetus hasn't moved."

"Shall I increase the pull to four Gs?" Naydrad asked, looking at Prilicla. But it was Cha Thrat who replied.

"No," she said. "Give it two Gs alternating as rapidly as possible between normal and reverse pull. You've got to try to shake Junior loose."

Now she was being knocked from side to side, as if by the soft, invisible paws of some great beast, while the patient was suffering the same maltreatment in the vertical plane. She managed to keep her head and the hands gripping Khone's fur steady, but she was feeling a growing nausea that reminded her of childhood bouts of travel sickness.

"Friend Cha Thrat, are you all right?" Prilicla asked. "Do you wish to stop?"

"Can we spare the time?"

"No," the empath replied, then: "The fetus is moving! It is—"

"Reverse, two Gs steady," Cha Thrat said quickly, effectively standing Khone on its head again.

"—now pressing against the upper womb," Prilicla continued. "The umbilical is no longer being compressed, and pressure on the blood vessels and nerve linkages in the area has been relieved. The muscles are beginning rapid, involuntary contractions..."

"Enough to expel the fetus?" she broke in.

"No," it replied. "They are too weak to complete the

birth process. In any case the fetus is still not in the optimum position."

Cha Thrat used a swear word that was definitely not Sommaradvan, and said, "Can we reposition and refocus the gravity grids so as to pull the fetus into the proper position for—"

"I would need time to—" Naydrad began.

"There isn't any time," said Prilicla. "I'm surprised friend Khone is still with us."

This was not going nearly as well as the remembered case in the Tralthan maternity ward had gone, and there was no consolation in telling herself that, in this instance, the life-form was strange and the operating facilities virtually non-existent. Khone's mind was no longer sending or receiving impressions, so that she could not even make the Last Apology to it for her failure.

"Please do not distress yourself, friend Cha," the Cinrusskin went on, beginning to tremble violently. "No blame can be attached to you for attempting a task that, because of the peculiar circumstances, none of us were able to do. Your present emotional radiation is worrying me. Remember, you aren't even a member of the medical team, you have no authority, and the responsibility for allowing you to try this procedure is not yours... You have just thought of something?"

"We both know," Cha Thrat said, so quietly that her voice reached only Prilicla, "that I have made it my responsibility. And yes, I've thought of something."

In a louder voice she went on quickly. "Naydrad, we need a rapid one-G push-pull this time, just enough to keep the fetus moving. Danalta, the muscle wall around the womb is thin, and relaxed due to the patient's unconsciousness. Will you produce some suitable limbs and hands? Prilicla will tell you the size and shape needed, and use the scanner to direct your movements of the fetus into the proper position. Murchison, will you stand by to help withdraw it, if or when it is born?"

Apologetically she added, "I cannot assist you. For the time being it would be better if I retained the closest possible physical contact with the patient. My feeling is that, unconscious or not, it will derive a greater measure of emotional comfort from my doing so."

"Your feeling is correct," Prilicla said. "But time is short, friends. Let's do it."

While Naydrad kept the fetus twitching slowly within the womb, and Danalta, using appendages whose shape and movements would give Cha Thrat bad dreams for many nights to come, tried to press and turn it into optimum position, she tried desperately to get through to her deeply unconscious mind-partner.

You will be all right. Your child will be all right. Hang on, please don't die on me!

It was like thinking into a black and bottomless pit. For an instant she thought there was a flicker of awareness, but it was probably that the feeling had come because she wanted it to be so. She turned her head slightly, so as not to break contact with the long, silvery tendrils, and wished that she was in a position to see the scanner display.

"It's in optimum position now," Prilicla said suddenly. "Danalta, move your hands lower. Be ready to press when I tell you if the fetus starts turning again. Naydrad, two Gs steady, down!"

For a moment there was silence except for the whistling of the distorters, which now seemed to be wavering in intensity as they labored like the patient, on reduced power, to perform their function. Time was running out for both of them. Everyone's attention was on Khone, and even Prilicla was watching the scanner display too intently to describe what it was seeing.

"I see the head!" Murchison said suddenly. "The top of the head only. But the contractions are too weak, they aren't helping very much. The legs are at maximum spread, but the fetal head is moving down, then back again, by a fraction of an inch with each contraction. Shall I try surgical enlargement of the—"

"No surgery," Cha Thrat said firmly. Even if the patient survived it, she had shared Khone's mind and knew that serious psychological damage would result from the inflicting of a surgical wound—not to mention the aftermath when close physical contact would be necessary to provide treatment and change dressings—on one whose species was virtually untouchable. The brief physical and mental contact with Conway and Cha Thrat had knocked a large hole in Khone's Gogleskan conditioning, but psychologically it was still a strong and very rigid structure.

But there was no time to explain her feeling or argue her point of view. Murchison had straightened up and was looking questioningly at Prilicla, who shook in the emotional winds blowing from all sides but said nothing.

"It would be better if we tried to assist the natural process," Cha Thrat went on. "Naydrad, I want alternating positive and reverse gravity again, this time between zero and three Gs down, initially for the next five contractions. And watch out for major displacement of other organs. This species has never been subjected to increased G forces—"

"I see the whole head now!" Murchison broke in excitedly. "And shoulders. Dammit, I've *got* the wee bugger!"

"Naydrad," Cha Thrat said quickly, "maintain three

Gs down for a moment until the afterbirth is out, then return to normal gravity conditions. Murchison, place the newborn between the digital clusters just to the left of my head. My feeling is that Khone will derive greater reassurance from holding on to its little one than from me holding on to its parent."

She watched as Khone's digits curled instinctively around the tiny form, which looked to the Sommaradvan part of her mind like a slimy, twitching little horror and which the Gogleskan portion insisted was a thing of indescribable beauty. Reluctantly she lifted her head from Khone's and released her grip on its fur.

"Your feeling is accurate, Cha Thrat," Prilicla said, "The patient, although still unconscious, is already emoting more strongly."

"But wait," Murchison said worriedly. "We were told that it must be conscious if it was to take care of the newborn properly. We've no idea what . . ."

She broke off because Cha Thrat, who now knew everything that the Gogleskan healer had known, was busily doing all that was necessary. It was contrary to her Sommaradvan upbringing to tell a deliberate lie, but the situation was fraught with all sorts of interpersonal difficulties and was too complicated for her to take the time needed to tell the truth.

Instead, Cha Thrat waited until the umbilical had been neatly severed and sealed off and the patient's lower limbs disposed more comfortably, then said smoothly, "There are a number of physiological similarities between the FOKT life-form and my own and, in any case, we females have certain instincts in these matters."

The Earth-human shook its head doubtfully and said,

"Your female instincts are a lot stronger, and more precisely directed, than mine."

"Friend Murchison," Prilicla said, its voice sounding loud because all but two of the distorters had ceased their whistling, "let us discuss female instincts at a more convenient time. Friend Naydrad, replace the litter canopy, turn up the internal heating three points, and maintain a pure oxygen atmosphere and watch out for signs of delayed shock. The emotional radiation indicates a condition of grave debility, but it is stable, there is no immediate danger, and circulation and mobility are returning to the lower limbs. We will all feel better, and especially the patient, when it has the ship's intensive-care equipment looking after it. Please move quickly.

"All except Cha Thrat," it added gently. "With you, my Sommaradvan friend, I would like private words."

Driven by Naydrad and with Danalta and Wainright flanking it, the litter was already moving off. But Pathologist Murchison was hanging back, its face deep pink and wearing an expression that Cha Thrat could now read and understand.

"Don't be *too* hard on it, Prilicla," Murchison said. "I think it did a very good job, even if it is inclined to forget who's in charge at times. I mean, well, let's just say that with Cha Thrat, Maintenance Department's gain was the medical staff's loss."

As Murchison turned abruptly to hurry after the litter, Cha Thrat watched it from three different and confusing viewpoints and with three sets of very mixed feelings. To her Sommaradvan mind it was a small, flabby, and unlovely DBDG female. To the Gogleskan mind it was just another off-planet monster, friendly but frightening. But from her Earth-human viewpoint it was an altogether different entity, one that for many years she had known to be highly intelligent, second only to Thornnastor in its professional standing, friendly, sympathetic, fair-minded, beautiful, and sexually desirable. Some of these aspects of its personality had just been demonstrated, but the sudden physical attraction Cha Thrat felt toward it, and the associated mind-pictures of horrible alien grapplings and intimacies, frightened her so badly that the Gogleskan part of her mind wanted to call for a joining.

Murchison was a female Earth-human and Cha Thrat was a female Sommaradvan. She *had* to stop feeling this stupid attraction toward a member of another species who was not even male, because in that direction lay certain madness. She remembered the discussion about Educator tapes with the wizard, O'Mara, and her own experience of sharing her mind with those of Kelgians, Tralthans, Melfans among others.

But that was not *her* experience, she reminded herself firmly. She was and would remain Cha Thrat. The Gogleskan and Earth-human who seemed to be occupying her mind were guests, one of them a particularly troublesome guest where thoughts of the entity Murchison were concerned, but they should not be allowed to influence her personal feelings. It was ridiculous to think, or feel, otherwise.

When the disturbing figure of Murchison had disappeared into the middle distance and Cha Thrat was feeling more like herself than two other people, she said, "And now, I suppose, comes the pinning back of the ears of a big-headed and grossly insubordinate technician with delusions of medical grandeur?"

Prilicla had alighted on the roof above Khone's doorway so that its eyes would be on a level with Cha Thrat's. It said gently, "Your emotional control is excellent, friend Cha. I compliment you. But your supposition is wrong. However, your obvious understanding of the Earth-human terms you have just used, and your earlier behavior during a very tricky clinical situation, leads me to speculate about what might possibly have happened to you.

"I am merely thinking aloud, you understand," it went on. "You are not required, in fact you are expressly forbidden to say whether my speculations are accurate or not. In this matter I would prefer to remain officially ignorant."

It was evident from the first few words that the empath knew exactly what had happened to Cha Thrat, even though its certainties were mentioned as suspicions. It suspected that Cha Thrat had shared minds with Khone, that the Gogleskan's mind had previously been shared with that of Conway, and it was the Diagnostician's medical expertise and initiative that had surfaced before and during the birth of Khone's child. For this reason the Cinrusskin was not offended by the incident —a Senior Physician was far outranked by a Diagnostician, even one who was temporarily in residence within the mind of a subordinate. And neither would the other team members feel offended if they were to suspect the truth.

But they must not suspect, at least until Cha Thrat was safely lost in the maintenance tunnels of Sector General.

"From your recent emotional radiation," Prilicla went on, "I suspect that you had strong if confused feelings of a sexual nature toward friend Murchison that were not pleasant for your Sommaradvan self. But consider the intensity of Murchison's embarrassment if it suspected that you, an entity of a completely different physiological classification forced by circumstances to work in close proximity with it, were regarding it with the eyes and the same strength of feeling as that of its life-mate. And if the others were to suspect as well, the emotional radiation from the team would be extremely painful and distressing to me."

"I understand," Cha Thrat said.

"Pathologist Murchison is highly intelligent," the Cinrusskin continued, "and in time she will realize what has happened, if she doesn't learn it from Khone first. That is why I would like you to explain this delicate situation to friend Khone at the first opportunity, and ask for its silence in this matter.

"Friend Khone," Prilicla added gently, "has the memories and feelings of Cha Thrat as well as Conway."

For a moment Cha Thrat could not speak as the Gogleskan healer's mind threatened to engulf her own with its peculiar mixture of fear, curiosity, and parental concern. Finally she said, "Will Khone be able to speak?"

"I have the feeling, not a suspicion, that both our Gogleskans are doing well," Prilicla replied, shaking out its wings in readiness for flight. "But now, if we don't end this conversation soon, the others will wonder what I am doing to you, and will be expecting you to arrive back bruised and bleeding."

The idea of Prilicla inflicting any kind of injury on anyone was so ridiculous that even a Gogleskan as well as a Sommaradvan and Earth-human considered it funny. Cha Thrat laughed out loud as, with the downdraft from the empath's wings stirring her hair, they followed the others back to the lander.

"You realize, friend Cha," the empath said, its trembling limbs a visible apology for the words that would diminish her pleasure, "that O'Mara will have to be told."

Chapter 15

BY the time they had been transfered from the lander to the special FOKT accommodation of *Rhabwar*'s casualty deck, both patients were fully conscious and making loud hissing noises. The sounds that the younger one was making did not translate, but Khone's were divided into repeated expressions of gratitude for its survival and weak but very insistent reassurances about its clinical condition. The healer's self-diagnosis was supported by the biosensors and confirmed by the less tangible but even more accurate findings of the emotion-sensitive Prilicla. And now that it was separated from its friendly off-world monsters, and its subconscious fears thereby allayed, by a thick transparent partition, Khone was quite happy to speak to anyone at any time.

That included the nonmedical crew members who, with Captain Fletcher's permission, left their positions in Control and the Power Room briefly to congratulate the patient and tell complimentary lies about the obvious intelligence, parental resemblance, and great beauty of the new arrival, a male child of greater than average weight. In spite of Prilicla's urgings that it should rest and refrain from overexcitement, the atmosphere around Khone's accommodation more closely resembled a birthday party than the casualty deck of an ambulance ship.

When Captain Fletcher arrived, they did not need an emphatic faculty to feel the atmosphere change. To Khone the Earth-human made a perfunctory inquiry about its health, then turned quickly to Prilicla.

"I need a decision, Senior Physician," it went on, "one that only you people can make. The hospital signaled us a few minutes ago, saying that an emergency beacon had been detected in this sector. The distressed ship is about five hours subspace flight away; the distress beacon was not one of the types used by the Federation, so the casualties might be a species new to us. That makes it difficult to estimate the time needed for the rescue. It could take a couple of days rather than hours.

"The question is," it ended, "do your patients require hospitalization before or after we respond to this distress call?"

It was not an easy decision to make because their patients, although stable and not in need of urgent treatment, belonged to a life-form about which little was known clinically, so that unexpected complications might arise at any time. Surprisingly the discussion, which was animated but necessarily brief, was ended by Khone itself.

"Please, friends," it said during one of the rare lulls, "Gogleskan females recover quickly once the birth trauma is over. I can assure you, both as a healer and a parent, that such a delay will not endanger either of us. Besides, here we are receiving much better attention than would be possible anywhere on Goglesk."

"You're forgetting something," Murchison said quietly. "We may be going into a disaster situation possibly involving a life-form completely new to us. It is conceivable that they might horrify or scare even us, much less a Gogleskan leaving its planet for the first time."

"They might," Khone replied, "but they would almost certainly be in a worse condition than I am."

"Very well," Prilicla said, turning back to the Captain. "It seems that friend Khone has reminded us of the priorities and of our duty as healers. Tell the hospital that *Rhabwar* will respond."

Fletcher disappeared in the direction of Control, and the Cinrusskin went on. "We should now eat and sleep, since there might not be an opportunity to do either for some time. The patients' biosensors will be monitored automatically and any change in condition signaled to me at once. They need rest, too, and they wouldn't get it if I left a team member on duty. Come along, everyone. Sleep well, friend Khone."

It flew gracefully into the gravity-free central well and up toward the dining and recreation deck, followed in more orthodox fashion by Naydrad, Danalta, Murchison, and Cha Thrat. But just before they began their weightless climb, Murchison gripped the ladder with one hand and placed the other on one of her medial limbs.

"Wait, please," it said. "I would like to speak to you."

Cha Thrat stopped but did not speak. The sensation of alien digits gently enclosing her arm and the sight of the flabby, pink Earth-human face looking up at her were giving rise to feelings that no Sommaradvan, much less a female one, had any business harboring. Slowly, so as not to give offense, she disengaged the limb from the other's grip and sought for emotional control.

"I'm worried about this ship rescue, Cha Thrat," it said, "and the effect on you of the casualties we may have to treat. Disaster injuries can be pretty bad, colli-

sion fractures and explosive decompressions for the
most part, and as a rule there are very few survivors.
You don't seem to be able to keep your Sommaradvan
nose out of the medical area, but this time you must
try, try really hard, not to get involved with our casualties."

Before Cha Thrat could reply, it went on. " You did
some very nice work with Khone, even though I'm still
not sure what exactly was going on, but you were very
lucky. If Khone or the infant or both of them had died,
how would you have felt? More important, what would
you have done to yourself?"

"Nothing," Cha Thrat said, trying hard to tell herself
that the expression on the pink face below her was one
of friendly concern for an other-species subordinate and
not something more personal. Quickly she went on. "I
would have felt very bad, but I would not have injured
myself again. The code of ethics of a warrior-surgeon is
strict, and even on Sommaradva there were colleagues
who did not observe it as I have done, and who envied
and disliked me for my own strict observance. To me the
code remains valid, but in Sector General and on Goglesk there are other and equally valid codes. My viewpoints have changed . . ."

She stopped herself, afraid that she had said too
much, but the other had not noticed that she had used
the plural.

"We call that broadening the mind," Murchison said,
"and I'm relieved and pleased for you, Cha Thrat. It's a
pity that . . . Well, I meant what I said about you being
the Maintenance Department's gain and our loss. Your
superiors find you a bit hard to take at times, and after
the Chalder and Hudlar incidents I can't imagine you
being accepted for ward training by anyone. But maybe
if you waited until the fuss died down, and didn't do

anything else to get yourself noticed, I could speak to a few people about having you transfered back to the medical staff. How do you feel about that?"

"I feel grateful," she replied, trying desperately to find a way of ending this conversation with a being who was not only sympathetic and understanding as a person, but whose physical aspect was arousing in her other feelings of the kind usually associated with the urge to procreate. Most definitely, she thought, this was a problem that could only be resolved by one of O'Mara's spells. Quickly she added, "I also feel very hungry."

"Hungry!" Murchison said. As the Earth-human turned to resume climbing to the dining area, it laughed suddenly and said, "You know, Cha Thrat, sometimes you remind me of my life-mate."

She was able to rest after the meal but not sleep and, after three hours of trying, she made the excuse to herself that Khone's life-support and synthetic food delivery systems needed checking. She found the Gogleskan awake, as well, and they talked quietly while it fed the infant. Soon afterward they were both asleep and she was left to stare silently at the complex shapes of the casualty deck equipment, which looked like weird, mechanical phantasms in the night-level lighting, until the arrival of Prilicla.

"Have you been able to speak with friend Khone?" the Cinrusskin asked, hovering over the two Gogleskans.

"Yes," Cha Thrat replied. "It will do as you suggested, to avoid embarrassing us."

"Thank you, friend Cha," Prilicla said. "I feel the others awake and about to join us. We should be arriving at any—"

It was interrupted by a double chime that announced their emergence into normal space, followed a few minutes later by the voice of Lieutenant Haslam speaking from Control.

"We have long-range sensor contact with a large ship," the communications officer said. "There are no indications of abnormal radiation levels, no expanding cloud of debris, no sign of any catastrophic malfunction. The vessel is rotating around its longtitudinal axis as well as spinning slowly end over end. We are locking the telescope into the sensor bearing and putting the image on your repeater screen."

A narrow, fuzzy triangle appeared in the center of the screen, becoming more distinct as Haslam brought it into focus.

It went on. "Prepare for maximum thrust in ten minutes. Gravity compensators set for three Gs. We should close with it in less than two hours."

Cha Thrat and Khone watched the screen with the rest of the medical team, who were making Prilicla tremble with the intensity of their impatience. They were as ready as it was possible to be, and the more detailed preparations would have to wait until they had some idea of the physiological classification of the people they were about to rescue. But it was possible for the ship ruler to draw conclusions, even at long range.

"According to our astrogation computor," Fletcher said, "the nearest star is eleven light-years distant and without planets, so the ship did not come from there. Although large, it is still much too small to be a generation ship, so it is highly probable that it uses a form of hyperdrive similar to our own. It does not resemble any vessel, past, current, or under development, on the Federation's fleet list.

"In spite of its large size," the Captain went on, "it has the aerodynamically clean triangular configuration typical of a vessel required to maneuver in a planetary atmosphere. Most of the star-traveling species that we know prefer, for technical and economic reasons, to keep their combined atmosphere-and-space vessels small and build the larger nonlanders in orbit where streamlining is unnecessary. The two exceptions that I know of build their space-atmosphere ships large because the crews needed to operate them are themselves physically massive."

"Oh, great," Naydrad said. "We'll be rescuing a bunch of giants."

"This is only speculative at the moment," the Captain said. "Your screen won't show it, but we're beginning to resolve some of the structural details. That ship was not put together by watchmakers. The overall design philosophy seems to have been one of simplicity and strength rather than sophistication. We are beginning to see small access and inspection panels, and two very large features that must be entry locks. While it is possible that these are cargo locks that double as entry ports for personnel who are physically small, the probability is that these people are a very large and massive life-form—"

"Don't be afraid, friend Khone," Prilicla broke in quickly. "Even a demented Hudlar couldn't break through the partition Cha Thrat put around you, and our casualties will be unconscious anyway. Both of you will be quite safe."

"Reassurance and gratitude are felt," the Gogleskan said. With a visible effort it added, more personally, "Thank you."

"Friend Fletcher," the empath said, returning its attention to the Captain, "can you speculate further about this life-form, other than that it is large and probably lacks digital dexterity?"

"I was about to," the Captain said. "Analysis of internal atmosphere leakage shows that—"

"Then the hull has been punctured!" Cha Thrat said excitedly. "From within or without?"

"Technician," said the ship ruler, reminding her of her position and her insubordination with the single word. "For your information, it is extremely difficult, expensive, and unnecessary to make a large, space-going structure completely airtight. It is more practical to maintain the vessel at nominal internal pressure and replace the negligible quantity of air that escapes. In this case, had escaping air not been observed, it would almost certainly have meant that the ship was open to space and airless.

"But there are no signs of collision or puncture damage," Fletcher went on, "and our sensor data and analysis of the atmosphere leakage suggests that the crew are warm-blooded oxygen-breathers with environmental temperature and pressure requirements similar to our own."

"Thank you, friend Fletcher," Prilicla said, then joined the others who were silently watching the repeater screen.

The image of the slowly rolling and spinning ship had grown until it was brushing against the edges of the screen, when Murchison said, "The ship is undamaged, uncontrolled, and, the sensors tell us, there is no abnormal escape of radiation from its main reactor. That means their problem is likely to be disease rather than traumatic injuries, a disabling or perhaps lethal illness affecting the entire crew. Under illness I would include the inhalation of toxic gas accidentally released from—"

"No, ma'am," said Fletcher, who had maintained the communicator link with Control. "Toxic contamination of the air supply system on that scale would have shown up in our leak analyses. There's nothing wrong with their air."

"Or," Murchison went on firmly, "the toxic material may have contaminated their liquid or food supply, and been ingested. Either way, there may be no survivors and nothing for us to do here except posthumously investigate, record the physiology of a new life-form, and leave the rest to the Monitor Corps."

The rest, Cha Thrat knew, would mean carrying out a detailed examination of the vessel's power, life-support, and navigation systems with the intention of assessing the species' level of technology. That might provide the information that would enable them to reconstruct the elements of the ship's course before the disaster occurred and trace it back to its planet of origin. Simultaneously, an even more careful evaluation of the nontechnical environment—crew accommodation and furnishings, art or decorative objects, personal effects, books, tapes, and self-entertainment systems—would be carried out so that they would know what kind of people lived on the home planet when they succeeded in finding it, as they ultimately would.

And eventually that world would be visited by the Cultural Contact specialists of the Monitor Corps and, like her own Sommaradva, it would never be the same again.

"If there are no survivors, ma'am," Fletcher said regretfully, "then it isn't a job for *Rhabwar*. But we'll only know when we go inside and check. Senior Physician, do you wish to send any of your people with me? At this stage, though, getting inside will be a mechanical rather than a medical problem. Lieutenant Chen and Technician Cha Thrat, you will assist me with the entry— Wait, something's happening to the ship!"

Cha Thrat was very surprised that Fletcher wanted her to help with such important work, badly worried in case she might not be able to perform to his expectations, and more than a little frightened at the thought of what might happen to them when they got inside the distressed ship. But the feelings were temporarily submerged at the sight of what was happening on the screen.

The ship's rate of spin and roll were increasing as they watched, and irregular spurts of vapor were fogging the forward and aft hull and the tips of the broad, triangular wings. She suffered a moment's sympathetic nausea for anyone who might be inside the vessel and conscious, then Fletcher's voice returned.

"Attitude jets!" it said excitedly. "Somebody must be trying to check the spin, but is making it worse. Maybe the survivor isn't feeling well, or is injured, or isn't familiar with the controls. But now we know someone is alive in there. Dodds, as soon as we're in range, kill that spin and lock on with all tractors. Doctor Prilicla, you're in business again."

"Sometimes it's nice," Murchison said, speaking to nobody in particular, "to be proved wrong."

While Cha Thrat was donning her suit, she listened to the discussion between the medical team members and Fletcher that, had it not been for the presence of the gentle little empath, would have quickly developed into a bitter argument.

It was plain from the conversation that the Captain was *Rhabwar*'s sole ruler so far as all ship operations were concerned, but at the site of a disaster its authority had to be relinquished to the senior medical person on board, who was empowered to use the resources of the ship and its officers as it saw fit. The main area of contention seemed to be the exact point where Fletcher's responsibility ended and Prilicla's began.

The Captain argued that the medics were not, considering the fact that the distressed ship was structurally undamaged, on the disaster site until it got them into the ship, and until then they should continue to obey its orders or, at very least, act on its advice. Its advice was that they should remain on *Rhabwar* until it had effected an entry, because to do otherwise was to risk becoming casualties themselves if the injured or ill survivor—who had already made a mess of checking its ship's spin with the attitude jets—decided to do something equally unsuccessful and much more devastating with the main thrusters.

If the medical team was waiting outside the distressed ship's entry lock when thrust was applied, they would either be smashed against the hull plating or incinerated by its tail flare, and the rescue would be aborted because of a sudden lack of rescuers.

Fletcher's reasons for wanting the medics to remain behind until the other ship had been opened were sound, Cha Thrat thought, even though they had given her a new danger to worry about. But the medical team had been trained for the fastest possible rescue and treatment of survivors, and they were particularly anxious not to waste time in this case when there might only be one. By the time she was leaving for the airlock, a compromise had been worked out.

Prilicla would accompany Fletcher, Chen, and herself to the ship. While they were trying to get inside, the empath would move up and down the outer hull and try to pinpoint the locations of survivors by their emotional radiation. The rest of the medical team would hold themselves ready for a fast recovery of casualties as soon as the way was open.

She had been waiting only a few minutes in the lock antechamber when Lieutenant Chen arrived.

"Good, you're here already," the Earth-human said, smiling. "Help me move our equipment into the lock, please. The Captain doesn't like to be kept waiting."

Without giving the impression that it was lecturing her, Chen discussed the purpose of the equipment they were moving from the nearby stowage compartment to the lock, so that Cha Thrat felt her level of ignorance was being reduced without the feelings of stupidity and inferiority that so often accompanied that process. She decided that the Earth-human was a considerate and helpful person, in spite of its rank, and one with whom she might risk a small insubordination.

"This is in no sense a criticism of the ship ruler," she said carefully, "but I am concerned lest Captain Fletcher is giving me credit for more technical experience than I in fact possess. Frankly, I'm surprised it wanted me along."

Chen made an untranslatable sound and said, "Don't be surprised, Technician, or worried."

"Regrettably," Cha Thrat said, "I am both."

For a few minutes the Lieutenant went on talking about the sections of portable airlock they were carrying that, when deployed and attached with fast-setting sealant around the entry port of the other ship, would enable *Rhabwar*'s boarding tube to join the two vessels and allow the medics to do their work unhampered by spacesuits.

"But rest your mind, Cha Thrat," Chen went on. "Your maintenance chief, Timmins, spoke to the Captain about you. It said that you are pretty bright, learn quickly, and we should give you as much work to do as possible. We should do this because, once the FOKT's accommodation was finished, you would have nothing to do and might fret. It said that, with your past performance in the hospital, the medical team wouldn't allow you anywhere near one of their patients."

It laughed suddenly and went on. "Now we know how wrong Timmins was. But we still intend to keep you busy. You have four times as many hands as I have, and I can't think of a better tool-carrier. Do I offend you, Technician?"

The question had been asked of the trainee technician and not the proud warrior-surgeon she had been, so the answer had to be "No."

"That's good," Chen said. "Now, close and seal your helmet, and double-check your safety-line attachments. The Captain's on his way."

And then she was outside, festooned with equipment and drifting with the two Earth-humans across the short distance to the distressed vessel, which was now held by the rigid, nonmaterial beams of *Rhabwar*'s tractors. While immobilizing the other ship, their own had acquired a proportion of its spin. But the countless stars that wheeled endlessly around the apparently motionless vessels aroused a feeling not of nausea but wonder.

Prilicla was already there when they arrived, having exited by the casualty deck's airlock, and was patrolling along the hull in its careful search for the emotional radiation that would indicate the presence of survivors.

Chapter 16

As soon as they were standing upright and held to the gray, unpainted hull plating by their boot magnets, and with the bulk of *Rhabwar* hanging above them like a shining and convoluted white ceiling, the Captain began to speak.

It said, "There are only so many ways for a door to open. It can hinge in or outward, slide vertically or laterally, unscrew clockwise or anticlockwise or, if the builders are sufficiently advanced in the field of molecular engineering, an opening could be dilated in an area of solid metal. We have yet to encounter a species capable of the latter and, if we ever do, we'll have to be very careful indeed, and remember to call them 'sir.'"

Before it had joined the Monitor Corps, she had learned, Fletcher had been a ruler-academic and one of Earth's foremost, and certainly most youthful, authorities on Extraterrestrial Comparative Technology, and the old habits died hard. Even on the hull of an alien ship that might apply thrust at any moment, it was lecturing —and remembering to include the occasional dry little joke. It was also speaking for the benefit of the recorders, in case something sudden and melodramatic happened.

"We are standing on a large door or hatch that is rectangular in shape with rounded corners," it went on, "so the probability is that it will open in or out. Below us, according to the sensors, is a large, empty compartment, which means that it has to be a cargo or personnel lock rather than an equipment access or inspection panel. The hatch is featureless, so the external actuator mechanism should be behind one of the small panels in the door surround. Technician, the scanner, please."

Because this particular scanner was designed to see into the vital organs of metal-encased machines rather than the softer structures of flesh and blood, it was much larger and heavier than its medical counterpart. In her eagerness to appear fast and efficient, Cha Thrat miscalculated the inertia and sent it crashing into the hatch cover, where it left a long, shallow dent before the Captain brought it to a halt.

"Thank you," Fletcher said drily, and added, "We are, of course, making no secret of our presence. A covert entry and our sudden appearance inside their ship might frighten the survivors, if there are any."

Chen made an untranslatable noise and said, "Whacking the hull with a sledgehammer would have been even better."

"Sorry," Cha Thrat said.

Two of the small panels concealed retractable lighting fixtures and the remaining one turned out to be a large rocker switch set flush with the hull plating. Fletcher warned them to stand clear, then pressed with its palm on both ends of the switch in turn. It had to press very hard, so hard that it had pushed its leg and arm magnets away from the hull, before anything happened.

A sudden rush of air from the edge of the slowly opening hatch sent Fletcher spinning away. Cha Thrat, who had the advantage of four foot-magnets holding her down, grabbed it by one leg and brought the Captain into contact with the hull again.

"Thank you," Fletcher said, as the fog of escaping air cleared, then went on. "Everyone inside. Doctor Prilicla, come quickly. The opening of the lock is sure to register on their control deck. If there are any survivors up there, now is the most likely time for them to get nervous and apply thrust..."

"There *are* survivors, friend Fletcher," the empath broke in. "One of them is forward, probably on the control deck, and several groups of them farther aft, but none in your immediate area. Out here I am too far from the sources to be able to detect individual emotional radiation, but the predominant feelings are of fear, pain, and anger. It is the intensity of the anger that worries me, friend Fletcher, so go carefully. I am returning to *Rhabwar* for the rest of the medical team."

With the scanner they were able to identify and trace the actuator wiring to a set of two rocker switches. The first one was locked in position, and when they pressed the second, the lock's outer seal closed behind them, after which the first one moved freely and opened the inner seal, simultaneously turning on the lighting.

Fletcher said a few words for the recorders about the intense greenish-yellow lighting that would, on later analysis, give useful information about the crew's visual organs and an indication of the type and proximity of their sun to the home planet. Then it led the way from the lock chamber into the corridor.

"The corridor is about four meters high, square in cross-section, well lit, unpainted, and gravity-free," the Captain went on. "We assume an artificial gravity system, currently malfunctioning or possibly switched off, because the inner surfaces are bare of ladders, climbing nets, or handholds that the crew would need to get about in the weightless condition. At this level the section of corridor visible to us follows the lateral curvature of the inner hull, and opposite the lock entrance there is a wide opening through which we can see two ramps, one ascending and the other descending, which lead, presumably, to other decks. We are taking the ascending one."

Consulting the analyzer strapped to its arm, the Captain went on. "Nothing toxic in the air, pressure low but still breathable, temperature normal. Open your visors so we can talk together without tying up the suit frequencies."

Fletcher and Chen launched themselves into the air above the ascending ramp. Less expertly, Cha Thrat did likewise and was halfway to the top when the others arrived—and dropped suddenly onto the deck with a muffled crash of equipment and a much less quiet burst of strong language. She had enough warning to be able to land on her feet.

"The artificial gravity system," the Captain said, when it had picked itself up again, "is still operating in this area. Move quickly, please, we're looking for survivors."

Large inward-opening doors with simple latch fastenings lined the corridor, and under Fletcher's direction, the search became a routine process. First unlatch the door, push it wide open while standing well back in case something nasty came through it, then search the compartment quickly for crew members. But the compartments held only racks of equipment or containers of various shapes and sizes whose labels they could not read, and nothing that in any way resembled furniture, wall decorations, or clothing.

So far, Fletcher reported, the ship's interior seemed incredibly spartan and utilitarian, and it was beginning to worry about the kind of people who would build and crew such a vessel.

At the top of the next ramp, in another section of

corridor that was gravity-free, they saw one of them. It was hanging weightless, spinning slowly and occasionally bumping against the ceiling.

"Careful!" Fletcher warned as Cha Thrat moved forward for a closer look. But there was no danger because she could recognize a cadaver when she saw one, regardless of its species. A hand placed on its thick, heavily veined neck confirmed the absence of a pulse and a body temperature that was much too low for a warm-blooded oxygen-breather who was alive.

The Captain joined her and said, "This is a big one, almost twice the mass of a Tralthan, physiological classification FGHI . . ."

"FGHJ," Cha Thrat corrected.

Fletcher broke off and took a deep breath, which it expelled slowly through its nose. When it spoke she could not be sure whether the Captain was being what Earth-humans called sarcastic, or simply asking a question of a subordinate who appeared to have more knowledge in a particular area than it had.

"Technician," it said, laying heavy emphasis on the first word, "would you like to take over?"

"Yes," she said eagerly, and went on. "It has six limbs, four legs and two arms, all very heavily muscled, and is hairless except for a narrow band of stiff bristles running from the top of the head along the spine to the tail, which seems to have been surgically shortened at an early age. The body configuration is a thick cylinder of uniform girth between the fore and rear legs but the forward torso narrows toward the shoulders and is carried erect. The neck is very thick and the head small. There are two eyes, recessed and looking forward, a mouth with very large teeth, and other openings that are probably aural or olfactory sense organs. The legs . . ."

"Friend Fletcher," Prilicla broke in gently. "Would

you please switch on your vision pickup and spotlight, and hold them very steady? We want to see what Cha Thrat is describing."

Suddenly every surface detail of the dead FGHJ was illuminated by a light even more intense than that of the corridor.

"You won't see a good picture," the Captain said. "The shielding effects of the ship's hull will cause fogging and distortion."

"That is understood," the empath said. "Friend Naydrad is preparing the large pressure litter. We will be with you very soon. Please continue, Cha Thrat."

"The legs terminate in large, reddish-brown hooves," she went on, "three of which are covered by thick, heavily padded bags fastened tightly at the tops, possibly to deaden the sound their feet make on the metal deck. Cylinders of metal, padded on the inner surfaces, encircle all four legs just below knee-level, with short lengths of chain attached to them. The links at the end of the chains have been broken or forced apart.

"The creature's hands are large, with four digits," she continued, "and do not appear particularly dexterous. There is a complicated harness suspended from and belted around the upper torso and flanks. Pouches of different sizes are attached to the harness. One of them is open and there are small tools scattered around the body."

"Technician," the Captain said, "remain here until the medic team arrives, then follow us. We're supposed to find and help the live ones and—"

"No!" Cha Thrat said without thinking. Then apologetically she added, "I'm sorry, Captain. I mean, be very careful."

Chen was already moving down the corridor, but the Captain checked itself as it was about to follow.

"I am always careful, Technician," it said quietly, "but why do you think I should be very careful?"

"I do not have a reason," she said, with three of her eyes on the cadaver and one on the Earth-human, "only a suspicion. On Sommaradva there are certain people, warriors as well as serviles, who behave badly and without honor toward their fellow citizens and, on rare occasions, grievously injure or kill them. These lawbreakers are confined on an island from which there is no escape. On the vessel that transports them to this island the noncrew accommodation lacks comfort, and the prisoners themselves are immobilized by leg restraints. With respect, the similarities to our present situation are obvious."

Fletcher was silent for a moment, then it said, "Let's take your suspicion a stage further. You think this might be a prison ship, in distress not because of a technical malfunction but because its prisoners have broken free and may have killed or injured all or part of the crew before they realized that they were unable to work the ship themselves. Perhaps some crew members are holed up somewhere, in need of medical attention, after inflicting serious casualties among the escapees."

Fletcher looked briefly at the cadaver, then returned its attention to Cha Thrat.

"It's a neat theory," it went on. "If true, we are faced with the job of convincing the ship's crew and a bunch of unruly prisoners, who are on less than friendly terms with each other, that we would like to help all of them without becoming casualties ourselves. But is it true? The leg restraints support your theory, but the harness and tool pouches suggest a crew member rather than a prisoner.

"Thank you, Cha Thrat," it added, turning to follow

Chen, "I shall bear your suspicions in mind, and be very careful."

As soon as the Captain had finished speaking, Prilicla said quickly, "Friend Cha, we can see wounds all over the body surface, but the details are indistinct. Describe them please. And do they support your theory? Are they the type of injuries that might be sustained by an entity being moved violently about inside a spinning ship, or could they have been inflicted deliberately by another member of the same species?"

"On your answer," Murchison joined in, "depends whether or not I go back for a heavy-duty spacesuit."

"And I," Naydrad said. Danalta, who belonged to a species impervious to physical injury, remained silent.

She looked closely at the brightly lit surfaces of the corridor for a moment, then gently rotated the cadaver so that its entire body was presented to the vision pickup. She was trying to think like a warrior-surgeon while at the same time remembering one of the basic physics tapes she had viewed as a trainee technician.

"There are a large number of superficial contusions and abrasions," she said, "concentrated on the flanks, knees, and elbows. They appear to have been made by grazing contact with the metal of the corridor, but the wound that caused its death is a large, depressed fracture located on and covering the top of the skull. It does not look as if it was caused by any type of metal tool or implement but by violent contact with the corridor wall. There is a patch of congealed blood, comparable to the area of the injury, on the wall where I am directing the vision pickup.

"Remembering that the cadaver's position in the vessel is approximately amidships," she went on, wondering if the Captain's lecturing manner was a psychological contagion, "it is unlikely that the spinning could have been responsible for such a grievous head injury. My conclusion is that the being, whose legs are very strong, misjudged a jump in weightless conditions and hit its head against the wall. The lesser wounds could have been caused while it was tumbling, unconscious and dying, inside the spinning ship."

Murchison's voice sounded relieved as it said, "So you're telling us that it had an accident, that no other antisocial type bashed in its skull?"

"Yes," Cha Thrat said.

"I'll be with you in a few minutes," it said.

"Friend Murchison," Prilicla began anxiously.

"Don't worry, Doctor," said the Pathologist. "If anyone or anything nasty threatens, Danalta will protect us."

"Of course," the shape-changer said.

While she was waiting for them to arrive, Cha Thrat continued to study the cadaver while listening to the voices of Prilicla, Fletcher, and *Rhabwar*'s communications officer. The Cinrusskin's empathic faculty had given it approximate locations for the survivors who, apart from the single crew member in Control, seemed to be gathered together in three small groups of four or five persons on one deck. But the Captain had decided that it would be better to make contact with a single crew member before approaching a group, and was heading directly for the survivor on the Control deck.

Cha Thrat steadied the cadaver and took one of its large, strong hands in two of her upper manipulators. The fingers were short and stubby and tipped with claws that had been trimmed short, and none of the digits were opposable. In this species' prehistory she could imagine those clawed hands conveying freshly killed food to the mouth that even now was filled with long and very nasty-looking teeth. It did not, she thought, look like a member of a species capable of building ships that traveled between the stars.

It did not look, well, *civilized*.

"You can't always judge by external appearance," Murchison said, making Cha Thrat realize that she had been thinking aloud. "Your Chalder friend from the AUGL ward makes this one look like a pussy-cat."

The rest of the medical team were following closely behind the Pathologist: Naydrad guiding the litter; Prilicla walking the ceiling on its six, sucker-tipped legs; and, as she watched, Danalta extruded a thicker, sucker-tipped limb of its own and attached itself to the wall like some watchful, alien vegetable.

Quickly Murchison attached its instrument pack to the wall with magnetic pads and used larger magnets and webbing to immobilize the cadaver. It said, "Our friend here was unlucky, but at least it is helping the others. I can do things to it which I would not think of doing to a living survivor, and without wasting time on—"

"Dammit, this is *ridiculous*!" a voice said in their suit phones, so distorted by surprise and incredulity that she did not recognize it at first as belonging to the Captain. Fletcher went on. "We're on the control deck and we've found another crew member, alive, apparently uninjured, occupying one of five control positions. The other four positions are empty. But the survivor is wearing restraints on all four legs and is chained to its control couch!"

Cha Thrat turned away and left without speaking. The Captain had told her that she should follow Chen and itself as soon as the medical team arrived, and she wanted to do just that before Fletcher had a chance to countermand the earlier order. Her curiosity about this strange, chained-up ship's officer was so intense that it was almost painful.

It was not until she had ascended two decks that she noticed Prilicla silently following her.

Fletcher was saying "I've tried communicating with it, with the translator and my making the usual friendly signs. *Rhabwar*'s translation computer is capable of converting simple messages into any conceivable language that is based on a system of word-sounds. It growls and barks at me but the sounds don't translate. When I approach closely it acts as if it wants to tear my head off. At other times its body and limb movements are erratic and uncoordinated, although it seems anxious to be free of its leg restraints."

Prilicla and Cha Thrat arrived at that moment, and the Captain added, "See for yourselves."

The Cinrusskin had taken up a position on the ceiling just inside the entrance, well away from the crew member's wildly flailing arms. It said, "Friend Fletcher, the emotional radiation disturbs me. There are feelings of anger, fear, hunger, and blind, unthinking antagonism. There is a coarseness and intensity in these emotions not usually found in beings possessing high intelligence."

"I agree, Doctor," the Captain said, moving back instinctively as one of the clawless hands stabbed out at its face. "But these couches were designed for this particular life-form, and the controls, switches, and doorhandles that we've seen so far in the ship are suited to those particular hands. At the moment it is completely ignoring the controls, and the sudden increase in spin we noticed during our approach was probably caused by it accidentally striking the keys concerned.

"Its couch, like the other four, is mounted on runners," Fletcher went on. "It has been moved back to the limit of its travel, which makes it very difficult for the being's hands to reach the control consoles. Have you any ideas, Senior Physician, because I haven't."

"No, friend Fletcher," Prilicla said, "but let us move to a lower deck where it cannot see or hear us."

A few minutes later it continued. "The levels of fear, anger, and antagonism have diminished, and its hunger remains at the same intensity. For reasons that aren't clear to me at the moment, the crew member's behavior is irrational and emotionally unstable. But it is in no immediate danger where it is, and it is not in any pain. Friend Murchison."

"Yes?" the Pathologist responded.

"When you are examining that cadaver," it went on, "pay special attention to the head. It has occurred to me that the cranial injury may not have been an accident, but was deliberately self-inflicted in response to acute and continuing cranial discomfort. You should look for evidence of an area of infection or cell degeneration affecting the brain tissues, which may have adversely affected or destroyed its higher centers of mentation and emotional control.

"Friend Fletcher," it went on without waiting for a reply, "we must quickly locate and check the condition of the other survivors. But carefully, in case they are behaving like our friend in Control."

With Prilicla's empathic faculty to guide them, they quickly found the three large dormitory compartments containing the remaining conscious survivors, five in one room and four in each of the others. The doors were not locked but the occupants had not used the simple latch system that would have opened them from the inside. The artificial gravity system was in operation, and the brief look they were able to catch before the occupants spotted and began to attack them showed plain, undecorated metal walls and flooring that was covered by disordered bedding and wrecked waste-disposal equipment. The smell, Cha Thrat thought, could have been cut with a knife.

"Friend Fletcher," Prilicla said as they were leaving the last dormitory, "all of the crew members are physically active and without pain, and if it wasn't for the fact that they are clearly no longer capable of working their ship, I would say that they are quite healthy. Unless friend Murchison discovers a clinical reason for their abnormal behavior, there is nothing we can do for them.

"I realize that I am being both cowardly and selfish," it went on, "but I do not want to endanger our casualty deck equipment and terrify friend Khone by moving in close on twenty oversized, overactive, and, at present, underintelligent life-forms who—"

"I agree," Fletcher said firmly. "If that lot got loose, they could wreck my ship and not just the casualty deck. The alternative is to keep them here, extend *Rhabwar*'s hyperspace envelope, and Jump both ships to Sector General."

"That was my thought as well, friend Fletcher," Prilicla replied. "Also, that you rig the boarding tube so that we can have rapid access to the survivors, that we gather samples of all packets and containers likely to hold this life-form's food or nutritious fluids. The only symptom these people display is intense hunger and, considering the size of their teeth, I would like to relieve it as soon as possible in case they start eating each other."

"And," the Pathologist's voice joined in, "you want me to analyze the samples so as to tell you which containers hold paint and which soup?"

"Thank you, friend Murchison," the empath said, and went on. "As well as your cranial investigation would you look at the cadaver's general metabolism with a view to suggesting a safe anesthetic for use on these people, something fast-acting that we can shoot into them at a distance. They must all be anesthetized very quickly because—"

"For fast work like that," Murchison broke in, "I'll need *Rhabwar*'s lab, not a portable analyzer like this one. And I'll need the whole team to help me."

"Because," Prilicla resumed quietly, "I have a feeling that there is another survivor who is not healthy and active and hungry. Its emotional radiation is extremely weak and characteristic of an entity who is deeply unconscious and perhaps dying. But I am unable to locate it because of the stronger, overriding emanations from the conscious survivors. That is why, as soon as the samples are gathered for friend Murchison, I would like every hole, corner, or compartment large enough to hold an FGHJ searched.

"It must be done quickly," the Cinrusskin ended, "because the feeling is very weak indeed."

Awkwardly Fletcher said, "I understand, Senior Physician, but there is a problem. Pathologist Murchison needs all of the medical team and extending *Rhabwar*'s hyperenvelope and realigning our tractors for the Jump and deploying the boarding tube will require all of the ship's officers . . ."

"Which leaves me," Cha Thrat said quietly, "with nothing to do."

" . . . So which should be given priority?" the Captain went on, seeming not to have heard her. "The search for your unconscious FGHJ, or getting it and the rest of them to Sector General as quickly as possible?"

"I will search the ship," she said, more loudly.

"Thank you, Cha Thrat," Prilicla said, "I felt you wanting to volunteer. But think carefully before you decide. The survivor, should you find it, will be too weak to harm you. But there are other dangers. This ship is large, and as strange to us as it is to you."

"Yes, Technician," the Captain said. "These aren't the maintenance tunnels at Sector General. The color codings, if present, will mean something entirely different. You can't make assumptions about anything you see, and if you accidentally foul a control link... Very well, you may search, but stay out of trouble.

Fletcher turned to look at Prilicla and added plaintively, "Or do you feel me feeling that I'm wasting my breath?"

Chapter 17

WITH the printouts from *Rhabwar*'s sensors providing information on the ship's layout, and in particular on the size and location of its empty spaces, Cha Thrat began a rapid and methodical search of the alien vessel. She ignored only the control deck, the occupied dormitories, and areas close to the ship's reactor that the sensor maps showed to be uninhabitable by the FGHJ life-form or, for that matter, any other species who were not radiation-eaters. She was very careful to check all interiors with sound sensors and the heavy-duty scanner before opening every door or panel. She was not afraid, but there were times when shivers marched like tiny, icy feet along the length of her spine.

It usually happened when the realization came that she was searching an alien starship for survivors of a species whose existence she could not have imagined a short time ago, at the direction of other unimaginable beings from a place of healing whose size, complexity, and occupants were like the solid manifestations of a disordered mind. But the unthinkable and unimaginable had become not only thinkable but acceptable to her, and all because a discontented and unloved warrior-surgeon of Sommaradva had risked a limb and her professional reputation to treat an injured off-world ship ruler.

At the thought of what her future would have been had she not taken that risk she shivered again, in dread.

Even though the first search was to be a fast, perfunctory one, it took much longer than Cha Thrat had expected. By the time it was completed, *Rhabwar*'s boarding tube was in position, and she could feel and hear the empty grumbling of both her stomachs.

Prilicla told her to relieve these symptoms before making her report.

When she arrived on the casualty deck, Prilicla, Murchison, and Danalta were working on the cadaver while Naydrad and Khone, its hairy body pressed against the transparent dividing wall, watched with an interest so intense that only the Cinrusskin sensed her arrival.

"What's wrong, friend Cha?" the empath asked. "Something disturbed you on the ship. I felt it even here."

"This," she replied, holding up one of the leg restraints that Murchison had removed from the cadaver and discarded before the dead FGHJ had been moved to *Rhabwar*. "The chain is not locked to the leg cuff, it is attached with a simple spring-loaded bolt that can be released easily when pressure is applied just here."

She demonstrated, then went on. "When I was searching the control deck area I looked at the crew member chained to its couch, without being seen, and noticed that similar fastenings hold the chains to all four of its leg cuffs. It and the cadaver here could have freed themselves simply by releasing the fastenings, which are within easy reach of its hands. It did not have to break free, and neither does the crew member chained to the control couch, who nevertheless continues to struggle violently against restraints that it could so easily remove. It is all very puzzling, but I think we must now discard the theory that any of these people were prisoners under restraint."

They were all watching her closely as she went on. "But what is affecting them? What is it that leaves a crew member normally a responsible, highly trained individual capable of guiding a starship, in such a state that it cannot unfasten its couch restraints? What has rendered the other crew members incapable of opening their own dormitory doors or finding food for themselves? Why has their behavior degenerated to that of unthinking animals? Could contaminated food, or the absence of specific foods, have caused this? And before you left me, the Senior Physician suggested that an organism might have invaded the brain tissues. Is it possible that—"

"If you will stop asking questions, Technician," Murchison broke in crossly, "I'll have a chance to answer some of them. No, the food supply is plentiful and contains nothing toxic to this life-form. I have analyzed and identified several varieties carried on the ship, so you will be able to feed them when you go back. As for the brain tissues, there are no indications of damage, circulatory impairment, infection, or any pathological abnormality.

"I found trace quantities of a complex chemical structure that, in the metabolism of this life-form, would act as a powerful tranquilizer. The residual material suggests that a massive dose was absorbed perhaps three or four days ago, and the effect has since worn off. A large supply of this tranquilizer was found in one of the cadaver's harness pouches. So it seems that the crew members tranquilized themselves before confining themselves to the control couch and their dormitories."

There was a long silence that was broken by Khone, who was holding up its offspring where the scrawny little entity could see all the strange creatures on the other side of its transparent panel. Cha Thrat wondered if the Gogleskan was already trying to weaken the young one's conditioning, even at the tender age of two days.

Impersonally it said, "It is hoped that the time of more intelligent and experienced healers will not be wasted by this interruption, but on Goglesk it is accepted that in certain circumstances, and against their will, otherwise intelligent and civilized beings will behave like vicious and destructive animals. Perhaps the entities on the other vessel have a similar problem, and must take strong and repeated doses of medication to keep their animal natures under control so that they can live civilized lives, and make progress, and build starships.

"Perhaps they are starved," Khone ended, "not of food but of their civilizing drug."

"A neat idea," Murchison said warmly, then matching the Gogleskan's impersonal tone it went on. "Admiration is felt for the originality of the healer's thinking but, regrettably, the medication concerned would not increase awareness and the ability to mentate, it would decrease it to the point where continuous use would cause these people to spend their entire lives in a state of semiconsciousness."

"Perhaps," Cha Thrat joined in, "the state of semiconsciousness is pleasant and desirable. It shames me to admit it, but on Sommaradva there are people who deliberately affect and often damage their minds with substances for the purely temporary pleasure they give the user..."

"Sommaradva's shame," Naydrad said angrily, "is shared by many worlds in the Federation."

"...And when these harmful substances are withdrawn suddenly from habitual users," she went on, "their behavior becomes irrational and violent and similar, in many respects, to that of the FGHJs on the other ship."

Murchison was shaking its head. "Sorry, no again. I cannot be absolutely certain because we are dealing with the metabolism of a completely new life-form here, but I would say that the traces found in the cadaver's brain was a simple tranquilizer that deadens rather than heightens awareness, and is almost certainly nonaddictive. Had this not been so I would have suggested using it as an anesthetic.

"And before you ask," the Pathologist went on, "progress with the anesthetic is slow. I have gone as far as I can go with the physiological data provided by the cadaver, but to produce one that will be safe to use in large doses I require blood and gland secretion samples from a living FGHJ."

Cha Thrat was silent for a moment, then she turned to include Prilicla as she said, "I could not find any trace of injured or unconscious survivors during my preliminary search, but I shall search again more diligently when the required samples have been obtained. Is the being still alive? Can you give me even an approximate guide to its location?"

"I can still feel it, friend Cha," Prilicla replied. "But the cruder, conscious emoting of the other survivors is obscuring it."

"Then the sooner Pathologist Murchison has its samples the sooner we'll have the anesthetic to knock out the emotional interference," Cha Thrat said briskly. "My medial digits are strong enough to restrain the arms of the FGHJ on the control couch while my upper manipulators take the samples. From which veins and organs, and in what quantities, must they be removed?"

Murchison laughed suddenly and said, "Please, Cha Thrat, let the medical team do something to justify its existence. You will hold the crew member tightly to its couch, Doctor Danalta will position the scanner, and I will obtain the samples while—"

"Control here." Fletcher's voice broke in from the wall speaker. "Jump in five seconds from ... now. The extra mass of the distressed ship will delay our return somewhat. We are estimating Sector General parking orbit in just under four days."

"Thank you, friend Fletcher," Prilicla said.

Suddenly there was the familiar but indescribable sensation, unseen, unheard, and unfelt but indisputably present, that signaled their removal from the universe of matter to the tiny, unreal, and purely mathematical structure that the ship's hyperdrive generators had built around them. She forced herself to look through the casualty deck's direct vision panel. The tractor and pressor beams that laced the ships rigidly together were invisible, so that she saw only the ridiculously flimsy boarding tube joining them and, at the bottom of the metal chasm formed by the two hulls, the heaving, flickering grayness that seemed to reach up through her eyes and pull her very brain out of focus.

She returned her attention to the solid, familiar if temporarily unreal world of the casualty deck before hyperspace could give her an eyestrain headache.

Cha Thrat had time for only a few words with Khone before following Murchison, Danalta, and Naydrad to the boarding tube. The Charge Nurse was helping her

carry packages of the material that Murchison had identified as food, and she had only to compare them with
the hundreds of others in the other ship's stores to be
able to feed all of the surviving crew members until they
bulged at the seams.

Her last sight of the casualty deck for a long time,
although she did not know it just then, was of Senior
Physician Prilicla hovering above the widely scattered
remains of the cadaver and interspersing its quiet words
to Khone with untranslatable cluckings and trillings to
the younger Gogleskan.

"If we can spare the time," Cha Thrat said to the Pathologist when they were standing around the control
couch and its agitated and weakly struggling occupant,
"we could feed it before taking your samples. That might
make the patient more contented, and amenable."

"We can spare the time for that," Murchison replied,
then added, "There are times, Cha Thrat, when you remind me of somebody else."

"Who do we know," Naydrad asked in its forthright
Kelgian manner, "who's that weird?"

The Pathologist laughed but did not reply, and neither
did Cha Thrat. Without realizing it, Murchison had
moved into a sensitive and potentially highly embarrassing area, and, if it ever did learn exactly what had happened to the Sommaradvan's mind on Goglesk, it should
be from its life-mate, Conway, and not Cha Thrat—Prilicla had been quite insistent about that.

There was surprisingly little variety in the FGHJs'
food containers—two differently shaped plastic bottles,
one holding water and the other a faintly odorous nutrient liquid, and there were uniform blocks of a dry,
spongy material wrapped in a thin plastic film with a
large ring for tearing it open. The liquid and solid foods
were synthetic, according to Murchison, but nutrition-

ally tailored to the requirements of the FGHJs' metabolism, and the small quantities of nonnutrient material present were probably there to excite the taste buds.

But when Cha Thrat tossed one of the packages into the crew member's hands, it began tearing at it with its teeth without removing the plastic wrapping. The simple, spring-loaded caps sealing the bottles were also ignored. It tore open the neck of the container with its teeth and sucked out the liquid that it had not already spilled down its chest.

A few minutes later the Pathologist made an untranslatable sound and said, "Its table manners certainly leave a lot to be desired, but it doesn't appear to be hungry anymore. Let's get started."

Feeding the crew member made no perceptible difference to its behavior except, perhaps, to give it more strength to resist them. By the time Murchison had withdrawn its samples, Naydrad, Cha Thrat, and the Pathologist itself were displaying several areas of surface bruising and Danalta, whose body could not be injured or deformed except by the application of ultrahigh temperatures, had been forced into some incredible shape-changes in order to help them immobilize the brute. When the task was done, Murchison sent Naydrad and Danalta ahead with its test samples while it remained, breathing rapidly, and with its eyes fixed on the crew member.

"I don't like this," it said.

"It worries me, too," Cha Thrat said. "However, if a problem is restated often enough, in different words, a solution sometimes emerges."

"I suppose some wise old Sommaradvan philosopher said that," Murchison said drily. "I'm sorry, Technician. What were you going to say?"

"An Earth-human Lieutenant called Timmins said it,"

she replied. "And I was about to restate the problem, which is that we are faced with a ship's crew who are apparently suffering from a disease that leaves them completely healthy, but mindless. Not only can they not operate their own undamaged and fully functioning ship, they do not remember how to unfasten their leg restraints, unlatch doors, or open food containers. They have become like healthy animals."

Murchison said quietly, "The problem is being restated, but in the same words."

"The living quarters are bare and comfortless," Cha Thrat went on, "which made us think at first that this was a prison ship. But is it possible that the crew members, for reasons that may be psychological and associated with space-travel, or a disease that affects them during space travel, know that bodily comforts, pleasant surroundings, and valued personal possessions would be wasted on them during a voyage because they *expect* to become animals. Perhaps the condition is brief, episodic, and temporary, but on this occasion something went wrong and it became permanent."

"Now," Murchison said, twitching her shoulders in the movement that Earth-humans called a shiver, "the words are different. But if it is of any help to you, among the samples Naydrad brought me for analysis there was medication as well as food. The medication was of one kind only, the tranquilizer capsules of the type found on the cadaver, in a form intended for oral self-administration. So you may be right about them expecting the condition and taking steps to reduce accidental damage to themselves during the mindless phase. But it's strange that Naydrad, who looks very carefully for such things, found only this one type of medication, and no sign of any instruments for the purposes of examination, diagnosis, or surgery. Even if they knew in advance that they were going to take sick, it looks as if the ship's crew did not include a medic."

"If anything," Cha Thrat said, "this new information increases the problem."

Murchison laughed, but the pallor of its normally pink face showed that it found nothing humorous in the situation. It said grimly, "I could not find anything wrong with the being I examined, apart from the accidental head injury that killed it, nor can I see anything clinically wrong with the other crew members. But *something* has tracelessly destroyed their higher centers of intelligence and wiped their minds clean of all memory, training, and experience so that they are left with nothing but the instincts and behavior patterns of animals.

"What kind of organism or agency," it ended with another shiver, "could cause such a selectively destructive effect as that?"

Cha Thrat had a sudden urge to wrap her medial arms around the Pathologist and comfort it, and an upsurge of the kind of emotion that no Sommaradvan, male or female, should feel for an Earth-human. With difficulty she controlled the feelings that were not her own and said gently, "The anesthetic might give you the answer. We are seeing patients in whom the disease, or whatever, has run its course. If they are knocked out and we found the other one, isn't it possible that the disease might not have run its course with this survivor, or the survivor has natural resistance to it? By studying the disease and the resistant patient you might discover the cure for all of them."

"The anesthetic, yes," Murchison said, and smiled. "Your tactful way of reminding a stupid Pathologist of the elements of her job would do credit to Prilicla itself. I'm wasting time here."

It turned to leave, then hesitated. Its face was still very pale.

"Whatever it is that is affecting these people," it said grimly, "is outside my clinical experience, and possibly that of the hospital. But there should be no danger to us. You already know from your medical lectures that other-species pathogens can effect only life-forms that share a common planetary and evolutionary background, and have no effect on off-planet organisms. But there are times when, in spite of everything we know to the contrary, we wonder if we will someday run into the exception that proves the rule, a disease or a clinical condition that is capable of crossing the species barrier.

"The mere possibility that this might be that exception," it went on very seriously, "is scaring the hell out of me. If this should be our bacteriological bogeyman, we must remember that the disease does not appear to have any physical effects. The onset and symptomology of the condition are more likely to be psychological rather than physical. I shall discuss this with Prilicla, and we shall be watching you for any marked behavioral changes, just as you must keep a watch on your own mental processes for uncharacteristic thoughts or feelings."

The Pathologist shook its head in obvious self-irritation. "Nothing can harm you here, I'm as sure of that as I can possibly be. But please, Cha Thrat, be very careful anyway."

Chapter 18

SHE did not know how long she spent watching the mindless struggling of the FGHJ on its couch, and its strong, blunt-fingered hands that had guided this great vessel between the stars before she left the control deck, feeling depressed and angry at her inability to produce a single constructive idea, to begin collecting food for the other, still-hungry crew members. But when she entered the nearest food storage compartment a few minutes later, she was startled to find Prilicla already there.

"Friend Cha," the empath said, "there has been a change of plan..."

The anesthetic that Murchison was producing would have to be tested, in minute but gradually increasing doses, initially on the FGHJ in Control. That process could take anything up to three days before the Pathologist could pronounce it safe for use. Prilicla felt sure that the survivor did not have three days and another method of pacifying the crew members, not as effective as anesthesia, must be tried. Adequate supplies of the crew's own tranquilizers were available, and large doses of these would be added to the crew's food and drink in the hope that, heavily tranquilized and with their hunger satisfied, the intensity of their emotional radiation would be reduced to a level where the empath could isolate and locate the remaining and seriously ill or injured survivor.

"I would like all of the crew members to be fed and tranquilized as quickly as possible," Prilicla went on. "Our friend's emotional radiation is characteristic of a mind of high intelligence presently degraded by pain, rather than one in the condition of its crew-mates, but it grows steadily weaker. I fear for its life."

At Prilicla's direction she heavily dosed the liquid food and water, then distributed it quickly to the dormitories while the Cinrusskin moved from deck to deck, with its empathic faculty extended to its maximum range and sensitivity. With full stomachs and dulled minds— some of them even went to sleep—the crew members' emotional radiation became less obtrusive, but otherwise the results were negative.

"I still can't get a fix," Prilicla said, its body trembling to its own as well as Cha Thrat's disappointment. "There is still too much interference from the conscious survivors. All we can do now is return to *Rhabwar* and try to assist friend Murchison. Your charges will not grow hungry again for some time. Coming?"

"No," she said, "I would prefer to continue the normal, physical search for your dying survivor."

"Friend Cha," Prilicla said, "must I remind you again that I am not a telepath, and that your secret, inner thoughts remain your own property. But your feelings are very clear to me, and they are of low-intensity excitement, pleasure, and caution, with the excitement predominating and the caution barely detectable. This worries me. My guess is that you have had an idea or come to a conclusion of some kind, which will involve personal risk before it can be proved or disproved. Would you like to tell me about it?"

The simple answer would have been "No," but she

could not bring herself to hurt the empath's hypersensitive feelings with such a verbal discourtesy. Instead she said carefully, "It may be that the idea came as a result of my ignorance regarding your empathic faculty, hence my reticence in mentioning it until I was sure that it had some value and I would avoid embarrassment."

Prilicla continued to hover silently in the center of the compartment, and Cha Thrat went on. "When we first searched the ship you were able to detect the presence of the unconscious survivor, but not locate it because of the conscious emoting of the others. Now that they are pacified into near-unconsciousness, the situation is the same because our survivor's condition has worsened, and I fear that it will remain the same even when the anesthetic becomes available and the others, too, are deeply unconscious."

"I share that fear," the empath said quietly. "But go on."

"In my ignorance of the finer workings of your empathic faculty," she continued, "I assumed that a weak source of emotional radiation positioned nearby would be more easily detectable than a stronger source at a distance. If there had been any such variation in strength, I'm sure you would have mentioned it."

"I would," Prilicla said, "and you are right in many respects. In others, well, my emphathic faculty has limitations. It responds to the quality and intensity of feelings as well as their proximity. But detection is dependent on factors other than distance. There is the degree of intelligence and emotional sensitivity, the intensity of the emotions being felt, the physical size and strength of the emoting brain, and, of course, the level of consciousness. Normally these limitations can be ignored when I'm searching for just one source and my friends, usually the medical team, move away or control their emotions while I'm searching. That isn't the case here. But you must have reached some conclusions. What are they?"

Choosing her words carefully, Cha Thrat replied, "That, because of its location, the unconscious survivor's radiation is and will remain obscured, and that it is very close to, or surrounded by, the conscious sources. This narrows the volume to be searched to the dormitory deck and perhaps the levels above and below it, and I shall concentrate on that volume only. And you said just now that the physical size of the emoting brain is a factor. Could it be that the survivor is a very small, and young, FGHJ hiding close to the mindless parent?"

"Possibly," Prilicla replied. "But regardless of age or size, it is in very bad shape."

Controlling her growing excitement, she went on. "There must be small storage cabinets, systems inspection centers, and odd holes and corners where a crew member or child would not normally go, but where a barely conscious entity whose injuries caused it to act irrationally might have hidden itself. I feel sure than I will find it soon."

"I know," Prilicla said. "But there is more."

Cha Thrat hesitated, then said, "With respect, Cinrusskins are not a robust species, and for that reason are more sensitive to the risk of physical injury than beings like myself. I can assure you that I have no intention of placing myself at risk, for whatever reason. But if I was to tell you my plan in detail, the possibility exists that you would forbid me to carry it out."

"Would you obey me if I did?" Prilicla asked.

She did not reply.

"Friend Cha," Prilicla said gently, "you have many qualities that I find admirable, including that of moderate cowardice, but you worry me. You have shown yourself reluctant to obey orders that you personally feel to be wrong or unjustified. You have been disobedient in Sector General, on this ship, and, I suspect, on your home world. This is not a quality that people find admirable in a person of subordinate rank. What are we going to do with you?"

Cha Thrat was about to tell the little empath how sorry she felt at causing it mental distress, then realized that it already knew exactly how she felt toward it. Instead she said, "With respect, you could allow me to proceed, and ask the Captain to concentrate the sensors on the reduced search area I have indicated, and report any changes to me at once."

"You know that I was thinking in the longer term," Prilicla said. "But yes, I shall do as you suggest. I share friend Murchison's feelings about this situation. There is something very strange here, and possibly dangerous, but we cannot even guess where the threat, if there is a threat, will come from. Take great care, friend Cha, and guard your mind as well as your body."

Cha Thrat began the search as soon as Prilicla left her, starting with the level above the dormitory deck, then moving to the one below it. But from the start her principal intention had been to enter and search those occupied dormitories, and, as soon as she did so, she knew that there would be a reaction from whoever was watching the sensor displays.

When it came, the voice in her earpiece was that of the Captain itself.

"Technician!" it said sharply. "The sensors show a body of your mass and temperature entering one of the dormitories. Get out of there at once!"

It was possible to argue politely and be circumspect with a gentle little entity like Prilicla, Cha Thrat thought sadly, but not with the Captain. She had just been given a direct order that she had no intention of obeying, so she spoke as if she had not heard it.

"I have entered a dormitory and am moving sideways around the room with my back to the wall," she said calmly. "I am moving slowly so as not to disturb or frighten the occupants, who seem to be half asleep. Two of them have turned their heads to watch me but are making no threatening movements. There is a small door, tight-fitting and mounted flush with the wall, probably a recessed storage cabinet, that might be large enough for an FGHJ to force a way in to hide. I am opening the door now. Inside there are..."

"Switch on your vision pickup," Fletcher said angrily, "and save your breath."

"...shelves containing what appears to be cleaning materials for the waste-disposal facility," she continued. "In case a fast retreat is necessary, I have left the heavier equipment outside and am wearing only a headset. Now I'm moving toward the wall facing the entrance where there is another small door."

"So you *can* hear me," Fletcher said coldly. "And you heard my order."

"I've opened it," she went on quickly, "and the missing survivor isn't there. Beside the door at floor level there is a small, flat, rectangular flap. Possibly it conceals a recessed handle for an upward-opening door. I will have to lie flat on the floor, and try to avoid the body wastes, to examine it."

She heard the Captain make an untranslatable but very unsympathetic sound, then she said, It is a tight-fitting flap, hinged on the top side, and free to move in or out with gentle pressure. There is a layer of sponge around the edges that suggests that it is nearly airtight. I can't get my head close enough to the floor to see inside the flap, but when I open it there is a strong smell that reminds me of the Sommaradvan *glytt* plant.

"I'm sorry," she went on. "Quite apart from the fact that you don't know what a *glytt* plant smells like, one wonders whether the seal is intended to keep the unpleasant smell of FGHJ wastes in or the other smell out. Or maybe it is just an inlet point for some kind of deodorant..."

"Friend Cha," Prilicla broke in. "In the short time since you inhaled the odor, has there been any irritation of your breathing passages, nausea, impairment of vision, or dulling of sensation or intellect?"

"What intellect?" Fletcher murmured in a disparaging voice.

"No," she replied. "I am opening the door of the last remaining storage closet to be searched. It is larger than the others, filled with racked tools and what looks like replacement parts for the dormitory furniture, but is otherwise empty. The crew members are still ignoring me. I'm leaving now to search the next dormitory."

"Technician," Fletcher said quietly. "If you can reply to Prilicla I know you can hear me. Now, I'm willing to consider your earlier disobedience as a temporary aberration, a fit of overenthusiasm, and a minor disciplinary matter. But if you continue the search in direct contravention of my orders you will be in major trouble. Neither the Monitor Corps nor the hospital has time for irresponsible subordinates."

"But I take full responsiblity for my actions," Cha Thrat protested, "including any credit or discredit that may result from them. I know that I lack the training to investigate an other-species ship properly, but I am simply opening and closing doors and being very careful while I'm doing it."

The Captain did not reply and maintained its silence

even when the sensors must have been showing Cha
Thrat entering the second dormitory. It was Prilicla who
spoke first.

"Friend Fletcher," the empath said quietly, "I agree
that there is a small element of risk in what the technician is doing. But it has discussed some of its ideas with
me and is acting with my permission and, well, limited
approval."

Ignoring the tranquilized FGHJs and not speaking at
all, Cha Thrat was able search the dormitory much more
quickly, but with the same negative result. None of the
storage cabinets revealed the missing survivor, adult or
child, and the narrow, floor-level flap held nothing but
the smell of *glytt*, which never had been one of her favorite aromas.

But the Cinrusskin's attempts to divert the Captain's
anger from her aroused such a sudden emotional warmth
in her that she hoped the empath would feel her gratitude. Without breaking into the conversation, and hoping that Prilicla could not feel her growing
disappointment, she began searching the third and last
dormitory.

". . . In any case, friend Fletcher," the empath was
saying, "the responsibility for whatever happens on the
distressed ship until the survivors are treated and evacu-
ated is not yours, but mine."

"I know, I know," the Captain agreed irritably. "On
the site of a disaster the medical team leader has the
rank. In this situation you can tell a Monitor Corps ship
commander like myself what to do, and be obeyed. You
can even give orders to a Corps Maintenance Technician
Grade Two called Cha Thrat, but I seriously doubt if
they would be obeyed."

There was another long silence, broken by the subject
of the discussion. She said, "I've finished searching the

dormitories. All three contain identical arrangements of fittings and storage compartments, none of which contains the FGHJ we're looking for.

"But the first and second dormitories share a common wall," she went on, trying to sound hopeful, "likewise the second and third. But the first and third are divided by a short corridor leading inboard toward what must be another, fairly large storage compartment whose sides are common to the inner walls of the three dormitories. The missing FGHJ could be there."

"I don't think so," Fletcher said. "The sensors show it as an empty compartment, about half the size of a dormitory, with a lot of low-power circuitry and ducting, probably environmental control lines to the dormitories, mounted on or behind the wall surfaces. By empty we mean that there are no large metal objects in the room, although organic material could be present if it was stored in nonmetal containers. But a piece of organic material of the body mass and temperature of a living FGHJ, whether moving or at rest, would show very clearly.

"All the indications are that it is just another storeroom," the Captain ended. "But no doubt you will search it, anyway."

With difficulty, Cha Thrat ignored Fletcher's tone as she said, "During my first search of this area I looked into this corridor and saw the blank end-wall containing what I mistakenly thought to be a section of badly fitted wall plating. My excuse for making this mistake is that there is no external handle or latch visible. On closer examination I see that it is not a badly fitted plate but an inward-opening door that is very slightly ajar, and the scanner shows that it fastens only from the inside.

"The vision pickup is on," she added. "I'm pushing the door open now."

The place was a mess, she thought, with weightlessness adding to the general disorder so that floating debris made it difficult to see any distance into the room. There was a very strong smell of *glytt.*

"We aren't receiving a clear picture," said Fletcher, "and something close to the lens is blocking most of the view. Have you attached the pickup correctly or are we seeing part of your shoulder?"

"No, sir," she replied, trying to keep her tone properly subordinate. "The compartment is gravity-free and a large number of flat, roughly circular objects are floating about. They appear to be organic, fairly uniform in size, dark gray on one surface and with a paler, mottled appearance on the other. I suppose they could be cakes of preprepared food that escaped from a ruptured container, or they might be solid body waste, similar to that found in the dormitories, which has dried and become discolored. I'm trying to move some of it out of the way now."

With a sudden feeling of distaste, she cleared the visual obstructions from the front of the pickup, using her medial hands because they were the only ones still covered by gloves. There was no response from *Rhabwar.*

"There are large, irregular clumps of spongelike or vegetable material attached to the walls and ceiling," she went on, moving her body so that the pickup's images would let the others see, however unclearly, what she was trying to describe. "So far as I can see, each clump is colored differently, although the colors are subdued, and under each one there is a short length of padded shelf.

"At floor level," she continued, "I can see three narrow, rectangular flaps. Their size and positions correspond to those found in the dormitories. These pancakes, or whatever, are all over the place, but I can

see something large floating in a corner near the ceiling
...It's the FGHJ!"

"I don't understand why it didn't register on the sensors," Fletcher said. It was the kind of Captain who insisted on the highest standards of efficiency from its
crew and the equipment in its charge, and treated a malfunction in either as a personal affront.

"Good work, friend Cha," Prilicla said, enthusiastically breaking in. "Quickly now, move it to the entrance
for loading into the litter. We'll be with you directly.
What is the general clinical picture?"

Cha Thrat moved closer, swatting more obstructions
from her path as she said, "I can't see any physical injuries at all, not even minor bruising, or external evidence
of an illness. But this FGHJ isn't like the others. It
seems to be a lot thinner and less well muscled. The skin
appears darker, more wrinkled, and the hooves are discolored and cracked in several places. The body hair is
gray. I...I think this is a much older FGHJ. It might be
the ship ruler. Maybe it hid itself in here to avoid what
happened to the rest of its crew..."

She broke off, and Prilicla called urgently, "Friend
Cha, why are you feeling like that? What happened to
you?"

"Nothing happened to me," she replied, fighting to
control her disappointment. "I am holding the FGHJ
now. There is no need to hurry. It is dead."

"That explains why my sensors didn't register,"
Fletcher said.

"Friend Cha," Prilicla said, ignoring the interruption,
"are you quite *sure*? I can still feel the presence of a
deeply unconscious mind."

Cha Thrat drew the FGHJ toward her so that she
could use her upper hands, then said, "The body temperature is very low. Its eyes are open and do not react to

light. The usual vital signs are absent. I'm sorry, it is dead and . . ." She broke off to look more closely at the creature's head, then went on excitedly. "And I think I know what killed it! The back of the neck. Can you see it?"

"Not clearly," Prilicla replied quickly, obviously feeling her own growing excitement, and fear. "One of those disklike objects is in the way."

"But that's *it*," she said. "I thought at first that one of them had drifted against the cadaver and stuck to its head. But I was wrong. The thing attached itself deliberately to the FGHJ with those thick white tendrils you can see growing from the edge of the disk. Now that I'm looking for them, I can see that they all have the tendrils and, judging by their length, the penetration into the cadaver's spinal column and rear cranium is very deep. That thing is, or was, alive, and could have been responsible for—"

"Technician," Fletcher broke in harshly, "get out of there!"

"At once," Prilicla said.

Very carefully Cha Thrat released her hold on the dead FGHJ, removed her vision pickup, and attached its magnetic clips to a clear area of wall. She knew that the medical team would want to study this strange and abhorrent life-form that was infesting the ship before deciding how to deal with it. Then she turned toward the entrance, which now seemed to be very far away.

The disks hung thickly like an alien minefield between the door and herself. Some of them were still moving slowly in the air eddies caused by her entry or by the blows with which she had so casually knocked them aside, or perhaps of their own volition. They presented views from every angle—the smooth surface of the mottled side, the gray and wrinkled reverse side, and the edges with their fringe of limp white tendrils.

She had been so busy searching for an FGHJ survivor that she had scarcely looked at the objects she had mistaken for cakes of food or dried wastes floating in the room. She still did not know what they were, only of what they were capable, which was the utter destruction of the highly trained and intelligent minds of their victims to leave them with nothing but the basic and purely instinctive responses of animals.

The thought of a predator who did not eat or physically harm its prey, but gorged itself on the *intelligence* of its victim, made her want to seek refuge in madness. She was desperately afraid of touching one of them again, but there were too many of them for her to avoid doing so. But if any of them got in her way, Cha Thrat decided grimly, she would touch it, hit it, very hard.

The gentle, reassuring voice of Prilicla sounded in her earpiece. It said, "You are controlling your fear well, friend Cha. Move slowly and carefully and don't—"

She winced as a high-pitched, piercing sound erupted from the earpiece, signifying that too many people were talking to her at once and had overloaded her translator. But they realized immediately what was happening because the oscillation wavered and died to become one voice, the Captain's.

"Technician, *behind you!*"

By then it was too late.

All of her attention had been directed ahead and to the sides, where the greatest danger lay. When she felt the surprisingly light touch, followed by a sensation of numbness on the back of her neck, a cool, detached part of her mind thought that it was considerate of the thing to anesthetize the area before inserting its tendrils. She swung an eye to the rear to see what was happening, and instinctively raised her upper hands to push away the disk that had left the dead FGHJ and was attaching itself to her. But the hands fumbled weakly, their digits suddenly powerless, and the arms fell limply away.

Other parts of her body ceased working, or began twitching and bending in the random, uncoordinated fashion of a person with serious brain damage. The calm, detached portion of her mind thought that her condition was not a pleasant sight for friends to see.

"*Fight* it, Cha Thrat!" Murchison's voice shouted from her earpiece. "Whatever it's doing, fight it! We're on our way."

She heard and appreciated the concern in the Pathologist's voice, but her tongue was one of the organs that was not working just then because her jaw was clamped shut. Altogether, she was in a state of considerable physiological confusion as muscles continued to twitch uncontrollably, her body writhed in weightless contortions, and sensations of heat, cold, pain, and pleasure affected random areas of her skin. She knew that the creature was exploring her central nervous system, trying to find out how her Sommaradvan body worked so that it would be able to control her.

Gradually the twitchings and writhings and even her fear diminished and were gone, and her body was able to resume its interrupted journey. The lens of the vision pickup turned to follow her. When she reached the door, she slammed it closed and locked it with fastenings that had suddenly become familiar.

"Technician," Fletcher said sharply, "what are you *doing*?"

It was obvious that she was locking the door from the inside, Cha Thrat thought irritably. Probably the Captain meant why was she doing it. She tried to reply but her lips and tongue would not work. But surely her actions would tell all of them that she, it, both of them, did not wish to be disturbed.

Chapter 19

THEY were all talking at once again. She had to bend the earpiece back to reduce the sudden howl of translator oscillation that was making it difficult to think. The vision pickup was still following her and they must have realized the significance of her action because the babble died quickly and became one voice.

"Friend Cha," Prilicla said, "listen to me carefully. Some kind of parasitic life-form has attached itself to you and the quality of your emotional radiation is changing. Try, try hard to pull it off and get out of there before your condition worsens."

"I'm all right," Cha Thrat protested. "Honestly, I feel fine. Just leave me alone until I can—"

"But your thoughts and feelings aren't your own anymore," Murchison broke in. "*Fight*, dammit! Try to keep control of your mind. At least try to open that door again so we won't waste time burning through it when we get to you."

"No," the Captain said firmly. "I'm very sorry, Technician, they aren't leaving this ship..."

The argument that ensued immediately overloaded Cha Thrat's translator again, which made it impossible for her to talk to any of them. But there were parts of it, particularly when Fletcher was speaking in its ruler's voice, that she heard clearly.

The Captain was reminding them, and calling on Prilicla to support it, that the strictest possible rules of quarantine governed this situation. They had encountered a life-form that absorbed the memory, personality, and intelligence of its victims and left them like mindless animals. Moreover, judging by their recent observations of Technician Cha Thrat, the things were capable of adapting to and quickly controlling any life-form.

By then nobody was trying to interrupt Fletcher as it went on. "This could mean that they are not native to the planet of the FGHJs, that they may have come aboard anywhere, and are capable of doing this to the members of every intelligent species in the Federation! I don't know what drives them, why they're content to suck out the intelligence of their victims instead of feeding on the bodies, and I don't even want to think about it. Or about how, or how rapidly, they can reproduce themselves. There are dozens of them in the room with Cha Thrat, and they're so small that more of them could be hidden in odd corners all over the ship.

"Until we get a properly equipped and protected decontamination squad in there," Fletcher went on, "I have no choice but to seal and place a guard on the boarding tube. This is something completely new to our experience, and it may well be that the hospital will advise the complete destruction of the ship, and its contents.

"If you will all think about it for a moment," the Captain ended, sounding very unhappy with itself, "you will realize that we cannot take the slightest risk of that life-form getting onto this ship, or running loose in Sector General."

There was silence for several moments while they

thought about it, and Cha Thrat thought about the strange thing that had happened, and was still happening, to her.

While trying to help Khone she had experienced a joining, and with it the shock and disorientation and excitement of having her mind invaded, but not taken over, by a personality that was completely alien to her. The effect had been rendered even stranger and more frightening by the fact that the Gogleskan's mind had also contained material from a previous joining with a mind whose memories were even more confusing, those of the Earth-human Conway. But this sensation was entirely different. The approach and entry was gentle, reassuring, and even pleasant, giving her the feeling that it was a process perfected after a lifetime of experience. But like herself, this invader seemed to be badly confused by the contents of her part-Sommaradvan, part-Gogleskan, and part Earth-human mind and, because of that confusion, it was having trouble controlling her body. She was still not sure of its intentions, but quite certain that she was still herself and that she was learning more and more about it with every passing second.

Murchison was the first to break the silence. It said, "We have protective suits and cutting torches. Why don't we decontaminate that compartment ourselves and burn them all, including the one on the technician's neck, and get Cha Thrat back here for treatment while it still has some of its mind left? The hospital people can finish the decontamination when we—"

"No," the Captain said firmly. "If any of you medics go onto that ship, you won't be allowed back here."

Cha Thrat did not want to join in because speaking would involve a minor mental effort and consequent disruption in an area of her mind that she wished to remain receptive. Instead, she moved her lower arms in

the Sign of Waiting, then realizing that it meant nothing
to non-Sommaradvans, held up one hand palm forward
in the Earth-human equivalent.

"I am confused," Prilicla said suddenly. "Friend Cha
is not feeling pain or mental distress. It is wanting something very badly, but the emotional radiation is characteristic of a source trying very hard to maintain calm and
to control its other feelings . . ."

"But it isn't in control," Murchison broke in. "Look
at the way it was moving its arms about. You're forgetting that its feelings and emotions aren't its own."

"You, friend Murchison, are not the emotion-sensitive
here," Prilicla said in the gentlest possible of reproofs.
"Friend Cha, try to speak. What do you want us to do?"

She wanted to tell them to stop talking and leave her
alone, but she desperately needed their help and that
reply would have given rise to more questions, interrup-
tions, and mental dislocations. Her mind was a bubbling
stew of thoughts, impressions, experiences, and memories that concerned not only her own past on Sommaradva and Sector General, but those of Healer Khone and
Diagnostician Conway. The new occupant was blunder-
ing about like an intruder lost in a large, richly furnished
but imperfectly lit household, examining some items and
shying away from others. This, Cha Thrat knew, was not
the time to leave it alone.

But if she answered a few of their questions, said just
enough to keep them quiet and make them do what she
wanted, that might be the best course.

"I am not in danger," Cha Thrat said carefully, "or in
any physical or emotional distress. I can regain full control of my mind and body any time I wish it, but choose
not to because I don't want to risk breaking mental contact by talking for too long. As quickly as possible I want

Senior Physician Prilicla and Pathologist Murchison to join me. The FGHJs are not important right now. Neither is the anesthetic or the search for the other survivor because—"

"No!" Fletcher broke in, sounding as if it was about to be physically nauseous. "Those things are intelligent. Do you see the insidious way they are trying to get the technician to reassure us and then entice us over to them? No doubt when you two are taken over there will be even better reasons for the rest of us to join you, or you to return here and leave *Rhabwar*'s crew in the same condition as the FGHJs. No, there will be no more victims."

Cha Thrat tried not to listen to the interruption because it set off trains of thought in her mind that were unsettling the new occupant and kept it from communicating properly with her. Very carefully she lifted her rear medial arm and bent it so that the large digit was pointing at the thing clinging to the back of her neck.

"This is the survivor," she said, "the only survivor."

Suddenly the stranger in her mind was feeling a measure of satisfaction and reassurance, as if it had at last succeeded in making its need understood, and she found that she could speak without the fear of it going away, fading, and perhaps dying on her.

"It is very ill," she went on, "but it was able to regain mobility and consciousness for a short time when I entered the compartment. That was when it decided to make a last, desperate try to obtain help for its friends and the host creatures in their charge. The first, fumbled attempts to make contact were the reason for my uncoordinated limb movements. Only within the past few minutes has it realized that it is the only survivor."

None of them, not even the Captain, was saying a

word now. She continued. "That is why I need Prilicla to monitor its emotional radiation at close range, and Murchison to investigate its dead friends, in the hope of finding out what killed them and finding a cure before its own condition becomes terminal—"

"No," the Captain said again. "It sounds like a good story, and especially intriguing to a bunch of e-t medics, but it could still be a ruse to get mental control of more of our people. I'm sorry, Technician, we can't risk it."

Prilicla said gently, "Friend Fletcher makes a good point. And you yourself know that the Captain's arguments are valid because you observed the mindless condition of the FGHJs after these creatures left them. Friend Cha, I, too, am sorry."

It was Cha Thrat's turn to be silent as she tried to find a solution that would satisfy them. Somehow she had not expected the gentle little empath to be so tough.

Finally she said, "Physically the creature is extremely debilitated and I could quite easily remove it to demonstrate its lack of physical control over me, but such a course might kill it. However, if I was to demonstrate my normal physical coordination by leaving this compartment and descending four levels, where we would be clear of the emotional interference from the FGHJs, and if I were to urge the creature to remain conscious until then, would the Cinrusskin empathic faculty be able to detect whether its emotional radiation was that of a highly intelligent and civilized being, or the kind of mental predator that seems to be *scaring* you out of your wits?"

"Four levels down is just one deck above the boarding tube . . ." began the Captain, but Prilicla cut it short.

"I could detect the difference, friend Cha," it said, "if

I was close enough to the life-form concerned. I'll meet you there directly."

There was another howl of oscillation from her translator. When it faded Prilicla was saying "Friend Fletcher, as the senior medical officer present it is my responsibility to make sure whether the life-form attached to Cha Thrat is the patient and not the disease. However, my species prides itself in being the most timid and cowardly in the Federation, and all possible precautions will be taken. Friend Cha, set the vision pickup to show if any of those life-forms try to leave the compartment and follow you. If any of them do, I shall return at once to *Rhabwar* and seal the boarding tube. Is that understood?"

"Yes, Senior Physician," said Cha Thrat.

"If anything suspicious occurs while I am with you," it went on, "even if I am able to avoid capture and still appear to be my own self, friend Fletcher will seal the tube and put the quarantine procedure into immediate effect.

"We need as much information on this life-form as you can give us," it ended. "Please continue, friend Cha, we are recording. I'm leaving now."

"And I'm going with you," Murchison said firmly. "If this is the ship's only survivor, one of a newly discovered intelligent species and possible future member of the Federation, Thorny will walk on me with all six of its feet if I let it die. Danalta and Naydrad can stay here in case we have need of special equipment and to watch the vision pickup. And in case the little beastie isn't as friendly as Cha Thrat insists it is, I'll add a heavy-duty cutting torch to my instruments so that I can protect your back."

"Thank you, friend Murchison," Prilicla said, "but no."

"But yes, Senior Physician," the Pathologist replied. "With respect, you have the rank but not the muscles to stop me."

Impatiently Cha Thrat said, "if you want to be able to detect any conscious emotional radiation, please hurry. The patient needs urgent attention..."

There was an immediate objection from Fletcher regarding her unjustified use of the word "patient." She ignored it and, trying her best to describe the thoughts and images that had been placed with so much effort in her mind, went on to outline the case history of the survivor and the history of its species.

They came from a world that even the Sommaradvan, Gogleskan, and Earth-human components of her mind considered beautiful, a planet so bountiful that the larger species of fauna did not have to struggle for survival and did not, for that reason, develop intelligence. But from the earliest times, when all life was in the oceans, a species evolved capable of attaching itself to a variety of native life-forms. They formed a symbiotic partnership in which the host creature was directed to the best sources of food while the weak and relatively tiny parasite had the protection of its larger mount as well as the mobility that enabled it to seek out its own, less readily available food supply. By the time the host creatures left the oceans to become large and unintelligent land animals, the mutually profitable arrangement continued and the parasite had become very intelligent indeed.

The earliest recorded history told of vain attempts to nurture intelligence in many different species of host creature. The native, six-limbed FGHJ life-form with its ability to work in a wide variety of materials, when a parasite was directing its hands, was favored above all the others.

But more and more they had wished for mind-partners they could not control, beings who would argue and debate and contribute new ideas and viewpoints, rather than creatures who were little more than general-purpose, self-replenishing organic tools with the ability to see, hear, and manipulate to order.

With these tools they built great cities and manufacturing complexes and vessels that circumnavigated their world, flew in the atmosphere above it, and, ultimately crossed the terrible and wonderful emptiness between the stars. But the cities, like their starships, were functional and unbeautiful because they had been built by and for the comfort and use of beings without any appreciation of beauty, and whose animal needs were satisfied by food, warmth, and regular satisfaction of the urge to procreate. Like valuable tools they had to be properly maintained, and many of them were well loved with the affection that a civilized being feels for a faithful but nonintelligent pet.

But the parasites had their own special needs that in no respect resembled those of their hosts, whose animal habits and undirected behavior were highly repugnant to them. It was vital to their continued mental well-being that the masters escaped periodically from their hosts to lead their own lives—usually during the hours of darkness when the tools were no longer in use and could be quartered where they could not harm themselves. This they did in the small, quiet, private places, tiny areas of civilization and culture and beauty amid the ugliness of the cities, where their families nested and they were separated from the host creatures by everything but distance.

It had long been an accepted fact among them that no creature or culture could avoid stagnation if it did not go outside its family or its tribe or, ultimately, its world. In their continuing search for other intelligent beings like or totally unlike themselves, many extrasolar planets had been discovered and small colonies established on them, but none of the indigenous life-forms possessed intelligence and had become just so many sets of other-species tools.

Because of an intense aversion to allowing themselves to be touched by the proxy hands of a nonintelligent creature, their medical science catered chiefly to the needs of their hosts and did not include surgery. The result was that when one of their own-planet tools contracted a disease that, to it, was mildly debilitating, the effect on the parasite was often lethal.

Cha Thrat paused for a moment and raised one of her upper hands to support the weight of the parasite. Sensation had returned to her neck and she felt that the creature's tendrils were loosening and pulling free. She could hear Prilicla and Murchison on the deck below.

"That is what happened to their ship," she went on. "The host FGHJs caught something that caused a mild, undulant fever, and recovered. The parasites, with this one exception, perished. But before they returned to their own quarters to die, they placed their now-undirected host creatures in places where food was available and they would not injure themselves, in the hope that help would reach the host creatures in time. The survivor, who seemed to have a partial resistance to the disease, rendered the vessel safe and accessible to rescuers, released the distress beacon, and returned to the ship's Nest to comfort its dying friends.

"But the effort to do this work," Cha Thrat went on, talking directly to Prilicla and Murchison who were now coming up the ramp toward her, "was too much for its host, an aging FGHJ of whom it was particularly fond, and the creature had a sudden cardiac malfunction and died inside the Nest.

"The distress signal was answered not by one of their own ships, but by *Rhabwar*," she concluded, "and the rest we know."

Prilicla did not reply and Murchison moved to one side, keeping the thin tube of its cutting torch aimed at the back of Cha Thrat's neck. Nervously the Pathologist said, "I'd need to check it with my scanner, of course, but I'd say physiological classification DTRC. It's very similar to the DTSB symbiotes some FGLIs wear for fine surgical work. In those cases it's the parasite who supplies the digits and the Tralthan the brains, although there are some OR nurses who would argue about that . . ."

It broke off as Cha Thrat said, "I have been trying to relinquish control of my speech centers so that it would be able to talk to you directly through me, but it is much too weak and is only barely conscious, so I must be its voice. It already knows from my mind who you are, and it is Crelyarrel, of the third division of Trennchi, of the one hundred and seventh division of Yau, and of the four hundred and eighth subdivision of the great Yilla of the Rhiim. I cannot properly describe its feelings in words, but there is joy at the knowledge that the Rhiim are not the only intelligent species in the Galaxy, sorrow that this wonderful knowledge will die with it, and apologies for anxiety it caused us by—"

"I know what it is feeling," Prilicla said gently, and suddenly they were washed by a great, impalpable wave of sympathy, friendship, and reassurance. "We are happy to meet you and learn of your people, friend Crelyarrel, and we will not allow you to die. Let go now, little friend, and rest, you are in good hands."

Still radiating its emotional support, it went on briskly. "Put away that cutting torch, friend Murchison, and go with the patient and friend Cha to the Rhiim quarters. It will feel more comfortable there, and you have much work to do on its dead friends. Friend Fletcher, preparations will have to be made at the hospital to receive this new life-form. Be ready to send a long hypersignal to Thornnastor as soon as we have a clearer idea of the clinical picture. Friend Naydrad, stand by with the litter in case we need special equipment here, or for the transport of DTRC cadavers to *Rhabwar* for investigation—"

"No!" the Captain said.

Murchison spoke a few words of a kind not normally used by an Earth-human female, then went on. "Captain, we have a patient here, in very serious condition, who is the sole survivor of a disease-stricken ship. You know as well as I that in this situation, you do exactly as Prilicla tells you."

"No," Fletcher repeated. In a quieter but no less firm voice it went on. "I understand your feelings, Pathologist. But are they really yours? You still haven't convinced me that that thing is harmless. I'm remembering those crew members and, well, it might be pretending to be sick. It could be controlling, or at least influencing, the minds of all of you. The quarantine regulations remain in force. Until the Diagnostician-in-Charge of Pathology, or more likely the decontamination squad clears it, nothing or nobody leaves that ship."

Cha Thrat was supporting Crelyarrel in three of her small, upper hands. The DTRC's body, now that she knew it for what it was, no longer looked or felt repugnant to her. The control tendrils hung limply between her LF002digits and the color of its skin was lightening and beginning to resemble that of its dead friends in the Rhiim nest. Had it to die, too, she wondered sadly, because two different people held opposing viewpoints that they both knew to be right?

Proving one of them wrong, especially when the being concerned was a ruler, would have serious personal repercussions, and she was beginning to wonder if she had always been as right as she thought she had been. Perhaps her life would have been happier if, on Sommaradva and at Sector General, she had been more doubtful about some of her certainties.

"Friend Fletcher," Prilicla said quietly. "As an empath I am influenced by feelings of everyone around me. Now I accept that there are beings who, by word or deed or omission, can give outward expression to emotions that they do not feel. But it is impossible for an intelligent entity to produce false emotional radiation, to lie with its mind. Another empath would know this to be so, but as a nonempath you must take my word for it. The survivor cannot and will not harm anyone."

The Captain was silent for a moment, then it said, "I'm sorry, Senior Physician. I'm still not fully convinced that it is not speaking through you and controlling your minds, and I cannot risk letting it aboard this ship."

In this situation there was no doubt about who was right or about what she must do, Cha Thrat thought, because a gentle little being like Prilicla might not be capable of doing it.

"Doctor Danalta," she said, "will you please go quickly to the boarding tube and take up a position and shape that will discourage any Monitor Corps officer from sealing, dismantling, or otherwise closing it to two-way traffic. Naturally, you should try not to hurt any such officer, and I doubt that lethal weapons will be deployed against you, for no other reason than that anything powerful enough to hurt you would seriously damage the hull, but if—"

"Technician!"

Even though the Captain was on *Rhabwar*'s control deck and at extreme range for Prilicla's empathic faculty, the feeling of outrage accompanying the word was making the little Cinrusskin quiver in every limb. Then gradually the trembling subsided as Fletcher brought his anger under control.

"Very well, Senior Physician," it said coldly. "Against my expressed wishes and on your own responsibility, the boarding tube will remain open. You may move freely between there and the casualty deck, but the rest of this ship will be closed to your people and that . . . that thing you insist is a survivor. The matter of Cha Thrat's gross insubordination, with the strong possibility of a charge of incitement to mutiny, will be pursued later."

"Thank you, friend Fletcher," Prilicla said. Then, switching off its mike, it went on. "And you, friend Cha. You have displayed great resourcefulness as well as insubordination. But I am afraid that, even when it is proved that you acted correctly, the Captain's present feelings toward you are of the kind that I have found to be not only unfriendly but extremely long-lasting."

Murchison did not speak until they were in the Rhiim compartment, when it paused in its scanner examination of Crelyarrel to look at her. The expression and tone of voice, Cha Thrat knew from the Earth-human component of her mind, expressed puzzlement and sympathy as it said, "How can one being get into so much trouble in such a short time? What got into you, Cha Thrat?"

Prilicla trembled slightly but did not speak.

Chapter 20

CHA Thrat's arrival for her appointment with the Chief Psychologist was punctual to the second, because she had been told that O'Mara considered being too early to be as wasteful of time as being too late. But on this occasion the impunctuality, although indirectly her fault, was on O'Mara's side. The Earth-human Braithwaite, who was the sole occupant of the large outer office, explained.

"I'm sorry for the delay, Cha Thrat," it said, inclining its head toward O'Mara's door, "but that meeting is running late. Senior Physician Cresk-Sar and, in order of seniority, Colonel Skempton, Major Fletcher, and Lieutenant Timmins are with him. The door is supposed to be soundproof, but sometimes I can hear them talking about you."

It smiled sympathetically, pointed to the nearest of the three unoccupied console desks beside it, and said, "Sit there, you should find that one fairly comfortable while we're waiting for the verdict. Try not to worry, Cha Thrat, but if you don't mind, I'd like to get on with my work."

Cha Thrat said that she did not mind, and was surprised when the screen on the desk she was occupying lit up with Braithwaite's work. She did not know what the Earth-human was doing, but while she was trying to understand it the realization came that it was deliberately giving her something to occupy her mind other than the things they were probably saying about her in the next room.

As one of the wizard's principal assistants, Braithwaite was capable of working a few helpful spells of its own.

Since her return to the hospital, Cha Thrat had been relegated to a kind of administrative hyperspace. Maintenance Department wanted nothing to do with her, the Monitor Corps ruler she had so grievously offended on *Rhabwar* seemed to have forgotten her very existence, and the medical training people treated her with sympathy and great care, much as they would a patient who was not expected to be long among them.

Officially there was nothing for her to do, but unofficially she had never been busier in her whole life.

Diagnostician Conway had been very pleased with her work on Goglesk, and had asked her to visit Khone as often as possible because Cha Thrat and itself were the only people that the FOKT would allow within touching distance, although that situation was beginning to change for the better. With behind-the-scenes assistance from the Chief Psychologist and Prilicla, progress was being made toward breaking down the Gogleskan racial conditioning, and Ees-Tawn was working on a miniature distorter, permanently attached to the subject and triggered automatically during the first microseconds of a distress call, which would make it impossible for the wearer to initiate one of the suicidal joinings.

O'Mara had warned them that the final solution to the Gogleskan problem might take many generations, that Khone would never be completely comfortable at the close approach or touch of another person, regardless of species, but that its offspring was already giving indications of being quite happy among strangers.

Thornnastor and Murchison had been successful in isolating and finding a specific against the pathogen affecting Crelyarrel, although they had admitted to Cha Thrat that the principal reason for its survival on the Rhiim ship was its possession of a fair degree of natural resistance. Now the little symbote was going from strength to strength, and was beginning to concern itself about the health and comfort of the FGHJ host creatures. It wanted to know how soon new Rhiim parasites could be brought to Sector General to take charge of them.

Similar questions were being asked by the group of visiting Monitor Corps officers who seemed to be ignorant of, or perhaps disinterested in, her recent insubordination on *Rhabwar*. They were Cultural Contact specialists investigating the ship with a view to gaining as much information as possible about the species who had caused it to be built, including the location of their planet of origin, before making a formal approach to the Rhiim on behalf of the Federation. They badly wanted to talk to the survivor.

Crelyarrel was anxious to cooperate, but the problem was that its people communicated by a combination of touch and telepathy limited to their own species. It was not yet well enough to take full control of a host crew member and, until it was able to do so, the translation computer could not be programmed with the language used by their FGHJ hosts.

Even though it was now generally accepted that the parasitic Rhiim were a highly intelligent and cultured species, none of the hospital staff were particularly eager to surrender their bodies, however temporarily, to DTRC control—and the feeling was mutual. The only person that Crelyarrel would agree to take over and speak through, with her permission, of course, was Cha Thrat.

As a result of these unofficial demands on her time, there had been little of it left for Cha Thrat to worry about her own problems.

Until now.

The muffled sounds of conversation from the inner office had died away into inaudibility, which meant, she thought, that they were either speaking quietly to each other or not speaking at all. But she was wrong, the meeting was over.

Senior Physician Cresk-Sar silently led the way out, its hairy features unreadable. It was followed by Colonel Skempton, who made an untranslatable sound, then *Rhabwar*'s ruler, who neither looked nor spoke, and Lieutenant Timmins, who stared at her for a moment with one eye closed before leaving. She was rising from her seat to enter the inner office when O'Mara came out.

"Sit where you are, this won't take long," it said. "You, too, Braithwaite. Sommaradvans don't mind having their problems discussed before concerned witnesses, and this one certainly has a problem. Is that deformed bird-cage you're sitting on comfortable?

"The problem," it went on before she could reply, "is that you are an oddly shaped peg who doesn't quite fit into any of our neat little holes. You are intelligent, able, strong-minded yet adaptable, and have experienced, seemingly without any permanent ill effects, the levels of mental trauma and disorientation that would cause many beings severe psychological damage. You are well regarded, even respected, by some very important people here, by many with no influence at all, and disliked by a few. The latter group, chiefly Monitor Corps personnel and a few of the medical staff, feel very unsure of who or what you are, and who has the seniority, while working with you.

"Sometimes," Cha Thrat said defensively, "I'm not sure who or what I am myself. When I am thinking like a senior person I can't help behaving like a..." She stopped herself before she said too much.

"Like a Diagnostician," O'Mara said drily. "Oh, don't worry, this department never reveals anyone's deep, dark, and, in your case, peculiar secrets. Prilicla, when it wasn't enthusing over your behavior immediately preceding and during Khone's delivery and on the Rhiim ship, told me about the joining it feels you underwent on Goglesk. Being Prilicla, it is anxious to avoid any painful and embarrassing incidents between its friends Conway, Murchison, and yourself, and so are we.

"But the fact remains," the Chief Psychologist went on, "that you shared minds with Khone who, because of an earlier sharing with Conway, gave you much of the knowledge and experience of a Sector General Diagnostician as well as a Gogleskan healer. You also became deeply involved on the mental level with one of the Rhiim parasites, not to mention some earlier prying into the mind of your Chalder friend, AUGL-One Sixteen. I'm not surprised that there are times when you aren't quite sure who or what you are. Is there any doubt about that at present?"

"No," she replied, "you are talking only to Cha Thrat."

"Good," O'Mara said, "because it is Cha Thrat's problematical future that we must now consider. Since the business on *Rhabwar*, when you were not only insubordinate but completely right, the option of a career in Maintenance, even though Timmins speaks highly of you, is closed, as is any hope you may have had of service as a ship's medic with the Monitor Corps. Shipboard discipline is often invisible, but it is there and it is strict, and no ship commander would risk taking on a doctor with a proven record of insubordination.

"The Cultural Contact people you've been helping with the Rhiim parasite," it continued, "are less discipline-oriented than the others, and they are impressed with you and are grateful enough to offer you a spot on your home planet, after the disciplinary dust has had a chance to settle, of course. What would you say to re-, turning to Sommaradva?"

Cha Thrat made an untranslatable sound and O'Mara said drily, "I see. But the medical and surgical options are also closed to you. In spite of the respect in which are held by many of the senior staff, nobody wants a know-it-all trainee nurse on their wards who is likely to say or do something that will suggest that its Charge Nurse or doctor on duty are, well, clinically incorrect. And while you have influence in high places, that also could disappear if the truth about your Gogleskan mind-swap became common knowledge."

Cha Thrat was wondering if there was anything she could do or say that would halt the relentless closing down of her options, when Braithwaite looked up from its display.

"Excuse me, sir," it said. "But from my knowledge of the personalities involved, Conway, Khone, and Prilicla are unlikely to discuss it among anyone but themselves, and Murchison, who is a very intelligent entity indeed, will do likewise when she realizes the truth or learns it from her life-mate. Her psych profile indicates the presence of a well-developed sense of humor, and it might well be that the thought of an other-species entity, and another female at that, looking upon her with the same libidinous feelings as those of her life-mate, Conway, would be funnier than it was embarrassing. Naturally, I would not suggest that any of these misdirected feelings would be translated into action, but certain entertaining sexual fantasies could arise that would illuminate the whole area of interspecies—"

"Braithwaite," O'Mara said quietly, "it is talk like that which gives people the wrong impression about e-t psychologists.

"As for you, Cha Thrat," it went on, "I decided a long time ago that there was only one position here that suited your particular talents. Once again you will start as a trainee, at the bottom, and advancement will be slow because your chief is very hard to please. It is a difficult and often thankless job that will cause irritation to most people, but then you've become used to that. You will have a few compensations, like being able to poke your olfactory orifices into everyone else's business whenever you think it necessary. Do you accept?"

Suddenly Cha Thrat's pulse was clearly audible to her and she was finding it difficult to breathe. "I—I don't understand," she said.

O'Mara took a deep breath, then exhaled through its nose and said, "You *do* understand, Cha Thrat. Don't pretend to be stupid when you aren't."

"I do understand," she agreed, "and I am most grateful. The delay was due to a combination of initial disbelief and consideration of the implications. You are saying that I am to learn the skills of nonmaterial healing, the casting of spells, and that I am to become a trainee wizard."

"Something like that," the Chief Psychologist said. It glanced at the display on her desk and added, "I see that you've already been exposed to the senior staff psych chart amendment procedure. It is routine, unexciting but very necessary work. Braithwaite has been trying to unload the job on someone for months."

About the Author

JAMES WHITE was born in Belfast, Northern Ireland, and resides there, though he spent his early years in Canada. His first story was printed in 1953. He has since published well-received short stories, novellas, and novels, but he is best known for the Sector General series, which deals with the difficulties involved in running a hospital that caters to many radically different life-forms.

From the author of the dazzling Sector General Series...

JAMES WHITE